PRABE FOR: *TH*

"Filled with pulse-pounding action,   .d
a timely message about the state of our planet, *The Rise of Winter* soars."

— Joel A. Sutherland, author of *Summer's End* and *Haunted Canada*

"Both a hopeful, and harrowing, look at the future of the only planet we have
ever called home."

— Kevin Sylvester, author of *The Almost Epic Squad: Mucus Mayhem*

"A timely, thought-provoking page-turner."

— Heather Camlot, author of *Clutch*

"An environmental and metaphysical fantasy, *The Rise of Winter* is entertaining as it introduces a new world and leaves a great deal to explore."

— *Foreword Reviews*

PRAISE FOR: *FROM ANT TO EAGLE*

Winner — Silver Birch Fiction Award

Finalist — Red Cedar Award

Finalist — Rocky Mountain Book Award

Finalist — R. Ross Annett Award for Children's Literature

Silver Winner — Foreword INDIES

"Absolutely terrific." — Paulette Bourgeois, Author

"An honest portrayal of love, loss, and friendship." — *School Library Journal*

"This is a story of emotional truth that is sure to captivate readers of all ages."

— Ashley Spires, Author and Illustrator of *The Most Magnificent Thing*

"A moving and ultimately hopeful book." — *Booklist*

"Tender, direct, and honest." — *Kirkus Reviews*

TERRA PROTECTORUM

The Rise of Winter

ALEX LYTTLE

central
avenue
publishing

2019

This is a work of fiction. Names, characters, places and incidents either are the product
of the author's imagination or are used fictitiously and any resemblance to actual
persons, living or dead, business establishments, events or locales
is entirely coincidental.

Published by Central Avenue Publishing, an imprint of Central Avenue Marketing Ltd.
www.centralavenuepublishing.com

Published in Canada. Printed in United States of America on acid free paper.

Library and Archives Canada Cataloguing in Publication

Lyttle, Alex, author
The rise of winter / Alex Lyttle.

(Terra protectorum)
Issued in print and electronic formats.
ISBN 978-1-77168-158-2 (softcover).--ISBN 978-1-77168-159-9 (EPUB).--
ISBN 978-1-77168-160-5 (Kindle)

I. Title.

PS8623.Y88R58 2019   jC813'.6   C2018-905944-3
                                          C2018-905945-1

To my four children:

Amelia,
who "might" one day read this book,

Kipling,
who wishes this book were a video game,

Ireland,
who would read this book if it were made of chocolate,

and Huxley,
who would eat this book if he could only get his hands on it.

I love you more than words can express.

The Guardians

	LAND	WATER	SKY
STRENGTH	ARCTOS ~BEAR~ TERRIONA	CANO ~ORCA~ AQUANION	CATHARIA ~CONDOR~ VENTIOS
WISDOM	WINTER ~HUMAN~ IMPERIA	CHEELION ~TURTLE~ SENTAVITUS	PTERON ~BAT~ AMINOCULOUS
AGILITY	VULPEERA ~FOX~ SENSIUM	TULLY ~OTTER~ PETRAQUIM	AURORA ~HUMMINGBIRD~ EVANESTIUM
SPEED	FELINIA ~CHEETAH~ KANETIS	ISTEEL ~SAILFISH~ GRAVIDIUM	FANTOM ~FALCON~ FULGAREM

The earth speaks,

Her voice a ragged whisper.

Her lungs are choked with soot,

Her throat dry.

Do you hear Her?

It is the voice of an old woman,

though She is still young.

The
Rise
of
Winter

PART 1: THE COVE

High atop Mount Skire, a snowy owl sits perched on the side of a dark pool, hidden in the rocky crags. This is not a typical place for an owl to rest—but this is not a typical owl, nor is it a typical pool.

The owl looks up from the still water, her short neck craning sideways so she can watch as the sun puts its final touches on the day. Mount Skire is the tallest of the Great Barrier Mountains—a range of towering peaks stretching across the entire continent, separating the country of Nacadia from the Forgotten Lands. From her lofty vantage point, the owl can see most of Nacadia spread out before her like a patchwork quilt. To her left is a dense forest extending from the base of the mountains toward Grander's Bay and the Western Ocean; to her right, rolling foothills undulate toward the northern coast. Small towns connected by dirt roads dot the interior countryside, while a single cloud of smog hangs in the distance over the capital city of Olport. Miles away on the eastern coast, too far to be seen, the owl's home lies hidden in a sandy cove, waiting for her return.

Another stiff breeze blows, ruffling the owl's feathers, revealing hidden silver plumes that shimmer in the dying light. Daylight will soon be gone, and the owl will have the answers for which she has come.

As the minutes pass, it grows darker. The ocean glows a reddish hue as the sun slips behind the horizon, until the rich darkness that follows envelops everything like a dense fog. Even with her keen night vision, the owl can barely make out the pool beneath her.

So, she waits . . .

And waits . . .

Until it starts.

A single photon of light cuts through the sky before growing to a gentle yellowish-gold beam that brightens the side of the mountain. A large moon has begun to rise, bathing everything in soft gold light.

"Luna Aurum," the owl whispers.

In the distance, the ocean appears as a vibrant expanse of glittering waves, while the trees of the forest glow like copper and glass. Finally, when the moon is directly overhead, the owl sees what she has come for.

Thin ripples disturb the surface of the pond, although the mountain is still and the wind has stopped. An image begins to form within the ripples. The water settles and the vision becomes clear: an orca, powerful and black, cutting through rough ocean waves.

"Very well," the owl whispers to no one. "Cano it shall be—it is as expected."

The image disappears, leaving the glassy pond with only the reflection of the owl and the golden moon above. The bird stands watching, anticipating. The whale was not a surprise, but there will be more. She stays, waiting for the real reason she came to this pool.

The ripples appear and dissipate again as another image forms.

The face of a young girl. Her raven-black hair falls twisted beside a pale, freckled face. Framed by the ringed locks are two emerald-green eyes with pupils shaped not like an ordinary girl's, but oval—like those of a cat.

The owl closes her large, yellow eyes and nods. "So," she says, "it is to be the girl. Many will not be happy with the choice." She opens her eyes and sighs. "But if it is the heart's decision, I shall make it so."

With one last look at the girl's image, the owl spreads her wings and rises from her stony perch into the night sky above. The moonlight glistens off her silver feathers as she flies to the Cove to prepare for the ceremony.

Chapter 1

I NEVER KNEW MY FATHER. ASIDE FROM TELLING ME HE'D DIED when I was very young, Granny never spoke of him, which was odd because she spoke about my mother, who had died during childbirth. She told me that my mother had been sweet and kind, and loved my father immensely. But my father . . . not a word. Any time I'd try to ask questions she'd close up like a clam, with a tight-lipped frown. I knew something was odd that day when she finally did mention him.

Come to think of it, a lot was odd about that day.

For starters, I counted eleven cars on my walk to school, which was two more than I'd ever counted before. Every day, someone in town was trading in their horse and buggy for one of the Society's new Dorf Model Bs, and it felt like the whole town would soon be overrun by those metal beasts.

But I guess that wasn't *so* strange. The Society had built new roads, and the price of their cars had dropped. Plus, everyone said driving made getting around easier.

I suppose the first *really* unusual thing happened at lunch. Right around the time I was getting my butt kicked by Penny and her cronies.

"WHAT KIND OF name is Winter, anyway?" Penny asked, pushing me against the brick wall of the school. "Who names their daughter after a mythical season where cold stuff falls from the sky? Your parents must have been weird. It's probably a good thing they're both dead."

I tried to take a swing at Penny, but Carly and Marly—the Twin Terrors, as I liked to call them—grabbed my arms and pinned them to the wall.

"I bet your parents were freaks just like you," Penny continued. "They probably had the same weirdo eyes. What are you, some sort of cat?"

I gritted my teeth. Penny was right. Cat-like eyes *did* run in my family. My cousin Alectus had them, Granny'd had them before she went blind, and apparently, my father had had them, too (or so my uncle said).

Cat eyes.

A family trait.

Lucky me.

Nothing helps you fit in at school like being different. I could probably write a short book on all the names I'd been called. And I'd pretty much started answering to cat calls in the hallways.

"You know what I wish?" Penny asked, her face so close I could see every bump and boil on her skin.

"That the Society would invent a cure for acne?"

It was a stupid comment. Penny pummeled me in the stomach for it, and I felt the air leave my lungs. I should've kept my mouth shut, but I was never good at that.

"No," Penny growled. "I hate that they let a freak like you into my father's school. It makes us all look bad. Besides, grade nine is hard enough without having your eyes to give us nightmares."

Marly and Carly laughed right on cue. They were Penny's goons and followed her everywhere. Aside from the fact that Marly wore her blond braid over her left shoulder while Carly wore hers over her right, they were almost identical—like two giant, ugly bookends. They followed Penny around because her father was the principal of the school, and it basically gave them immunity; they could do whatever they liked.

"You think about my eyes while you're sleeping?" I said between gasps. "That's sort of creepy."

Penny's face contorted into an ugly scowl. She reminded me of a comic-book character, as if steam were about to pour from her ears. She punched me harder, and this time I crumpled.

"Any more funny comments?" she asked.

It took me a minute to stand back up, and I shook my head to concede. Penny turned to Carly and Marly. "What should we do with her today, girls?" she asked. "She's in a particularly hilarious mood. We'll have to fix that."

"We could take her behind the school and pound her," Marly suggested.

"Yeah, we could pound her," Carly agreed.

Poor twins, they were about as smart as two rocks.

"Nah, I've got a better idea," Penny said, grinning and turning around to face the sidewalk at the front of the school. "You see that group of boys over there?" She pointed to some kids from our class, standing by the road. "I want you to crawl over to them and purr like a kitty cat. Since you already look like one, you might as well act like one, too."

I groaned inwardly. I would have preferred the pounding. The last thing I wanted was to make a fool of myself in front of the boys.

When I didn't immediately get down on all fours, Marly and Carly pushed down on my shoulders. They were both almost six feet tall and stronger than anybody in the school. There was no resisting.

"Good," Penny said, once I was down in the crawling position. "Now start moving."

I slumped my head low so that my hair fell over my face, hoping it would hide my identity, and started crawling across the lawn. Penny's white sneakers followed closely beside, while the twins brought up the rear.

I crawled until I was a few feet away from the boys and stopped. I couldn't see their faces, but their shoes turned toward me and they stopped talking.

"Go ahead," Penny said.

When I didn't make any noise, Penny began shifting back and forth on the spot. She was always trying to impress the boys, but most of them thought she was either mean or annoying. Which was probably why she was always angry.

A low murmur spread through the boys, and Penny nudged me with her knee. She bent down so that her mouth was beside my ear.

"Purr," she ordered.

"What the heck are you doing, Penny?" one of the boys asked.

I could sense Penny's agitation growing as she straightened back up. "I'm just walking my pet around the school," she said. "What's the matter, Winter? Cat got your tongue?"

Marly and Carly forced a laugh, but none of the boys seemed to find this funny.

Penny bent down again and hissed, "*Purr*!"

When I still didn't make a sound, she kneed me in the side, sending a sharp pain through my ribs. I was about to give in and do what she wanted when suddenly the boys broke into laughter. And not just a chuckle—this was a full-force, stomach-clenching roar.

It was followed by the sound of Penny screaming.

I looked up to see two of the boys keeled over, while a third was practically in tears. The whole group was howling and pointing at Penny as if they'd just seen the funniest thing in the world.

I turned to see Penny standing a few feet away, her hands flapping as she jumped up and down frantically. The twins were desperately swiping at her forehead.

A small sparrow swooped down near Penny's head and she shrieked, pulling away from the twins and ducking. That's when I saw it: a large glob of bird poop running right down her face.

I couldn't help but laugh.

Marly—or maybe it was Carly—tried again to wipe Penny's face, but it only smeared the glob through her eyebrow.

A crowd began to form and Penny was hysterical. As much as I was enjoying myself, I decided it was a good time to slip away. I backed up slowly, preparing to make a run for it, when—

"Bombs away!"

The shrill voice came from above, and I turned to see a second glob of poop land on Penny's ear, dangling like an earring. There was another round of laughter and Penny took off, screaming, toward the school.

The sparrow swooped and pulled at Penny's hair as she went, causing her to trip over a stray backpack and face-plant on the lawn. The twins rushed to help her up, and the three of them went barreling toward the front doors of the school. All the while, the bird continued to dive at them.

Only when they had disappeared inside did the sparrow give up. It circled a few times before flying off over my head toward the trees beyond. As it passed I heard the same small, high-pitched voice say, "Serves her right!"

I looked around to see if anyone else had heard the voice, but no one seemed to have noticed.

Where had it come from? Had it been from another student? One of the boys? It seemed so clearly to have been coming from above. Almost as if it was from the sparrow. But birds couldn't talk!

Was my mind playing tricks on me?

Chapter 2

WHEN I GOT HOME FROM SCHOOL I WAS STILL THINKING ABOUT the bird. I paused briefly on our back porch, looking out at the orange grove in our backyard. We lived on the outskirts of Dunvy, a small town in the heart of Nacadia, nearly a five-hour trip to the coast or the capital. It was a quiet town, known for its oranges and sugar cane, but ever since the Society had extended their massive roadway up to the mountains, we'd had a lot more travellers passing through.

I rested my chin on my hands, leaning on the railing. I must have hit my head on the wall when the twins pushed me. Maybe I had a concussion and that's what made me think the bird was talking.

I shook my head.

Yes, I concluded, *I must definitely have a concussion.*

I took one last look across the yard, breathing in the rich scent of citrus before going inside.

I dropped my bag carelessly on the kitchen floor and walked into the living room.

"Granny?" I called.

Normally when I got home, Granny would be sitting in her worn-out armchair by the window, but the chair was empty.

That was unusual.

"Granny?" I called again, this time louder.

Granny was stone-blind but her hearing was better than anyone I knew. Besides, the house wasn't big. She should have heard me.

So, where was she?

I ran up the stairs to look in her room.

"There you are," I said, breathing a sigh of relief. She was sitting on the edge of her bed, facing the dresser and holding something in her hand. I moved around to see what it was. It looked like some sort of stone, only it was white, like pearl, with gold etchings carved into its surface. Granny was rubbing the face of the stone and mumbling under her breath. She appeared to be in a kind of trance, and still hadn't noticed me.

"Granny?" I said again.

I got close enough to see the object more clearly—it was a necklace with a circular stone pendant the size of my palm, mounted on a gold chain. The etchings were symbols, some running around the outside edge of the pendant like numbers on a clock, and more in the middle. I leaned in closer to see what they were.

As I did, I brushed against Granny's shoulder and she jumped.

"Great Terra!" she yelled, while at the same time I jumped higher and yelled something less appropriate.

Granny turned around. "I didn't see you," she said with an embarrassed grin.

It was her favourite joke. Of course she hadn't seen me—she had lost her vision in a farming accident a long time ago, or so she said. Two large scars ran straight down her face, passing through each of her eyes.

"What is that?" I asked, reaching out to touch the necklace.

She yanked it back abruptly, knowing, even without vision, exactly what I was doing.

I pulled my hand away, irritated. Why was she always so secretive? I didn't doubt that she loved me—she'd looked after me since I lost my parents—but sometimes she still treated me like a child.

"Why can't I look at it?" I asked.

Granny hesitated. I could see that she was thinking hard about something. She turned back toward me and held out the necklace.

"Really?" I said, reaching to take it.

The moment my fingers touched the smooth rock, a jolt shot through my hand and up my arm.

"Ouch!" I yelled, yanking my hand away.

One of the gold etchings around the edge of the stone glowed a deep green, and Granny's mouth twisted into a frown.

"So it is," she whispered.

"So what is?" I asked, shaking my hand and inspecting it. There didn't appear to be any marks or burns.

Granny stood up and held out the necklace again. I hesitated to take it, the pain in my fingers still lingering, but like the glowing green of the symbol, it faded quickly. I reached out and took the necklace, and this time there was no jolt.

It was smooth like glass and heavier than I'd expected. I turned it around in my hand and looked at the symbols. There were twelve around the edge, each in the shape of a different animal. In the middle were three more: a drop of water, mountains, and three swirling lines.

"What is this?" I asked.

"Old," Granny replied.

I rolled my eyes. "No, I mean, where did it come from?"

Granny exhaled slowly as if carefully choosing her words.

"Your father had it the day he died."

I was shocked. Granny never spoke about my father. *Ever.* And suddenly she was offering information?

"It was my father's?" I exclaimed.

Granny shook her head adamantly. "I did not say it was your father's. I said he had it the day he died."

I was suddenly filled with an overwhelming need to ask questions. "Where did he get it? What do you mean it wasn't his? Did he steal it?"

Then another thought crossed my mind: *If my father had it the day he died, then Granny must have had it for years.* Why had she never shown it to me?

Granny took the necklace back and tucked it into a blue velvet pouch before putting it into the top drawer of her dresser.

"What are you going to do with it? If my father had it last, maybe it should be passed down to me."

"Maybe," Granny said, "but right now I'm hungry. Let's go eat."

And just like that, the discussion was over. It was the longest conversation we'd ever had about my father.

Chapter 3

As Granny set about making dinner, I gathered the garbage and went to take it out back. The evening air was warm and the sun was already hidden behind the trees, causing shadows to wash over the porch. With the rainy season over, the air felt dry. It probably wouldn't rain again for weeks.

The bag was heavy and banged noisily as I dragged it down the stairs to the bin. I opened the top and threw it in.

CRASH!

On my way back to the porch, the thought of that strange necklace troubled me.

Why had Granny kept it from me for so long? I didn't have any siblings, so shouldn't my father's treasures be mine? I hated how secretive she was about him. She still hadn't told me how he'd died! Sometimes I wished—

"Woo-wee, dinner is served!"

I spun around mid-thought. Someone had spoken behind me.

I scanned the backyard quickly, but didn't see anyone. "I-is someone there?" I called.

The orange grove was shadowy and dark—was someone hiding there? Maybe my mind was playing tricks on me again, like with the sparrow.

I climbed the porch steps to go inside, and the voice spoke again.

"Sure would be easier if I were a little taller," it said.

This time I was sure I'd heard it. I turned and went back down the stairs, looking around. Again, I saw no one—only the fat raccoon that lived under our deck, who had apparently come out to sniff through the garbage. He was sitting on top of the garbage can trying to pry off the lid.

"Did someone say something?" I called out.

Nobody answered me, but I'd obviously startled the raccoon. Its ears twitched and it turned around to face me, then craned its neck left and right as if searching for something.

"Doesn't look like there's anyone here but me," the voice said, and this time I was certain it had come from the raccoon.

"You—you can talk?" I asked.

The raccoon's jaw dropped and its eyes widened. "You—you can understand?"

We stood staring at each other for what felt like an hour.

"I must be dreaming," I finally muttered, backing away from the raccoon but tripping on the bottom stair and falling on my butt in the process.

"Oh, Terra, I've finally done it," the raccoon said, jumping from the top of the garbage can and shaking its head. "One too many cans of

Meatys! And I knew it, too! I kept saying to myself, 'Don't do it, Proctin, don't eat the Meatys, it's not real food.' But did my stomach listen? Noooo. It kept on growling and saying, 'More, more, more!'" The raccoon placed its tiny paws over its eyes and fell over backward. "Look what I've done! My poor brain, the largest of its kind, ruined! I mean, take my beauty, sure, but my brain? Oh, not my brain!"

The raccoon lay on the ground, smacking its paws against the sides of its head, tail swishing back and forth in the air, wailing over and over, "My brain! My brain! My brain!"

Dream or no dream, I couldn't help but laugh. I walked over and looked down at the raccoon while it continued its fit.

"I beg your pardon," I said.

"And I begged for more Meatys!" cried the raccoon.

"No, I beg your pardon, as in, excuse me."

"You're excused," said the raccoon. "But I'm not. How can I excuse myself when I've gone and ruined everything?"

A little frustrated, I reached down and touched the raccoon on its shoulder.

Immediately it stopped its woeful cries and looked up at me.

"You touched me!" it said, shooting up from the ground onto its paws.

I pulled my hand back. "I'm sorry. I was just trying to get your attention."

"No, no, you touched me," it said again, this time with excitement in its voice. "Do it again!"

I was confused, but reached my hand forward and felt the soft fur behind the raccoon's neck.

"Aha!" cried the raccoon. "You're real!" It jumped toward me and wrapped its little arms around my leg. "Absolutely, physically real! I can touch you!"

I shook my leg slightly, trying to get it off me without seeming rude.

The raccoon stepped backward and lifted its paw into the air with a flourish. "My name's Proctin," it said.

Alright, so it wasn't my mind playing tricks on me after all, I thought.

I reached my hand forward, quite aware that if anyone saw me at that moment they'd think I'd lost my mind. "Winter," I said, shaking the raccoon's paw. "Pleased to meet you."

"To think I've lived in your house for ten years and we're only just learning each other's names," said the raccoon.

"Under," I said.

"Under?"

"You've lived *under* my house for ten years. I hear you going through our garbage at night. You live under there." I pointed beneath the deck.

"If you knew where I lived, why didn't you ever say hello?"

"I didn't know you could talk."

"Of course I can talk," Proctin said, indignant. Then his head drooped and his eyes looked sad. "My mother used to say I talked too much."

"Well, until now, I guess I never understood you," I said.

As I spoke, I mulled this over in my head. I had never spoken to an animal before, had I? I mean, I'd spoken to the odd dog passing on the street, but as far as I knew they had never understood me.

"Do you talk with any other humans?" I asked, but the raccoon was no longer listening. He had crept back over to the garbage and was standing on his hind legs, trying to reach the lid. He hopped and managed to lift it slightly before it fell back in place.

"Here, let me help you," I said, walking over and lifting it for him. "Just try not to make too much of a mess. You *do* know I'm the one who has to clean up after you in the morning?"

"Sorry about that," Proctin said. "I'll do my best." He hopped on top of the garbage and started tearing through the debris.

His mood seemed to have changed at the mention of his mother and he no longer appeared interested in continuing the conversation. I watched for a moment before going back into the house.

I didn't say anything about the raccoon to Granny over dinner. In fact, I barely said anything at all. I was in a daze and worried she would think I was crazy. But something about the thin-lipped smile on her face made me think that maybe she already knew.

That night when I climbed into bed, I sat absently staring at my geography textbook. I couldn't focus. There was too much to think about— the laughing sparrow, the necklace in Granny's dresser, but mostly, the talking raccoon that had called himself Proctin.

What a weird day, I thought, putting the textbook aside and grabbing my journal off the bedside table. It had been an eventful one and it would take me a while to write it all down.

Better get started.

Chapter 4

IT FELT LIKE I'D ONLY JUST CLOSED MY EYES WHEN I WAS wrenched from sleep by a scraping sound on glass.

The room was black, except for a tunnel of golden light projecting through the window onto the opposite wall. In the centre of that projection was the shadow of a bird—tall and rigid with a short neck and a curved beak.

I climbed from my bed and looked outside. A large, golden moon hung over the distant mountains, illuminating the orange trees and yard. A tree branch swayed gently by the window—but there was no bird on it.

I spun around to the light on the wall to find the bird's shadow had disappeared.

Or had it even been there in the first place?

I rubbed my head, worrying about the long-term damage from my likely concussion. I was tired, but too unsettled to sleep, so I stood staring at the moon—full, clear, and golden. It was bigger than I'd ever seen it and gave the odd impression that it was sitting on top of the mountains.

The mountains . . .

For as long as I could remember, I'd felt a weird pull toward the mountains, as if they were the north end of a magnet and I was the south. At night, I'd sit by my window and watch them. It sounds odd, but it felt as if they were saying my name. I didn't know why; I'd never been to the mountains, never even been close. I spent my school days with Granny in Dunvy and the rest of the year on Pitchi, an island off the coast of Olport. My Uncle Farlin lived there with his son, Alectus. It wasn't always a pleasant experience—my cousin saw to that—but it was the only other home I'd known.

So why did I feel as though the mountains called me?

No one lived up there, as far as I knew, and there was nothing beyond them but the Forgotten Lands. There were rumors about what existed in the Forgotten Lands—endless sand, swamps with toxic air, landscapes torn apart by windstorms and earthquakes—but they were all exactly that: rumors. No one had ever gone to the Forgotten Lands. No one was crazy enough to try. Except, perhaps, the Society. Kids at school said the Society was planning an expedition. But kids were always making up things about the Society. Some even joked that the Society would one day go to the moon. As if *that* were possible. Still, it was hard to put anything past the Society, with all they'd invented in such a short time. "The future is forward," or so their slogan said.

Something howled in the distance, low and forlorn.

Coyote, I thought. Common to the area.

I climbed back into bed. If I didn't sleep soon I'd probably not wake for my alarm. I smiled at that thought. There was a good chance I'd sleep through it anyway.

I don't know how long I was out before I was awoken by another noise. This time it was a loud thump, and I sprang from my bed.

Okay, that time I definitely heard something.

I stood in the middle of the room, breathing quickly, waiting for something to happen. The house was silent and the air was crisp. I started to shiver in my pajamas and was feeling a bit silly when I saw something moving outside the bedroom window.

I crossed the room to get a better look.

The moon was now half hidden behind a wall of clouds, but despite the dim light, I saw that I was right—something *was* moving outside. Many things. Large, skulking shadows were creeping across the lawn toward the house. I squeezed my eyes shut and reopened them to be sure I wasn't dreaming, but the shadows remained. I couldn't make out exactly what they were, but they appeared to be some sort of animal. Some sort of very large animal. I tried to count them, but there were too many—ten, twenty, maybe thirty?

Something grabbed my shoulder from behind and I screamed.

I spun around to find Granny standing in her nightgown and robe, a fearful look on her face.

"You have to get out," she said.

I didn't have the chance to ask what was going on before she handed me a pair of jeans and a shirt. "Put these on. Hurry!"

I didn't question her. Something in her voice frightened me. Something was very wrong. I threw on my clothes and Granny took my arm, pulling me quickly down the stairs to the living room.

"Wait here," she said, disappearing into the kitchen. She moved faster than I'd known she could, and reappeared carrying my backpack.

"I've got everything you'll need in here," she said.

I stared at her in disbelief. "Everything I'll need for what?"

"Your journey to the Cove," said a voice from the shadows.

I jumped. I hadn't noticed anyone else in the room.

A low figure emerged from the darkened corner. It stood a little higher than my knees and seemed to glide across the floor rather than walk. Its body was sleek and long, with pointed ears and a bushy tail. A coat of well-groomed auburn fur shone in the pale moonlight while a streak of white ran from under its snout to its belly. It was a fox—a red fox—similar to the ones that hunted and played in the fields around our house.

"Did you just speak?" I asked.

The creature nodded. "My name is Vulpeera."

I turned and looked at Granny. "What's going on? Am I dreaming?"

Granny shook her head. "This is not a dream, though I wish it were. Vulpeera is here to take you to the Cove. Listen to her; she will explain everything on the way."

I couldn't decide what was crazier—the talking fox in the middle of my living room or the fact that Granny seemed to know the creature.

There was another loud crash like the one that had awoken me—this time from the kitchen. Wood creaked under the pressure of some immense weight. Something was trying to break through the back door.

Granny and Vulpeera exchanged nervous looks. "Quickly," Granny said, "this way." She moved to the far side of the room and opened the door to the basement. "Down here."

The fox moved toward the door, but I stood still. What was going on? What was outside? Everything around me was moving so fast.

Another crash echoed through the house, followed by the sound of splintering wood as a small piece of the door broke off. I turned to see a shadow run through the kitchen, and Vulpeera's back arched as she snarled.

The shadow darted around the fox and scurried between my legs. I recognized its black and grey pattern as it crossed through a stream of moonlight.

"Proctin!" I exclaimed.

"What's going on out there?" he panted. "There are hundreds of them!"

Another crash, this time followed by a scraping sound as whatever was outside tried to claw its way in.

"Quickly, Winter," Granny said, "we don't have much time."

As if to answer her, yet another crash resounded through the house as the door gave way. Two large shadows pounced into the kitchen, but I didn't wait to find out what they were. I sprinted to the open basement door and leapt through. Proctin and Vulpeera jumped after me, and Granny followed, slamming the door shut just as two loud thumps hit the other side.

"What are those?!" I cried, but no one answered. I was at the top of the stairs and it was completely dark—I couldn't see a thing. Proctin clung to my leg. Keeping my hand on the cold stone wall, I crept down the stairs and pulled the cord for the light.

The basement lit up and I saw Granny and Vulpeera already standing on the far side of the room, pushing against the washing tub.

Whatever was upstairs was now clawing and bashing at the basement door. Soon they would be through, and we'd have nowhere to go. Why had we come to the basement? There was no way to escape—we were locked in! My hands clenched in fear. Proctin was gripping my leg so tightly I could feel his claws digging through my pants. I tried to pry them free, but his grasp was unbreakable.

Granny and Vulpeera had managed to push the washing tub to the side, revealing a hole in the wall behind it, big enough to crawl through.

"Come on," Vulpeera said, jumping into the hole.

Proctin released my leg and scurried across the room. He peered inside. "I'm definitely not going in there," he said. "It looks muddy and dark and cold and—"

Vulpeera's face re-emerged from the darkness. "Not you," she growled. "Winter, hurry! Once they find out where we're going they'll move to cut us off at the other end."

I bent down and looked inside the hole. Proctin was right—it did look muddy and dark and cold, but another crash from upstairs gave me the courage to climb in.

"Hurry, Granny," I said, reaching my hand out to guide her in after me.

Granny bent down with a grave expression. Her eyes were forever closed but somehow, I felt like she was looking at me.

"I'm not coming," she said.

"What?!"

I started to crawl back out of the hole, but she held up a hand to stop me.

"Don't worry about me," she said. "I can handle whatever comes through that door. Besides, it's not me they're after—it's you."

"Handle what behind the door? Granny, they're huge! You can't—"

"I've still got some fight left in me," Granny said, smiling.

"What are you talking about? Fight? Granny, what's after me?"

"I should have told you a long time ago," Granny said, shaking her head. "I thought I was keeping you safe. I didn't think you'd be chosen, not after your father. I'm sorry, Winter." She reached out a hand and touched my face. "Vulpeera will explain everything. Trust her."

"Granny, I'm not going without you!" I was angry, and my throat tightened as tears began to form, but she stood and began pushing the tub back into place before I could stop her.

What was happening? What was my grandmother talking about?

24

What did she mean about me being chosen?

Before the washing tub was fully back in place, Proctin let out a cry. "Oh, for Terra's sake," he said, jumping in behind me.

The slit of light grew smaller, until it was no wider than my hand. Granny's face reappeared. "I almost forgot," she said. She reached into the pocket of her bathrobe, then held out her hand. In it was the necklace from the drawer. "Take this. And remember that I love you."

"I don't care about the necklace!" I said, as the crack closed. I should have told her I loved her, too, or one of a hundred other things. Instead I sat there in the darkness, wondering if those would be the last words I would ever say to my grandmother.

Chapter 5

"COME ON," VULPEERA SAID, PULLING MY SHIRT FROM BEHIND with her teeth. "Lillian will be fine."

I would have refused to leave except . . . *Lillian?* I hadn't heard anyone call Granny by her first name since . . . well, since ever. It was weird enough talking to a fox, but even weirder for it to be on a first-name basis with my grandmother.

"How do you know Granny?" I asked, but there was no answer. The fox had disappeared ahead through the tunnel, though I hadn't heard her leave.

I looped the necklace over my head and crawled after her, while Proctin followed closely behind.

The ground was wet and cold under my knees and seemed to be sloping downward. I tried not to think about how only a few minutes before I'd been tucked in my warm bed. I tried not to think about Granny. I tried not to think about anything.

"Hurry," Vulpeera said, her voice in front of me again. It was too dark to see anything, and it seemed as if the fox were flying through the tunnel. I couldn't hear a single noise from her except when she spoke. Proctin, on the other hand, sounded as if he were dragging a bag of bricks behind me, and made an odd wheezing sound when he breathed.

"You humans are very slow on all fours," he said.

"We humans don't normally crawl."

"We raccoons can walk just as well on two legs as on four." He let out a little grunt and I heard him lift his front paws off the ground, only to fall back with a wet thud. "Okay, maybe not just as well, but pretty close." He tried again with the same result. "I'll work on it."

As we moved deeper into the tunnel, Proctin continued to practice walking on two legs while I picked up my pace the best I could. It was difficult; the tunnel was narrow, with roots that slapped at my face and rocks that stabbed my knees.

"Vulpeera, how much farther?"

"Not much," she replied.

My hands were numb and my neck was stiff. I couldn't see anything, so I focused on listening and was surprised to hear a faint sound ahead, like rushing water.

"What's that noise?" I asked.

"We're getting close to Pteron's cave," Vulpeera said.

"Cave? I thought we were going to a cove."

"We'll catch a ride from the cave to the Cove."

"That's confusing. How will we—" My face smacked into the side of the tunnel as it took a hard turn left. The sound of rushing water had grown to a low rumble, and for the first time I saw a dim light.

Finally, an end to the stabbing pain in my knees, I thought.

I crawled about twenty more feet before exiting the tunnel into a large cavern with a dark river running through the middle. A light coming from one end cast jagged shadows on the walls as it passed through the stalactites and stalagmites, making it look like we'd entered the mouth of some overgrown crocodile.

"It's nice to be on two feet again," I said, as I stood and stretched.

"Two feet, she said two feet!"

I looked around. Someone had spoken, but it wasn't Proctin or

Vulpeera. The raccoon had tucked itself between my feet like a third shoe while the fox stood rigidly, looking into the dark cave like a bloodhound pointing toward a scent.

"Who's there?" I asked.

"She wants to know who's here."

"Tell her!"

"No, you tell her."

"Let Pteron tell her."

The cave had suddenly become an amphitheater of tiny voices echoing off the walls, drowning the sound of rushing water. Eyes—hundreds of small, yellow eyes—looked down at me from the walls and ceiling and stalactites.

"Is it her?"

"It must be her."

"The chosen one!"

"She looked at me!"

"No, she looked at me!"

"I can hear you," I said. "Who's there?"

My voice seemed to shake the sides of the cave, and the black walls began to shudder and move as if they were made of running water.

The voices became deafeningly loud.

"Enough!" bellowed a deep, resonant voice, and all the others faded away.

Two new eyes appeared up above, the same yellow as the others but much larger. They were like bodiless globes, hanging in midair as they stared down at me. I began to back away when they suddenly broke free from the ceiling and dropped toward me. I let out a yelp and covered my face as I stumbled backward. The gigantic yellow eyes stopped a few feet in front of me as the creature perched and spread itself out on a stalagmite: an enormous bat with a long, slender nose and tall, pointed ears. Its unfurled wings must have spanned a metre as it clung to the rock. Around its head, a crest of golden fur shimmered in the trickle of light coming from the far end of the cave.

"So," the bat said, "you must be Winter."

I nodded—still afraid, but slightly reassured by the calmness of its voice.

"Those eyes," he continued. "I have seen them before. And your hair. You have so much of your parents in you."

In this messed-up world of talking animals it was *my eyes* that were fascinating? "Wait—you knew my parents?"

The bat's mouth spread into a smile. "Of course," he said, nodding his head, "we all did. Your grandmother, Lillian, is a good friend of mine."

I thought about Granny and a lump suddenly formed in my throat, but I fought it back down. The last thing I wanted to do was start crying in front of these animals—especially if they had information about my parents.

"Who are you?" I asked.

"My name is Pteron," the bat said, "and I am the Sky Guardian of Wisdom."

He said this as if I should know what it meant.

"And you knew my parents how?"

The bat looked at Vulpeera with a confused expression.

Vulpeera shook her head. "Lillian has told her nothing."

"Nothing?" the bat questioned, his eyes momentarily widening.

"Nothing," Vulpeera repeated.

"I see," Pteron said, nodding solemnly. "Well, she will have to be brought up to speed quickly—the ceremony is in two days."

"Yes, I will do that once we are on the river. Forgive my urgency, but we shouldn't stay. Lupora already had the house surrounded when I arrived. It won't be long before—"

Vulpeera stopped talking. A sound had come from deep within the cave—a growling, scraping sound like dogs running on pavement.

Pteron's eyes narrowed to small slits. "How could they have known already?" he asked, shifting himself higher on the rock to look deeper into the cave. "I suppose it doesn't matter. They're here. Quickly, Cheelion is waiting by the entrance."

Vulpeera nodded. "Follow me, Winter," she said, and ran toward the light coming from the entrance of the cave, bounding over the rocks and stalagmites as if they were nothing more than a well-marked path.

"Who's coming?" I asked, looking back toward the scraping sound. "Why won't anyone tell me what's going on?"

Proctin took off after Vulpeera. "I'd rather not wait to find out," he yelled.

"Go with Vulpeera," the bat said. "She will explain everything. I will see you at the ceremony."

The noise was growing louder—whatever was coming was getting closer.

I turned and ran after Vulpeera, but tripped over the first stalagmite in my path. Cat-eyes or not, I wasn't very good at seeing in the dark.

In a heartbeat Vulpeera was by my side, helping me to my feet with her wet nose nuzzled against my arm. "Careful," she said. "Quickly but carefully."

Following the river, we ran toward the entrance of the cave. The ledge of rock grew narrower as the river widened, and I had to focus on the ground to avoid tripping. Behind us, the sound of growling and snarling grew louder.

"Hurry!" Vulpeera said, the urgency now rising in her voice.

I made the mistake of looking back. Dark silhouettes rushed toward us, and on the walls of the cave were shadows that resembled dogs.

"Are those—"

"Wolves!" Vulpeera shouted. "Come on—over here!" She leapt onto a large rock in the river, and motioned for me to follow.

"There?" I yelled. "Not there! We need to keep running!"

Panic was starting to take over.

"Get on!" Vulpeera cried. "Trust me!"

I remembered what Granny had said about trusting the fox, and jumped onto the rock. When I looked back, the wolves were only twenty metres behind—large, greyish beasts with wide, snarling mouths and sharp canine teeth. Their muscular shoulders flexed with every stride as they tore through the cave, bounding over the rocks and closing the gap between us.

I was going to die sitting on a rock like a meal on a dinner plate!

Just as that thought crossed my mind, the rock began to move. Not quickly by any means, but the shore was definitely getting further away.

"Hurry, Cheelion!" Vulpeera yelled. "They're closing in!"

The distance was growing but we weren't far enough. It was going to be an easy jump for the wolves.

The largest wolf pulled out in front and I braced for impact. It was only ten metres away . . .

Four metres . . .

Two . . .

Strands of drool dangled from its open mouth as it pounced.

31

It soared through the air, only to be engulfed by a black cloud that fell from the ceiling of the cave. With a splash it toppled into the water, howling as thousands of bats swarmed it from above. The wolves behind gave up their pursuit as bats continued to pour from the ceiling and walls. In seconds, the whole cave had become a frenzy of flying creatures so thick it was impossible to see.

Our rock gained speed as if caught in a current. The wolves jumped and snapped and howled in rage before the river banked sharply, and we left the cave behind.

Chapter 6

WE FLOATED DOWN A WIDE RIVER LINED WITH ROCKS AND BRAM-
bles and brush. Large, wilting trees reached out over the water, their
sinewy branches like fingers grabbing at us from above. It was night,
but the sky was brighter than any night I could remember. The same
golden moon I'd watched from my window now hung directly above,
illuminating the river in a yellowish hue as its light passed through the
branches.

We had slowed considerably when the river widened, drifting at a
leisurely pace. It was strangely peaceful, the noise of snarling wolves and
squealing bats now far behind us.

I realized I'd been tensing every muscle in my body and let myself
relax, loosening my grip on the rock below me.

The rock?

Somehow we were floating along the river on a rock—every few
moments propelled faster by some unseen current. In front of us was
a log, sticking upright in the water, leading us as we went. I tried to
make sense of it but was too exhausted to think. Everything had been
so strange. And with my adrenaline now gone, my body was devoid
of anything that might keep it going. I wanted to stay awake, to ask
Vulpeera about everything that had happened, but the urge to close my
eyes was overwhelming. I took off my backpack and laid my head on it
as Proctin curled his warm, soft body against mine.

"Vulpeera," I said, with a large yawn, "can you tell me about my parents?"

"Not now," Vulpeera said. "Get some rest. You're tired. When you wake, I will tell you everything. We have a long journey before we reach the Cove."

I thought about protesting, but Proctin's little body was comforting and sleep overtook me.

Voices floated above the gurgling of the river as I passed in and out of consciousness.

"Nothing?" came a voice, slow and soothing.

"Nothing at all," came another, not unlike Vulpeera's.

"Her father? The Guardians? The Cove? Why has Lillian kept it from her?"

"Shh—you will wake her. Let her sleep, poor thing. We will tell her everything tomorrow."

"But the ceremony is in two days."

"Shh . . . there will be time. There will be time."

WHEN I AWOKE, the sun shone bright and warm overhead, and we drifted between fields of wildflowers and long grasses. The world was still green from the recent wet season, but before long, the dry months would parch the landscape and paint it with yellows and browns. The mountains stood strong in the distance—the same mountains I'd seen so many times before, yet somehow these seemed different. We must have been far from home because I didn't recognize any of the peaks.

"Where are we?" I asked, sitting up and rubbing my head. Proctin stirred but didn't wake.

"About a day's journey from the ocean," came the voice from my dreams, the slow, drawling voice that seemed to pause between every word.

I looked over the front of our rock to see two black eyes staring back at me. They belonged to what I'd thought was a log the night before, but now realized was the head of a sea turtle. The rock on which I was sitting was its shell, complete with faded green plates that were chipped in several places, giving the impression the turtle was very old. I felt ashamed I hadn't realized sooner. But who was this turtle? And—

"Cheelion," the turtle said, reading my mind. "Water Guardian of Wisdom."

"Winter," I replied. "Grade nine at Dunvy High."

I knew as soon as the words were out of my mouth that it was a silly thing to say, but the turtle just nodded slowly.

"And the raccoon?" he asked, looking toward Proctin, now waking with a stretch.

"A sycophant," Vulpeera said. "He followed us from the house and managed to sneak aboard during our scuffle with the wolves."

I thought back to where I'd heard the word "sycophant." Biology class—Mr. MacPherson had said a sycophant was a parasite that lived off another creature.

"He's not a sycophant!" I said, looking angrily from Vulpeera to Cheelion.

Proctin's eyes widened and he quickly jumped between us. "Oh, yes I am!" he exclaimed. "Definitely a sycophant! One hundred percent sycophant! Left my colony a long time ago and haven't seen or spoken to them since. I live with the humans now."

Cheelion seemed to contemplate this momentarily. He had drifted toward the bank of the river and stopped in a calm pool next to a rock. "Sycophant or not," he said, "your kind made your loyalties clear a long time ago. This is the end of the ride for you."

Proctin clung to me as Vulpeera tried to push him off the shell with her nose.

"But, but, but . . . I assure you, I have no association with my kind anymore. I'm barely even a raccoon. I—I'm more human than anything. Yes, that's it, more or less human. I live with Winter. We're family!" He turned to me with pleading eyes. "Right?"

Vulpeera wasn't listening and continued to push, loosening Proctin's grip on my leg.

"Stop this," I said, putting my hand between them. "He's right—we're family. He lives under my house, and we share dinners most nights."

Proctin nodded forcefully. "Yes! Yes, we do! Dinner!"

Vulpeera looked questioningly at Cheelion.

The turtle shook his head. "Dinner or not, we will need to discuss private matters and can't have spying ears about. He must get off."

"Then I'm leaving too," I said, picking up Proctin with a heave and moving toward the edge of the shell. He was much heavier than I'd expected.

Cheelion looked deep in thought, and we stared at each other for a few moments before he turned back toward the river.

"Fine," he said. "Just don't get too comfortable, raccoon. Your ride ends when we get to the Cove."

I sat back down cross-legged on the shell, and Proctin climbed on my lap.

"Well," I said, "now that we've got that resolved, can someone tell me exactly where we're going and what this ceremony is?"

Vulpeera sat down beside me, her tail swishing back and forth. "Yes, we have a lot to cover before we reach the Cove. Best get started. Am I right to suppose Lillian has told you little about the Guardians?"

"Nothing," I said. "I don't even know what a Guardian is."

"And what of the amulet you're wearing?"

I instinctively touched the heavy stone around my neck. "She only said that it belonged . . . er . . . that my father had it when he died."

Cheelion and Vulpeera exchanged a look.

"Okay," Vulpeera said, "well, I suppose we must start from the beginning. To understand the Ceremony of Guardians, you must first know what a Guardian is."

"I'm listening," I said. Vulpeera stood and began pacing back and forth across the shell.

"The Guardians," she began, "are an ancient group sworn to protect the very thing that brings us life. In accepting our Guardianships, we take an oath dedicating our lives to protecting Terra."

"Terra? You mean the planet?"

Vulpeera nodded. "Yes, I mean the planet. But also, I mean more than the planet. Terra is the soil and the rocks and the creatures you can see and touch, but She is also the energy that flows in and between and around us all. She is as much our Mother as She is a part of us—the substance that binds and brings us together."

I mulled this over. "So, Terra is the earth but also some sort of life force? And you protect Her from what, exactly?"

"Anything that threatens to destroy Her," Vulpeera said.

"Destroy the whole planet?"

Vulpeera nodded.

I couldn't help but laugh. "What could possibly destroy the whole planet?"

Cheelion turned to me with an irritated expression. "Terra is more fragile than you think," he said. "She exists in a fine balance—upset that balance, and you destroy Her."

Vulpeera nodded her agreement. "We know this to be true because, long ago, it nearly happened."

"It did? When?"

"We refer to it as the Almost End. It was many years ago, and some of the details have been lost with time, but it is said that Terra was different back then. There were no Forgotten Lands and there were four seasons instead of two."

"Winter, spring, summer, and autumn," I murmured.

Vulpeera nodded.

"But those are stories from fairy tales. They're not true. There are only two seasons—dry and rainy."

Cheelion shook his head as Vulpeera continued. "There are only two seasons now, but before, when the world was cooler, there were four. Back then, Terra was healthier. Nearly all of Her land was inhabitable and the animals flourished."

"What happened?"

"As Vulpeera said," Cheelion interjected, "many of the details have been lost, but legend states that back then, the humans were even more advanced than they are today. They had learned ways to extract Terra's energy and used it for their machines and tools and weapons. They harvested Her energy and resources without thought for the future. They were greedy. And as Terra's resources dried up, fighting broke out. A war ensued. A Great War that destroyed most of the humans along with much of the land they lived on."

"But that doesn't make sense. We're still here."

"A few survived. And those who did swore to change their ways. They met with Terra and heard Her counsel. A Guardianship was formed—a group of animals given abilities and tasked with maintaining the balance."

"So, you and Vulpeera are both Guardians?"

Cheelion nodded.

"And how many of you are there?"

Vulpeera lifted her front paw, pointing at my chest. "Look at the symbols on the amulet. What do you see?"

I took the amulet in my hand and examined it. "They're animals," I said, counting them. "Twelve."

"Correct. Twelve animals, each representing one of the Guardians."

I pointed to the symbols in the middle—mountain peaks, a water droplet, and three swirling lines. "And what are these symbols?"

"They signify the three domains of Terra—earth, water, and sky," Vulpeera said. "Within each domain there are four Guardians, one for each of the four primary attributes: strength, speed, agility, and wisdom."

I found the symbol of the fox next to the mountain peaks. "Does this mean you are the Land Guardian of Speed?" I asked.

Vulpeera laughed. "No, not speed. Felinia would have a good chuckle if she heard you say that. I am the Land Guardian of *Agility*. And Cheelion is the Water Guardian of Wisdom."

"Oh right, agility," I said, remembering how Vulpeera seemed to glide rather than walk. "And the bat said he was the Sky Guardian of

Wisdom."

"Yes," Vulpeera nodded, "Pteron is the Sky Guardian of Wisdom."

I scanned the rest of the symbols, running my finger around the outside of the amulet. "In the water there's a whale, turtle, otter, and swordfish."

"Not a swordfish—a sailfish," Vulpeera corrected. "The fastest fish in the sea."

I nodded and continued, "And in the sky, there's a hummingbird, bat, and . . . um, what are these other two symbols? Birds of some sort."

"A falcon," Vulpeera said, "for the Sky Guardian of Speed, and a condor, for the Sky Guardian of Strength."

"Oh, a condor and a falcon," I said, tracing the symbols. "That makes sense. And on land there's a fox, a cheetah, a bear, and—"

I paused, looking up at Vulpeera. She nodded, as if she knew my question before I'd asked it.

"A human?" I said.

"Yes," Vulpeera confirmed, "the Land Guardian of Wisdom."

I swallowed hard. "And who's that?"

Vulpeera smiled.

Chapter 7

"ME?!" I SAID. "*Me?!* WHY ME?"

"Because Terra has chosen you," Vulpeera replied. "It is an honor."

My heart raced. "But I don't know anything about being a Guardian. Why would Terra choose me?"

"We do not claim to understand Terra's decisions," Cheelion said. "We are but servants to our Mother. She tells us Her wishes and we carry them out."

"That's right," Vulpeera agreed. "We do not question Terra. We trust in Her guidance."

"But shouldn't *I* have some choice in this? I mean, it seems like a lot to just say, 'Hey, guess what, you've been chosen to protect the earth or whatever—good luck!'"

"You do have a choice," Cheelion said, sounding somewhat annoyed. "The ceremony for the new Guardians is tomorrow night. There, you can choose either to accept your Guardianship or refuse."

"The ceremony is tomorrow night?! That's a little rushed, isn't it?"

"We have waited years for this ceremony," Cheelion said. "I would hardly call it rushed. Lillian has done you no favour by keeping you in the dark."

"Then can't it wait a little longer? Do I have to choose now? Can't I—"

"It cannot wait," Cheelion said. "It has been far too long as it is. Until all the Guardianships are restored, a new Terra Protectorum cannot be chosen. And right now, we need a Terra Protectorum more than ever. Terra is hurting. With each passing year, She grows weaker. A decision must be made. Whether it is you or someone else, a Guardian must sit on the humans' throne."

I looked at Vulpeera, hoping for some clarification. The turtle wasn't making much sense. "Terra Protectorum?" I asked. "What's that?"

But Vulpeera was no longer looking at me. Instead, she stared over the side of the shell at the passing riverbank, ears perked, back stiff, nose high in the air.

"What is it?" I asked, looking in the same direction.

We had drifted into a forest, and the riverbank was now lined with thick cypress trees that blocked the sun. It was eerily quiet but for the gurgling of the river. I had a feeling we were being watched.

"Vulpeera?" I prompted, lowering my voice to a whisper.

"Leave the girl be!" Vulpeera shouted at the woods, her voice startling me. "It is not your place to cast judgment. Terra has decided and we must trust in Her decision."

It looked as if Vulpeera was calling out to no one in particular, until a dark shadow emerged from the woods. At first I thought it was a wolf, but quickly realized it was far too big. It was enormous—easily four or five times as big as the wolves. It had thick brown fur with a grey sheen, and walked on four legs the width of tree trunks. When it reached the side of the river it sat back on its hind legs, staring at us. Even sitting, it was nearly half the height of the trees. Its head was like a wrecking ball, with a powerful snout and piercing red eyes that glared at me. It was a bear, but not like any I'd ever seen; it appeared to be the king of all bears.

A deep, powerful growl came from the back of its throat, and it flared its lips, revealing a row of yellow-white teeth. I'm not sure what I was thinking—I *wasn't* thinking, because I gave a sheepish wave.

This seemed to anger the bear, and it flung its head backward, roaring so loudly the trees shook.

I made a note to myself: don't wave at angry bears.

As the river carried us away, the bear's eyes never left me. I was only vaguely aware of the wolves that had emerged from the trees around it, standing guard like puppies next to their mother.

I was so entranced that I barely caught the urgency in Cheelion's voice when he spoke in his not-so-urgent sort of way. "Vulpeera," he said, "we have a problem."

I spun around to find a tree fallen across the river. But this was a minor issue. The real problem was the row of angry, growling wolves perched along the top of the log, watching as we approached.

Chapter 8

"CHEELION, CAN YOU TURN AROUND?" VULPEERA ASKED, A slight panic to her voice.

Cheelion turned upriver, but we continued to drift slowly toward the log. It seemed only to draw out the process of getting eaten.

"The current is too strong with this much weight," he said, and he and Vulpeera looked at Proctin.

Proctin's eyes went wide, and he hid behind my legs.

"Don't even think about it," I said, standing firmly in front of Proctin.

Vulpeera turned away. "We need to think quickly," she said.

The tree was only thirty metres away, and though we were drifting more slowly, we still didn't have much time before we reached the wolves.

"Maybe we can fight them off," I suggested, looking around for something to use as a weapon. I spotted a piece of wood floating a few feet away, and lay on my stomach. I managed to grab the stick, but it was waterlogged and flimsy. Besides, me with a stick against a pack of angry wolves wasn't exactly great odds.

Vulpeera circled the shell, scanning the riverbank. "What about the other side?" she said, but as she did, more wolves emerged from the trees on the opposite bank. We were trapped—funneled toward the waiting wolves.

I scanned the water for something else to use as a weapon, but there was nothing.

"Fetch!" I yelled, and threw the soggy stick toward the riverbank. The wolves didn't flinch. They just growled and looked angrier.

"What are we going to do?!" I cried, turning to Vulpeera.

"Catharia!" she said.

"What?"

"Catharia!" she repeated.

"I have no idea what you're talking about!"

She pointed up to the sky with her paw, where a giant bird flew above the trees, followed by four smaller birds. They dipped toward us and I saw that they were condors—bald-headed, black-bodied, grey-white talons glistening in the sun like scythes. I had seen similar birds living in the cliffs near my uncle's home, but this bird—the one in front— looked ten times bigger than any condor I'd ever seen.

They swooped low to the river with their talons raised in attack. The front bird's wingspan stretched half the river's width, and I froze in panic, my legs locking in place like rusted bucket handles. All I could do was watch as the birds swept toward us, ready to cut us like ribbons. My life suddenly had two foreseeable endings—diced like a salad by the condor's talons or chewed like a steak by the wolves. Neither was appealing.

I closed my eyes and braced for impact as the condors rapidly approached. They would be there before the wolves. Salad. My life would end as a chopped salad.

Soft feather tips brushed past my hands, and I opened my eyes to see the condors passing around us. The largest bird grabbed one of the wolves from the log and lifted it by its scruff like a kitten. The wolf yelped and cried as it was carried into the sky, before being dropped back down into the rushing water. The other birds weren't large enough to lift the wolves, but their talons scraped through fur and flesh and sent the wolves running for the woods.

Those claws were as sharp as they looked.

The birds turned to make a second pass but it wasn't necessary; the wolves had scattered and we passed unharmed under the fallen log. We rounded another turn in the river to find the huge condor perched on a tree trunk by the riverbank.

"Excellent timing, Catharia," Vulpeera said.

The condor nodded once, a quick dip of its head.

The powerful-looking bird had a collar of white feathers around its neck and over the tips of its wings. The rest of its body was black, and it stood nearly as tall as me. It stared, its eyes golden halos surrounding black pupils. If it hadn't just saved my life I might have jumped off the far side of the turtle and swum for it. The fierceness of its glare made me feel as if I'd done something wrong.

The bird said nothing as we continued to drift along the river. When we had twisted around another bend and the condor was out of sight, I pulled the amulet from beneath my shirt.

"Let me guess—that condor is the Sky Guardian of Strength?" I said, tracing the symbol of the condor with my finger.

"Yes," Vulpeera nodded. "That was Catharia, the Sky Guardian of Strength."

"She definitely looks the part."

"Catharia is a powerful Guardian."

"Doesn't exactly give off the friendly vibe, though, does she?"

Vulpeera smiled. "We all have our strengths and weaknesses."

"Speaking of strength," I said, looking further along the amulet to the symbol of the bear. "I'm guessing that wasn't just your basic country bear."

Vulpeera and Cheelion exchanged a quick glance.

"No," Vulpeera said, "that was Arctos, the Land Guardian of Strength."

"Then why wasn't he trying to fight off the wolves? Isn't he on our side?"

Again, Vulpeera and Cheelion looked at each other. "Yes, he is on our side," Cheelion said.

"Then why did I get the feeling he wanted to tear off my head and use it as a volleyball? Believe me, I have a pretty good instinct for when someone doesn't like me."

I thought about Penny and the Twin Terrors.

"He, well—" Vulpeera started to say something but stopped.

"He what?" I pressed. "Why do the wolves want to hurt me? Why are they so angry?"

Vulpeera sighed and looked away from me, toward the riverbank.

"How much did Lillian tell you about your father?" she asked.

Chapter 9

"My father?" I said. "Granny hardly told me anything. Why? What does this have to do with him?"

"Did she ever tell you what happened to him?"

"No! Never! She said he died of a broken heart." My hands were suddenly sweating. Vulpeera was finally going to tell me what I'd waited my whole life to know. "D-did you know my father?"

"Vulpeera," Cheelion warned, "this isn't for you to tell. If Lillian has kept secrets, there must be a reason. It is not your place to go behind Lillian's back."

"No!" I said, "I want to know! Please, tell me!"

Vulpeera's soft brown eyes looked at me with pity. "I'm sorry. Cheelion is right. When the ceremony is over you will go home, and you can ask Lillian yourself."

"But she won't tell me! I've tried asking a hundred times."

"Then she must have a reason," Cheelion said again.

I was beginning to dislike the turtle. He reminded me of Granny, all secretive and stubborn. Vulpeera, though—if I could get her alone, I might be able to find out something. She had obviously known my father. What was the big secret? What was it that Granny had been hiding from me for so long? And what did it have to do with the wolves trying to kill me?

I went to the far side of the shell and sat down. "This really isn't fair."

Vulpeera's soft fur brushed my arm. "Don't be disappointed. Things will soon start to make sense. Why don't you have something to eat? You must be hungry."

She was right. I was hungry. *Starving*, actually. Proctin appeared by my side as I rummaged through my backpack. Inside I found a change of clothes, a flashlight (which would have been useful in the cave), and some food—crackers, cheese, dried meat, apples, oranges, nuts, and a canteen of water.

I ate the crackers and cheese, sharing with Proctin, who drooled like a dog beside me. He gobbled down things faster than I could hand them over, until his cheeks were stuffed like a chipmunk's, while Vulpeera watched with a scornful glare. When she decided she'd seen enough, she walked to the other side of the shell and snatched a fish from the river with her snout before sitting down to enjoy her own dinner.

"Vulpeera, please," I whispered across the shell, hoping Cheelion wouldn't hear me. "Can't you tell me just a little?"

Vulpeera glanced back at me with sad eyes but made it obvious the conversation wasn't going anywhere. I turned with a humph toward the river and sat watching the ripples of the current and the fish beneath. The shoreline slowly changed from dense forest to open fields, and I occupied my mind by thinking about everything that had happened. The cave, the river, the wolves, the condor, the bear . . . So much had happened so quickly—or maybe not so quickly, since it felt like only a short while before the sky grew dark and I fell asleep with my backpack for a pillow.

WHEN I AWOKE, something felt different.

It was just beginning to grow light, the horizon a bright streak like the rind of an orange, and Proctin was no longer lying beside me. Instead, I found him watching Vulpeera picking the meat off a fish skeleton.

We were no longer on the river. The moment I sensed it, I sat up to find a vast expanse of turquoise and green water to my right, while a white-sand beach ran along the coast to my left.

"The ocean," I said, smelling the briny air and tasting salt on my lips.

"Yes," Vulpeera said, turning to face me.

I knew the smell well. I had spent a large part of my childhood on an island surrounded by the ocean.

"When did we leave the river?" I asked, watching the shore longingly. My back hurt from sleeping on the shell, and I desperately wanted to get off and walk along the sandy beach.

Vulpeera came to sit beside me, allowing Proctin to swoop in for her leftover fish. "We left the river a few hours ago," she said. "It won't be long before we reach the Cove."

The word "cove" pierced me like a knife. I'd forgotten where we were heading, and all my fears came rushing back.

Vulpeera read my expression. "You're worried," she said.

I nodded. "I still don't understand what the ceremony is. Like, I get that I'm supposed to be some new Guardian, but what *exactly* is going to happen?"

"The ceremony will have two parts," Vulpeera said. "First, the new Guardians will be sworn in, making their oaths to Terra. Once all the Guardianships have been restored, Luna Aurum—the Golden Moon—will reveal our new Terra Protectorum."

"Terra Protectorum—Cheelion said that before. What is it?"

"The Terra Protectorum is our leader, chosen from the Guardians."

I thought this through. "So, it's sort of like the class president and the student council?"

Vulpeera looked confused. "Class president?"

"Uh, never mind. So, what happens if I say no?"

"If you were to say no, there would be no Land Guardian of Wisdom, and a Terra Protectorum could not be chosen."

"Oh."

I looked at Cheelion, trying to gauge his reaction, but he showed none.

"And is there any chance that either of you might be the Terra Protecto—or whatever you call it?"

"The Terra Protectorum," Vulpeera said, emphasizing the words as she repeated them. "Cheelion is likely to be selected. He is the oldest and wisest of all the Guardians and would make a good Terra Protectorum."

"Thank you, Vulpeera," Cheelion said with a slow nod.

"As for me—it would be very unlikely. It is usually a Guardian of Strength or Wisdom that is chosen, though I have heard there have been foxes in the past." Vulpeera grinned as she said this.

"Well, I think you would be a great leader," I said.

"That's kind of you to say, but as it stands, it will likely be either Cheelion or Arctos."

"Arctos! As in, the bear that wants to kill me?"

Vulpeera grimaced. "Well, yes. *That* bear."

"But why would Terra choose him?"

"Arctos is misguided in his anger toward you, but he has shown himself to be a good leader these past few years. He could also be a good Terra Protectorum," Vulpeera said.

Cheelion nodded. "Yes, Arctos would be a strong leader."

Vulpeera lifted a paw and rested it on my knee. "Don't worry, once you become a Guardian, Arctos won't lay a paw on you."

This was meant to be comforting, but all I could think was: *And what if I choose not to be a Guardian? Then what?*

"Remember, it is in your blood to be a Guardian," Vulpeera said.

"In my blood?"

She glanced sideways at Cheelion. "Your father—"

"Vulpeera!" Cheelion cautioned, his normally calm voice making us both jump.

"Er, I was just going to tell her—"

"Now is not a good time to be telling anyone anything," Cheelion said. "We've got company."

"Company?" Vulpeera and I exclaimed together.

I looked over the side of the shell to see five black fins sticking out of the water, circling like sharks around our raft.

Oh great, I thought. *Here we go again.*

Chapter 10

THE BLACK THINGS STICKING OUT OF THE WATER WERE FINS—I'd
got that much right—but they weren't sharks. Sharks might have been
better.

Around and around they went, gradually making tighter circles so
that large waves rocked us back and forth, washing over the side of
Cheelion's shell.

"Cano!" Vulpeera growled. "Stop this at once!"

Four of the fins broke away while one continued to make slow, lazy
circles before stopping right in front of Cheelion's face, blocking our
way. A huge head popped up from the water in front of the fin, slick
and black with a white patch on either side. It was the face of an orca—
a killer whale—and it looked exactly the part: killer.

The orca glared at me as it spoke. "Give me the girl and you can pass
freely," it spat.

Vulpeera looked furious. "We will not give you the girl!" she
growled. "She has been summoned by Terra to be sworn in as the new
Land Guardian of Wisdom. Let us pass!"

The orca threw back its head and wailed a high-pitched cry. "You
would have this child—this daughter of a murderer—sit beside you as
Guardian?"

"What happened to your father was a tragedy," Vulpeera said. "We
all loved Orcavion. But this girl is not to blame. You cannot hold her
accountable for the mistakes of her family."

"I *can* hold her accountable, and I will!" screeched Cano. "Someone must pay! I will not have her sit beside *me* as Guardian while the blood of my father stains her hands!" He slammed his massive tail against the water. The wave it created washed over the shell like a small tsunami.

"You are not yet a Guardian," Vulpeera lashed, the agitation in her voice growing. "You would be wise to remember that."

"True," said the orca, "but then, neither is she. Until we reach the Cove, we are but two creatures with ties to no one. The humans have no reservations about killing, so why should I?"

The orca sank back beneath the water and started circling again. The other fins rejoined the effort, and with their size and speed, the waves grew. Cheelion's shell rocked back and forth as the water washed over it.

"Can we make it to the shore?" Vulpeera asked, turning to Cheelion.

"I will try," the turtle drawled.

Cheelion turned toward the shore but the orcas cut him off, brushing only inches from his beak. One of the orcas broke away from the others and made a wide, sweeping circle before rushing toward us.

"We're going to die!" Proctin shrieked, clinging to my shoulder. "Of all the ways to go—eaten by a giant fish—oh, the irony! If I live, I swear I'll never eat another fish again!"

The orca dipped below us at the last second, and a giant wave crashed over Cheelion's shell, knocking me backward.

Before I could recover, a second whale charged, and this time the wave flipped Cheelion over, sending me plummeting into the water.

I could see nothing but bubbles and rolling turtle, while shrill cries echoed like sirens in my ears. I managed to figure out which way was up and kicked hard for the surface, breaching and taking a huge gasp of air. Vulpeera was still atop Cheelion, somehow not even wet, and she reached toward me with her paw.

"Grab on!" she yelled, and I pulled myself back up onto the shell with her help.

Proctin climbed up on the other side, looking terrified and drenched.

I rubbed my eyes to stop the sting from the salt water, but before I could say a word, Cheelion was flipped again and I was flung back into the water.

This time I was sure it was the end. I forced my eyes open under water—I was too far from the shell to make it safely back. A whale would grab me and drag me to the bottom of the ocean, and that would be that. So, I waited for them to come . . .

But seconds passed and nothing happened.

My lungs ached for air, so I spun around and pushed for the surface. I emerged, sputtering and coughing, trying to get rid of the water in my lungs. Cheelion was ten feet away, but I didn't have a hope of reaching him. Not with the black fin cutting through the water toward me like a saw about to chop me in half.

Despite the hopeless situation, I frantically swam toward the shell, kicking and flailing, thinking about the sharp teeth that would sink into my legs at any second.

But they never came.

Miraculously, I made it back to the shell and pulled myself on board.

My body ached and I coughed until my throat hurt. I knew the whales would come again, and I would not be able to pull myself back up a third time. Proctin was lying beside me looking equally defeated—his chest rising and sinking deeply with every breath as he worked to suck air through wet lungs.

I lay on my back looking up at the sky, where a small flock of seagulls circled. This would be the last thing I would see. At least it was nice. Relaxing, almost, with the gentle rocking of the shell and the—

I sat upright. The waves had stopped, and the orcas now circled at a much safer distance. Something was keeping them away.

I looked around the turtle's head to find a row of sharp-looking white poles sticking up from the water like a fence.

"Isteel," Vulpeera called, "can you hold them off until we reach the shore?"

One of the long sticks protruded further from the water, revealing the head of a swordfish. No, a sailfish.

"I will try," the sailfish said.

As Cheelion swam toward the beach, the orcas continued to make passes, but the wall of swords banded together to form an impenetrable shield, repelling the whales in any direction they came. Again and again they were driven back, until the water became too shallow and they were forced to retreat.

"We will have to make the rest of the journey on foot," Vulpeera said. "It isn't far."

I jumped from the shell and landed in knee-high water. Vulpeera followed and we took off running. Even when we were safely on the sand, I didn't stop. It felt too wonderful. I was finally free of the shell.

"You see that hill up ahead?" Vulpeera asked, running beside me.

I looked down the beach and spotted a steep hill of rough black rock a few hundred metres ahead.

"Yeah?"

"That's the Cove. Once you are beyond that hill, you will be safe."

Safe? Wasn't I already safe? The whales couldn't go on land.

As soon as this thought crossed my mind, three large wolves appeared on a sand dune overlooking the beach, and my stomach clenched. The wolf in the middle lifted its head and howled before leading the other two in a charge toward us.

"RUN FASTER!" Vulpeera shouted.

Chapter 11

LET'S GET SOMETHING STRAIGHT: I WAS NOT AN ATHLETE. BUT I could have been one at that moment—that's how hard I ran. It's amazing what the threat of three hungry-looking wolves will do.

My feet pounded the ground as I followed Vulpeera toward the hill. It had been nice to stretch my legs, but now I wished I was back on the shell. No, strike that, I wished I was back in my home—pre-wolf invasion.

Vulpeera glided over the sand while my feet sank with each step, ruining any chance of a quick getaway.

The wolves moved along the dune above us, positioning themselves to cut us off.

"We're not going to make it!" I panted.

"Come on," Vulpeera called. "Keep running!"

When the wolves were fifty metres ahead, they cut straight down the beach and stopped in front of us. Our only route to safety was now completely blocked. I thought about running into the water, or up the sand toward the trees.

"Keep going!" Vulpeera yelled, so I stopped thinking, and just ran. "Whatever you do, keep running toward the Cove!"

With a burst of speed that made me realize how discouragingly slow I was moving, Vulpeera darted out in front. She charged toward the wolves and the largest one licked its lips. Vulpeera was like a small puppy compared to the massive beasts.

"Vulpeera!" I yelled, but she didn't stop. She leapt directly at the wolves, and they pounced.

The first wolf opened its jaws like a baby bird receiving a worm from its mother and closed them to find nothing but air. Somehow Vulpeera had changed direction mid-flight, dancing like a leaf in the wind as she passed over the wolf's head, tearing at its ear.

The wolf howled in anger and spun to grab her, but the fox slipped away, dropping from its back and darting between its legs. Vulpeera snapped at the wolf's ankles and pulled at its tail, sending the wolf into a spinning frenzy. A second wolf tried to help but it was no more successful than the first. It was as if Vulpeera were a ghost, or a shadow, or the wolf's own tail. Soon, all three wolves were turning and thrashing and snapping at everything and nothing, never coming close to catching the ruddy blur that darted among them.

I continued running, cutting toward the water to take a wide route around the distracted wolves, sprinting as fast as I could in the soft sand.

The hill was only about thirty metres away. I was beginning to think I would make it when I heard the yelping stop and turned to see one of the wolves streaking toward me. It was only a few feet away when it was caught by a red blur from behind, jumping on its back and pulling it over sideways. But while Vulpeera slowed the one wolf, the others weren't far behind.

I ran for my life.

I kept expecting to get knocked on my face by a wolf landing on my back, but it didn't happen. I made it to the hill and looked up. It was steep and rough and sharp, made from the same volcanic rock my science teacher had shown us.

I crawled up the slope, ignoring the pain of the rock cutting into my hands and knees.

I was nearly at the top when my foot was yanked backward, and my face slammed hard against the stone. Blood filled my mouth and bright lights flashed through my field of vision. The wolves' snarling was replaced by a high-pitched ringing in my ears as I lay face down on the rocks.

Whatever had grabbed me had let go, but I was too dazed to get up.

"Winter! Climb!" a voice yelled from behind.

I placed my hands—wet with blood—beneath me, and pushed myself up.

"Hurry!" the voice called again.

I pushed harder, lifting my body so I could crawl. The rocks shifted beneath me as I moved my grip higher, pulling myself upward.

One hand, then the other, I told myself. *Ignore the pain in your knees. Don't think about your hands. Keep going. Keep—*

Again I was yanked back. This time it was my side that scraped along the rock, pulling skin and flesh away from my ribs.

One of the wolves bit at my leg. It was odd—I saw the wolf's teeth sinking through my pants but the pain as they grazed the skin beneath felt distant.

I kicked with my other foot and it connected with hard skull. The wolf fell backward, stunned.

Keep going.

I pulled myself to the crest of the hill, waiting for the wolf to pounce again. And it did—this time lunging for my throat. It got within inches before abruptly stopping, like a dog at the end of its leash. Behind, Vulpeera held its tail between her teeth while gripping the rock with her paws.

"Jump!" she yelled through gritted teeth.

Jump? Jump where?

My head was still dazed. I turned and looked down the other side of the slope. It was steeper than the side I'd climbed, but at the bottom was soft white sand.

Jump there? I thought. It was too far down!

I looked back at Vulpeera but instead of one, there were now two wolves.

One leapt toward me.

It must have knocked me backward because suddenly I was falling, the jagged rock tearing at me as I went. The pain was excruciating, worse than anything I'd ever felt. I suppose it was a blessing when my head hit something hard at the bottom and everything went black.

Chapter 12

You're going to be okay now, Winter. It's safe here. Just relax.

I had never met my mother; she died shortly after my birth, but sometimes I'd hear her voice—soft and sweet and kind.

Don't worry, it's just a bruise. You hit your head, but you're going to be alright.

She was always looking out for me. Sometimes after a particularly bad day at school, I'd go home and lie with my face deep in my pillow and listen to my mother's reassuring voice in my head.

Open your eyes, Winter. It's nearly time.

I knew I should listen to my mother, but I was too content. I could hear the soft lapping of waves against sand, and a gentle breeze blew over my face, warm and soothing. I was having the most wonderful nap. I didn't want to open my eyes.

Winter! Open your eyes! We have much to talk about before the ceremony!

My mother's voice had changed—she sounded irritated. She was never irritated.

I opened my eyelids a crack but clenched them shut when a bright glare burned my retinas. I had briefly seen a silhouette but couldn't make out my mother's face.

I tried again. This time I squinted, keeping them open for a few seconds. They still hurt—come to think of it, my whole body hurt.

"Mom?" I said, trying to sit up but feeling a sudden stabbing sensation in my side. I lay back down.

"No, it's me—Vulpeera," the voice said.

"Vulpeera?" I opened my eyes to see a long nose and two gentle brown eyes staring back at me.

"You must have hit your head harder than I thought," Vulpeera said, an uneasy look on her face.

Ugh. So it wasn't just one big, horrible nightmare.

I was at the bottom of the rock hill, lying in soft sand. My head throbbed and I put my hand to where it hurt most, feeling a sticky wetness.

At least I had made it. And clearly Vulpeera had made it, too. I wondered if Cheelion was okay and if—

"Proctin! Where's Proctin?"

I hadn't looked back after I'd jumped off Cheelion's shell. Proctin would have been too slow to keep up, and the wolves—oh, the wolves— why hadn't I thought about him sooner?

"Don't worry," Vulpeera said. "Last I saw that raccoon he was high- tailing it up a tree beyond the beach."

"So, he's okay?"

"If the branches hold him, he'll be fine." Vulpeera chuckled.

"Good," I said, relieved. I looked around. "Is this the Cove?"

We were on a wide expanse of white-sand beach, enclosed by the black volcanic hill I had climbed over. Well, more like toppled over.

"This is the Cove," Vulpeera said. "Our sanctuary and ceremonial gathering place."

I stood up to get a better view. One of my knees must have been knocked out of joint because it popped as I stood, and a jolt of pain shot up my leg. I hurt all over and my clothes were shredded and bloodied. I'm sure I looked as if I'd just been mauled by a pack of wolves—which was fitting, I guess.

"This is where Terra chooses Her new Guardians?"

"Not exactly," Vulpeera said. "Terra's decisions are communicated through Mount Skire. The ceremonies take place here."

The cove was circular, about the size of the infield of the baseball diamond behind our school. A third of the circle was occupied by the ocean waves crashing toward the centre, where a large marble pillar stood like a monument. One side of the pillar—the side facing the waves—had a smooth slope to it, while the other side had stairs carved into the stone. It looked like a giant waterslide, and if I hadn't been so sore I might have given it a try.

Next to the pillar stood a nearly leafless silver birch tree with twisted branches and a knotted hole in one side. Scattered around the cove were enormous slabs of grey rock.

I hobbled toward the rocks to get a better look. They weren't placed randomly—twelve of them were arranged around the cove like the numbers on a clock. Four of the rocks jutted from the ocean. The stones were flat and round and all different sizes, and the ones on land each bore either a marble chair or a wooden perch.

Twelve rocks arranged in a circle . . . four in the water . . . four with perches . . .

I pulled out the amulet from beneath my shirt and looked at it carefully, then back at the stones.

One for each of the Guardians.

My legs ached with every step, but I managed to get to the closest rock—the largest by far. The grey rock itself stood as high as my chest, and on top was a gigantic black marble chair. It looked like a throne for some sort of king—some massive sort of king.

"The bear," I whispered to myself.

"Yes," Vulpeera said. I hadn't noticed her following me.

I started walking around the cove clockwise.

The next stone slab was a quarter of the size but otherwise the same, and a smaller black throne sat on top.

I looked at the amulet. "The cheetah?"

Vulpeera nodded. "Felinia, the Land Guardian of Speed."

"And this must be yours," I said, continuing around the circle to an even smaller throne.

"Yes," Vulpeera answered, following closely by my side.

I looked out to the rocks in the water. Each had a smooth, sloping side similar to that of the pillar in the centre. The sizes varied, but the amulet told me which Guardians they were for: the sailfish, the otter, the turtle, and—I looked nervously at the last—the orca. I shuddered at the thought of Cano's black eyes and deafening shrieks.

On the opposite side of the pillar were the Sky Guardian thrones. The hummingbird's was not much larger than my foot and had a slender stick for a perch, while the condor's was enormous and had a thick tree shaped like an upside-down 'L' on top. The branch had deep scars cut into the wood, presumably from the condor's claws. The falcon's and the bat's perches were similar but smaller.

When I'd completed my circle, there was only one throne left to look at. It was a quarter the size of the bear's, but even so, the chair was much too large for me.

"And this one must be—"

"Yours."

I spun around. The voice was not Vulpeera's.

"Who said that?" I asked, scanning the area but seeing only sand and stones.

"Up here," came the voice again, and I followed it to the top of the birch tree, where a white snowy owl sat staring at me.

Had it been there all along?

It wasn't a large bird—not like Catharia—and its white feathers shimmered silver in the breeze. Its faded yellow eyes were rimmed with black, its head rotated so that its body faced the opposite direction. It turned slowly, righting itself on the branch, watching me continuously.

"So," the owl said, "the young Winter Wayfair has arrived at the Cove despite the best efforts of a few. We are glad for it. Terra is glad."

The owl's voice had a resonant quality, as if it were bouncing off every wall of the cove.

"How do you know my name?" I asked nervously. There was something powerful about the owl, something that made me uneasy.

"I know much more than that," the owl said, puffing out its chest. "I know you are the daughter of Gregor and Autumn Wayfair. I know you have lived with Lillian since you were an infant and that every night you write in a journal. I know you spend your school year in Dunvy and your holidays on the island of Pitchi. I know you are bullied by your peers and tormented by your cousin. I know that in the evenings you watch the mountains endlessly. But most importantly, I know you are having doubts about accepting your Guardianship."

I stood with my mouth open. I wasn't sure if I should be impressed, or worried that I had a stalker.

"My name is Scanda," the owl continued. "I am the Guardian of the Guardians, Messenger of Terra, Keeper of the Cove."

The owl spread her wings and dropped from the tree, landing neatly on the sand in front of me.

"The amulet," she said, bowing her head.

It took me a moment to realize what the owl was asking. I reached up and felt the necklace between my fingers, the polished surface smooth beneath my skin.

Give it to the owl? But it was my father's.

Granny's words returned to me—it hadn't belonged to my father. Still, wearing it made me feel closer to him, as if it connected us. I didn't want to give it up, but I didn't want to deny the owl, either. I'd already had enough trouble with animals hating me that day. Besides, the necklace hadn't exactly brought me any luck.

I slipped the amulet from around my neck and laid it at the owl's feet.

Scanda grasped the chain with her talon, turned, and flew back up to the tree, where she placed the amulet around a high branch. It swung back and forth, glinting in the sun.

Vulpeera nudged my hand gently with her nose. "Come on," she said, "let's go rinse your wounds in the water and prepare for the ceremony."

Chapter 13

I STOOD IN THE SHALLOW WATER, RINSING THE BLOOD AND SAND from the gashes covering my body. The salt water stung like wasps, but Vulpeera assured me it would help the cuts heal. I hoped so—otherwise it was a really mean prank.

As I washed, I thought about everything that had happened. Two days before, I had been an ordinary girl attending Dunvy High (okay, maybe not *ordinary* with eyes like mine, but close enough), and now here I was, sitting in the middle of a sandy cove next to a talking fox after escaping both a pack of angry wolves led by an overgrown bear *and* a pod of angry killer whales. Truthfully, I didn't understand.

I took a deep breath and let it out slowly, feeling it catch in my throat. Vulpeera's soft fur rubbed against my leg.

"What's wrong?" she asked.

I took another deep breath, trying to hold myself together and keep my voice steady. "I just . . . I just feel completely overwhelmed. I've got you and Cheelion telling me I should become the next Land Guardian of Wisdom, and at the same time, there's a bear and an orca trying to kill me so that I don't. And I've got no idea what it actually means to be a Guardian. I appreciate that you've been trying to explain it to me, but, well, shouldn't there be some sort of handbook for all this?"

Vulpeera nodded. "I see how scary it all must seem, and no doubt Arctos and Cano have not made it any easier, but try to remember that it is Terra you will serve, not them. Our Mother's selection comes with both honor and faith. She is careful. She would not have chosen you if you were not ready. And from everything I have seen thus far, you are ready."

"*Ready*?" I lifted my arms to show the gashes. "Look at these! I'm one cut away from a missing limb."

"You don't give yourself enough credit," Vulpeera said, pacing back and forth in the wet sand of the surf. "You could have given up in the cave, or on the river, or on the beach. You could have stopped running and let yourself be killed, but you didn't, you kept going. It is a testament to your character that you are here. You need to trust in yourself. But more importantly, you need to trust in Terra."

I sighed, looking out across the ocean. "I don't mind trusting Terra—it's just that bear I have trouble trusting."

"Arctos is . . . misguided. As I said before, he will not touch you once you have taken your oath. And if he is made the Terra Protectorum, he will need you to teach him your ability."

"Ability?"

Vulpeera smiled. "Once you are made a Guardian, Terra will grant you an ability, to help protect Her and all of Terra Creatura."

"Terra Creatura? Do you purposely talk gibberish?"

Vulpeera laughed. "Terra Creatura is what we call the creatures of the earth. From the great condors and bears, right down to the tiniest of insects. As a Guardian, you are sworn to protect all of Terra Creatura."

"And I'm given some ability to help me do this?"

Vulpeera nodded. "Long ago, before the Almost End, there were no Guardians, and the balance of life was maintained by Terra Herself. But without responsibility, Terra Creatura grew reckless. They showed no concern for the balance and in doing so, they nearly destroyed our Mother. When it came time to start over and the Guardianship was created, Terra decided to grant control of Her balance to the Guardians. It was Her hope that with responsibility would come diligence. The many facets of Terra were divided, and each group of Guardians was given a piece to protect. The Guardians of Strength would protect Her elements, the Guardians of Speed would protect Her forces, the Guardians of Agility would protect Her fluidity, and the Guardians of Wisdom would be granted the most important responsibility of all—that of protecting Terra's energy."

"I'd be responsible for protecting Terra's energy with this ability She gives me? And then I'd have to teach that ability to the bear?"

"If Arctos is made the Terra Protectorum, then yes. It is the responsibility of each of the Guardians to teach their ability to the Terra Protectorum, whomever that may be."

"Why?"

"So that the Terra Protectorum may reach Unomnis, a state of oneness with our Mother."

"And then what happens?"

Vulpeera shrugged. "Honestly, I'm not certain. No one has ever mastered all twelve of the abilities, so this is all based on legend. But it is said that once a Terra Protectorum has mastered all of the abilities, they will reach a state of completeness. From this state, the Terra Protectorum will have the power to heal all. They will be omniscient and omnipotent—all-knowing, all-seeing, all-powerful. Everywhere and nowhere. Or so the legend goes."

I mulled this over as Vulpeera continued to pace, noticing that her paws made no prints in the wet surf.

"What exactly will my ability be?"

"For that, you must wait and see," Vulpeera said with a wink. "But I promise, you will not be disappointed."

"You and your secrets remind me of Granny," I said, rolling my eyes and walking from the water to my backpack.

Vulpeera was right—my cuts felt better. I sat down and took an apple from the bag, or at least the remnants of what looked like an apple. I tore off a bite of the bruised fruit, watching the sun make its final descent behind the horizon, the sky now a salmon colour.

A nagging question crept into my head as I sat. Since Cheelion wasn't around, I decided to ask it.

"Vulpeera," I said, cautiously choosing my words. "You said before that, um . . . that being a Guardian was in my blood. What did you mean?"

Vulpeera gave me a sly smile like she knew where this was going. "Guardianships are passed down through a bloodline. Whether it's to a son or a daughter or a niece or nephew, the next Guardian nearly always has some relation to the previous."

"My father was a Guardian?"

Vulpeera turned her head toward the water, scanning the waves. She didn't look back at me as she said, "Yes."

"And the whale—Cano—he called my father a murderer. That isn't true, is it?"

Vulpeera continued to stare out to the horizon, but for the briefest of seconds her eyes changed. What had that look been? I'd seen it before. Then it came to me: it was the same look my teachers gave me when they asked for something to be signed by my parents, only to find out I had none.

Pity—that's what it was.

"It's dusk," Vulpeera said, standing and turning toward the thrones. "We should take our places. The ceremony will soon begin."

Chapter 14

I sat on the throne of the Land Guardian of Wisdom, the marble cold and hard beneath me. It should have felt good to sit, but at that moment I felt anything but comfortable.

The sun had disappeared below the horizon until only a faint amber light trickled into the Cove, and in that light, shadows began to emerge. A cat-like silhouette, long and slender, crept over the wall and down toward the throne between Vulpeera and me. It climbed up and sat with a straight back, while its long tail swished back and forth behind it.

The cheetah, I thought. Vulpeera had called her Felinia, the Land Guardian of Speed.

A few seconds later, a streak of black fell from the sky like an arrow, weaving its way through the thrones twice before settling on a perch atop one of the Sky-Guardian stones. It was a sleek bird with brown wings and a white, speckled chest. I thought through the animals and recalled the falcon, the Sky Guardian of Speed.

It made sense—the bird had been only a blur until it landed.

I easily recognized the next two shadows from the sky: Catharia, the enormous condor, and Pteron, the bat, who flew as if he had the hiccups. Catharia sat on the largest perch, looking regal and intimidating, while Pteron hung upside down with his furry body half hidden beneath his wings.

The Water Guardians were harder to spot. One moment, the waves washed over empty rocks, and the next, they were occupied by shadows.

There was a small, pacing creature I recognized as an otter; a motionless mound that was Cheelion; a long spear pointing high above the water, Isteel. And lastly, a massive beast with black skin that gleamed in the dying light—Cano, the orca that had tried to kill me only a few hours before.

Cano was staring at me, his eyes like two burning coals. His hatred was unmistakable.

Why did he hate me so much? Had my father really murdered his?

I couldn't believe that. I wouldn't let myself.

The last Guardian appeared. My skin grew cold, and every hair stood on end as the enormous shadow lumbered over the wall. It suddenly felt hard to breathe, as if all the air had been sucked from the cove.

Arctos had appeared large at the river but when he walked toward me, stopping only a few feet from my throne, I saw how truly massive he was. His powerful shoulders were the same height as my head, even as I sat high on my throne.

The bear made no move to go to his seat; instead, he stood glaring at me, his face so close I could smell sour fish on his breath. His dark brown fur was tipped with grey, and on his right side was a bald patch of leathery black skin that bore an old scar. I couldn't help but notice his giant paws in the sand, claws half buried, but still visible enough to remind me how easily he could crush every bone in my body.

"Arctos, you are late!" a familiar voice boomed. Scanda did not sound pleased. "Take your seat!"

Arctos sniffed and gave an unconcerned shrug of his giant shoulders before turning and climbing onto his throne.

From her perch on the tree, Scanda glowered at the bear before swiveling her head completely around, looking at each of the animals in turn.

"Guardians of Terra," she said, "protectors of She Who Gives Us Life. May strength and agility and speed and wisdom forever hold us fair!"

"We live to protect," came a low chorus from around the cove.

"Tonight, we are gathered to accept two new Guardians sent by Terra, and to bear witness as they take their oaths of Guardianship."

There was a quiet murmur around the circle.

"For years, we have patiently waited while two of our thrones remained empty. They stood as reminders of Malum and its destruction. Tonight, balance will be restored. Tonight, we mend our circle. Tonight, we move past the destruction."

Again, there were murmurs, this time louder.

"I know some of you have concerns over Terra's selections," Scanda continued, "but I remind you to trust in your Mother. Trust in Terra, for She has been more careful than you presume."

The murmurs grew to grumblings of discontent.

The owl would have none of it. Her eyes changed, taking on a glow as she glared around the circle. The animals fell silent, one by one, as if their tongues had turned to stone.

When the cove was silent again, the owl continued, "Tonight, we call on Cano, son of Orcavion, to take his oath as the Water Guardian of Strength, and Winter, daughter of Gregor, to take her oath as the Land Guardian of Wisdom.

"Come forward, Cano. Come forward and take your oath."

The giant whale slid from his watery pedestal and swam to the centre of the circle. The moon had begun to rise, and golden light reflected off the water around the cove.

Once Cano had reached the pillar in the centre, swimming up the sloping edge so that his face was near the top, the owl raised her wings to the sky.

"Cano, son of Orcavion, Terra has selected you as the next Water Guardian of Strength, to protect all of Terra Creatura through your power and vitality, and above all, to pledge your life to protecting Her. In return, Terra will grant you the gift of Aquanios—the power to control the waves. Do you accept Her gift and honor Her request?"

Cano bowed his head and closed his eyes.

"I accept."

Scanda spread her wings wider and lifted them to the moon above. The plumes beneath shimmered a silvery-gold in the moonlight. As she chanted in words I couldn't understand, a vortex of water rose from the ocean around Cano. Higher and higher it went, until the podium and Cano were hidden behind a swirling water-tornado.

I stared in awe as the tower of water continued to climb, Scanda intoning to the moonlit sky all the while. The other animals' heads were bowed, their eyes closed. I considered doing the same but couldn't look away.

It lasted only a few minutes, then the owl lowered her wings and stopped chanting. The vortex sank back to the ocean and there rested Cano, looking somehow different. I couldn't quite pick out the difference—the sheen of his skin? The glow in his eyes? No, it was something more.

"May we welcome Cano, our new Water Guardian of Strength."

The animals barked and howled in applause while I sat quietly watching Cano, wondering what had changed. I was still trying to figure it out when the owl turned to me.

"Winter, daughter of Gregor, Terra has selected you as the next

Land Guardian of Wisdom, to protect all of Terra Creatura through your intelligence and foresight, and above all else, to pledge your life to protecting Her. In return, Terra will grant you the gift of Imperia—the ability to control Her energy. Do you accept Her gift and honor Her request?"

Everything was happening too quickly. I hadn't had a second to think. A million thoughts raced through my head at once. How was I supposed to agree to something when I didn't understand exactly what it meant? I looked over at Arctos, and he glared back at me with so much hate and malice I sank deeper into my throne.

My hands trembled. The cove was silent, all eyes on me.

"Well," Scanda prodded, "do you accept?"

I swallowed hard and took a deep breath.

"No," I said, "I do not accept."

Chapter 15

THE COVE ERUPTED INTO A CHORUS OF SQUAWKS AND SHRIEKS reminiscent of Grade Eight band class. I shifted back in the large stone chair until my spine pressed against the smooth rock. Across the circle, the birds fluttered their wings in agitation, the otter paced back and forth on its dimly lit podium, and to my left, Vulpeera looked at me with so much disappointment I could feel my heart breaking.

The only one who didn't seem phased was Arctos. He continued to stare straight ahead with a grin plastered beneath his black snout.

The noise was growing. Many of the animals had turned to those beside them and were talking in not-so-quiet voices.

"She said no," chirped one of the birds.

"What will happen?" came a voice over the waves.

"Has *anyone* said no before?" came another.

I felt like I was back at school, with Penny and the twins talking about me as if I weren't there. I needed to get away, but there was nowhere to run. I was trapped in a place far from home without the slightest idea of how to get back. If I ran, I'd be eaten by the wolves as soon as I climbed the wall, but judging by the looks I was getting, I'd probably be eaten if I stayed.

"Silence!" Scanda shouted from her perch.

A hush fell over the cove, until the wash of the ocean was the only sound.

The owl looked down at me as though deciding what to do. Throw me into the ocean for Cano and his pod to finish off? Or maybe it would be faster to let the bear crush me? I tried to swallow, but my throat was dry.

"Do you understand what it is you are saying?" Scanda asked. "You are turning down Terra—She who brings you food and water and air and life? You are turning down the greatest honor that can be bestowed upon a member of Terra Creatura."

I forced myself to look at the bird. "I just don't understand what is going on," I said, my voice shaking. "I don't get why I've been chosen. I don't get what being a Guardian means, and I don't think I'm the right person for the job."

"Terra would not have chosen you if you were not the right person," Scanda replied.

"Stop trying to convince her," Arctos's deep voice bellowed. "She has made her decision!"

"She has until Luna Aurum fades to decide," the owl said coldly.

"I don't care how long she has. She should never have been chosen in the first place. Malum courses through her veins, murder is in her blood. And I do not speak only of her father. Look what the humans have done to Terra. They strip Her forests, they blast Her mountains, they pollute Her air, all while one of them sits on that throne swearing to protect her. I ask you this—what good has come from the humans? What have they brought? We have seen this before. Destruction, that is what they bring. And she will bring it, too."

There was a mix of approval and disagreement from around the circle as the other animals voiced their opinions.

"If not her, then who?" Scanda replied. "Someone must occupy the throne. Balance must be restored. Without a Land Guardian of Wisdom, there can be no Terra Protectorum."

"Why must someone sit on that throne?" Arctos retorted. "Why can there be no Terra Protectorum without the humans? Have Terra choose another animal to stand as the Land Guardian of Wisdom. There are plenty of wise and willing creatures. Plenty who would not bite the hand that feeds them."

"But none as wise as the humans," the owl lamented. "As careless as they have become, they are a part of the balance."

"They are the destruction of balance!" the bear growled. "And Terra has chosen the worst of them. Have Terra choose another."

"If the girl refuses, we know the alternative," the owl said, and the cove fell silent. She took her time looking around before continuing. "I believe we are all in agreement that we do not want the alternative. The Guardianship must pass down the bloodline to Winter."

"I say we end the bloodline!" Cano yelled from across the cove.

"So you have already tried," shot Vulpeera. "Both of you!" She glared up at Arctos with more anger in her eyes than I would have thought possible from such a gentle creature. "Convincing Lupora and her wolves to hunt down Terra's selection? I would have thought hired work was beneath you."

Arctos's lips parted, and his teeth shone in the moonlight in an ugly snarl. "I did not hire Lupora," he said. "The wolf does as she pleases. I cannot help that she is attracted to power."

"You were there on the riverbank and did nothing to stop her."

Arctos shrugged. "I was there as an observer, nothing more. You forget that I was the one left to clean up the mess of this one's father." He pointed at me with a powerful claw. "If anyone besides Cano has the right to be angry, it is me."

"We cannot blame her for the actions of her father! She's only a child!" barked Vulpeera.

"She's *his* child!" Arctos retorted.

"And you are all children of Terra," Scanda bellowed. "Arctos, you are unwise to question Terra's judgment!" A sudden, icy chill fell over the cove, causing steam to rise from my lips. The owl glared at the bear so intensely, I half expected him to burst into flames. Or maybe that's just what I was hoping.

Arctos returned to his throne with a huff.

The iciness faded as quickly as it had arrived, and Scanda's eyes returned to normal. "Terra has made Her decision," she continued. "If Winter is willing, the Guardianship will pass down the bloodline to her. If she is not . . . well, let us not worry about the alternative just yet."

A chorus of murmurs followed.

Scanda turned on her perch and looked at me. "Winter, daughter of Gregor, hear me well. The choice is your own. I will not lie and say the path will be easy. But Terra has called on you because She believes in you. She needs you, just as She once needed Lillian."

"Granny?" I said. "Granny was a Guardian?"

It made sense. If Guardianships were passed down through a family, one of my father's parents had to have been a Guardian. It explained why Granny knew Vulpeera. It explained a lot.

"Lillian once sat on that very throne you now occupy, staring up at me with the same confusion and fear. She was a great and powerful Guardian—perhaps one of the greatest we have ever known. And I see much of her in you. Your father, too, despite the choices he made at the end, was one of the most powerful Guardians in the history of this order. It is in you to protect. Cast your fears aside and trust in yourself. But more importantly, trust in Terra. You have until the Golden Moon crests to make your decision."

I barely heard what the owl was saying. I was too caught up in thinking about Granny. She had been a Guardian? And she had kept it from me? Why had she kept *so much* from me? Once, years before, we had been sitting on the back porch after dinner, and I had asked her how my father died. I used to ask this question often, even though I knew the answers were always the same: "Not right now," or "I'm too tired to talk," or "One day, Winter, one day I'll tell you everything." But that day had been different. Maybe it was the glass of wine she'd had, or the warm breeze, but without turning toward me, she'd whispered seven words: "Your father died of a broken heart."

I had felt relieved at that time—silly, really, because it wasn't an answer. At least, not a real one. But it was more than I'd ever gotten before and somehow, it was enough. But there in the Cove, thinking back on that day, all I felt was cheated. Granny had kept secrets from me my whole life. She had kept me in the dark, and now I was surrounded by animals who knew more about my past than I did.

What would happen if I went back home?

More secrets, that's what.

I looked over at Vulpeera. She was standing on the side of her stone slab, staring at me, her eyes pleading. She was the closest thing I'd had to a friend in years. If I went back home, I'd continue to live in darkness, but if I stayed, she and the other Guardians might finally give me the answers I so badly needed.

And I could think of only one way to stay.

I turned and looked up at Scanda. "I won't need until the Golden Moon crests," I said, taking a deep breath and clasping my hands together to stop them from trembling. "I accept my Guardianship."

Chapter 16

SCANDA SPREAD HER BRILLIANT WINGS, AND THE SILVER BENEATH shimmered once more. I'd moved high up to the central podium and could see all around the Cove. The animals were waiting with their eyes closed and their heads bowed.

The wind picked up around me—a shrill whistle mixed with the sounds of sand and water rushing past. My hair whipped and my clothes rustled. I had to brace myself to keep from being blown off the podium. Around me the funnel rose, a great wall of ocean and rock, blurring my view of the cove. It was deafening. It was powerful. It was . . . gone.

As quickly as it had come, it vanished.

Or at least, the sound and the force of the wind had stopped.

But the funnel of water remained—high above me, trapping me inside. I was in the centre of the tornado, and it was eerily quiet. I didn't have much time to ponder this before my hands and feet began to tingle. It was an odd sensation. I suddenly felt weightless. I looked down to find my feet floating above the pillar. The wind was a solid wall of sand and water around me as I floated up into the night sky. I should have been scared with my body hovering precariously high above the stone pillar, but I felt completely at ease, like something was holding me—something soft and gentle.

A warm sensation spread through my chest and down into my legs, as if I were being submerged into a tepid bath, and my skin glowed a faint blue. As the warmth grew, the blue turned to a soft green. What had been comfortable at first began to hurt. I opened my mouth to scream, but nothing came out. The heat continued to grow. It spread from my chest down into my arms and fingertips, where it concentrated further. It was like having my hands on a hot stove and being unable to remove them. I wanted to cry, to yell, to fly away. My fingers burned a bright, searing yellow, and the pain became excruciating. I thought I was dying. I thought dying might be better. But then it vanished, leaving only a strange tingling sensation.

I drifted back down to the podium and landed softly. The wind died and the Cove reappeared. I could feel everyone looking at me, but I couldn't stop staring at my hands. What had just happened? They felt numb. I shook them to see if I could bring life back into them, but it didn't seem to help.

"May we welcome Winter, our new Land Guardian of Wisdom," the owl cried, and the gathering erupted into chirps and squawks and yelps. Everyone was cheering—everyone but Arctos and Cano. When the noises died down, the owl motioned for me to go back to my throne.

"Guardians of Terra," Scanda said, "our circle is whole. The balance has been restored."

My legs felt shaky as I walked down the sloping stairs of the podium and back to my throne.

"Let us move on to the second part of the ceremony—the choosing of a leader." Scanda tilted her head back and closed her eyes. The moon was now directly above her. "Heart of Terra," she called, "show the Guardians who will be their leader. Show them their guide in this time of turmoil and unrest. Show them their Terra Protectorum!"

The owl chanted in her unknown tongue, her face turned up to the moon above.

I looked around the circle. Vulpeera suspected either Cheelion or Arctos would be chosen. I prayed it would be Cheelion. If Arctos were chosen, it would be bad news for me. He clearly didn't want me sitting on a throne next to him. Vulpeera had said he wouldn't touch me once I was a Guardian, but I wasn't so sure. He didn't strike me as the honorable type.

The owl continued to chant and I heard the words "Terra Protectorum," but everything else was incomprehensible. On and on it went. I started wondering if maybe Terra had taken the night off. Maybe She wasn't going to choose anyone after all.

I looked at my tingling hands, searching for signs of injury. I was thinking that they looked pretty normal when, suddenly, they disappeared. Right in front of my eyes—there, then gone. I looked up and realized everything had disappeared. The whole cove had become pitch black. Had my eyes stopped working? Had all my senses stopped working? Everything had gone silent; even the waves had stopped, and I couldn't make out my hands even when I held them in front of my eyes. The only thing that told me I was still in the Cove was the hard stone beneath me.

What was happening?

I didn't have to wait long to find out.

The light came back with a searing glare. It shone right down on me, so brightly I had to clench my eyes to shield them.

Something touched my head—something hard and cold and metallic. It slid over my hair and down my chest. When I reached up to touch it, it felt familiar—smooth and heavy.

The amulet.

I opened my eyes, squinting to see, and found the rest of the animals staring back at me, slack-jawed. I had a sudden realization. The light—it wasn't shining on everyone; it was shining only on me.

Chapter 17

THE COVE WAS ONCE AGAIN THROWN INTO CHAOS. CHIRPS AND squawks of anger came from the Sky Guardians; fins smashing against water echoed from the Water Guardians; the cheetah chirruped; the otter whined; and all around, animals called out in confusion and alarm.

"This is madness," called the condor. "The child barely knows what it is to be a Guardian. How can she be expected to lead?"

"She hasn't even learned her own skill," added the cheetah.

"Scanda, what's going on?" asked Isteel, the sailfish.

But even the owl looked dumbfounded.

It was such a mess that nobody noticed Arctos.

Nobody except me.

The hulking bear had left his throne and was now standing on his hind legs beside me. He towered over my throne like a house.

"Terra has gone mad," he said, his lips curled into a snarl. "A Guardian, perhaps, but the Terra Protectorum? With the power of all the Guardians? You would be unstoppable. I will not stand by and watch our Mother condemn Herself."

Arctos lifted his large front paw like a hammer.

It was all I could do to raise my hands over my head in defense. My body tensed as I waited for the blow that would end my life, and I screamed so loudly it hurt. But not in my throat—it hurt in my chest. It burned. It burned the way it had when I'd been lifted off the ground in the funnel of water. The burning spread quickly into my fingertips.

A sudden flash erupted. A bolt of fire shot from my hands and struck the bear in the chest. He fell backward in the sand, fur ablaze as he howled in rage.

The cove went silent. All the other animals watched as the bear rolled around to put out the fire.

"I'm sorry," I said, looking around at the anxious faces. "Arctos, I-I didn't mean to . . ." but I couldn't finish my sentence. I had no idea what I'd just done.

Arctos put out the flames and stood, panting, his eyes wide.

"Hear me well, human," he growled, "this is not the end of this matter! I will not stand by and let you sit as the Terra Protectorum, growing stronger and stronger until one day you destroy us all." He looked around the cove at the other animals. "I, for one, will not give the usurper's child my power! I will not foster her family's conquest to destroy us all! To me, she will never be the Terra Protectorum!"

Arctos looked at me once more before turning and bounding over the black wall at a startling speed for something his size.

"Whoever stands beside her spits on the memory of my father!" Cano bellowed over the water. "I will not rest until she has paid for her family's treachery. Blood will be repaid with blood!" He slapped his tail against the water and slid from his pedestal, watching me with those haunting eyes as he sank beneath the waves.

Murmurs began to rise, but Scanda silenced them. "Guardians!" she bellowed, "I know you have questions. I know you have concerns. But you must have faith that Terra knows what is best. You must respect Her decision, as hard as it is to understand."

"Perhaps it will take a human to change the humans," Pteron said from his upside-down perch.

"True," called a small voice from the hummingbird's stone. "We are all in agreement that something must change. Terra cannot go on like this. We have all felt Her weakening. But we must be careful. Arctos may be quick-tempered, but he is no fool. There is some truth to what he says. The girl will grow to be powerful, and if she turns out like her father, there will be no stopping her."

"I have watched the girl grow since she was a child," Scanda said. "There is much of Lillian and her mother in her. If we guide her growth, teach her the ways of the Terra Protectorum, she may be the one to turn the tides of fate that have risen against us. She may breathe new air into our skies and fill our lakes and rivers with clean water. She may help undo the doings of her kind. But without your help, she will not succeed. You must stand behind Terra's decision and to do so, you must stand behind Winter."

A few murmurs of agreement came from the other guardians.

"I ask you this: who will stand behind Winter?"

"I will," said Vulpeera, jumping to her feet.

"As will I," said Felinia.

"Me, me, me!" chirped the otter.

"The strength of the sky will back her," said Catharia.

"As will its speed," said the falcon.

"I will help in any way—large or small," came the tiny voice of the hummingbird.

"I, for one, am honored to help Lillian's grandchild," said Pteron.

"The wisdom of the water will always do what is best for Terra," said Cheelion in his slow drone.

"The ocean's speed is here to serve," said Isteel.

Scanda nodded. "Good, then we are in agreement." She swiveled her head and looked down at me. "Winter, daughter of Gregor, there is much you have to learn, and in time it will all make sense. Terra is hurting and has called on you to aid Her. Even with the help of the Guardians, it will not be easy. There are many outside this circle who do not believe in the Guardians, dark creatures misguided by greed. For now, you will return home, where you will be safe under Lillian's protection. There, you will be visited by each of the Guardians to begin your training."

"And how do you propose we get her to Lillian?" called Isteel. "By now, Lupora and her pack will have surrounded the Cove. No doubt Arctos and Cano will have spread the word of the child's selection. Many will be angry. It will not be safe to simply walk or swim her out of here."

"Then she must be carried," Scanda said, looking toward the Sky Guardians. "Catharia, can you lift her?"

The large bird puffed out her chest and lifted her sharp bill toward the sky. "She will be heavy," said the condor, "but I can carry her. At least past the Red Woods."

"Good. That will be far enough. Fantom will travel with you as your scout. Lupora has allies in the sky," the owl said, and the falcon nodded its agreement. "Felinia can use her speed to follow on land and meet you past the Red Woods. From there, she will take Winter the rest of the way home."

The cheetah looked up from where she'd been cleaning herself.

"Me?" she said.

"Yes, you," Scanda said, turning her piercing yellow eyes toward her.

The cheetah's expression showed her disgust. "You want me to run through the Red Woods, with all the cobwebs and vines and—"

"Yes," Scanda repeated, her eyes glowing.

Felinia sighed. "Oh, alright."

"I will go too," Vulpeera said, stepping forward. "I may not be as fast as Felinia, but I can follow behind and keep up with Catharia." She jumped from her stone and glided across the sand toward me, where I sat with my legs dangling over the edge of my stone, trying to rub the pain out of my hands. Vulpeera nuzzled up against my legs.

"Don't worry," she whispered. "You'll be home soon."

PART 2: THE FOREST

An old woman sits alone in her bedroom, a torn picture in her hand, wondering if things could have been different.

She cannot see the photograph; her eyes are sealed by deep scars, but she knows what the picture shows, and holding it in her hands reminds her of the day the image was captured.

A young man and woman stand at the top of a grassy hill. The man is behind the woman, his arms around her waist, his hands cradling her pregnant belly. Not far behind sit a bear and a fox.

"They were so happy then," the woman reflects. "If only things could have turned out differently."

She returns the picture to the dresser before walking to the open window, where she can hear the wind outside. The cicadas sing and a coyote howls. The world is alive, yet it is dying.

"Was I wrong to lie?" the woman asks herself. "Was it selfish? I should have known that Terra would come asking. If I had told the truth, might I have prevented so much harm? They were lies—yes— but is it wrong to lie to protect the ones we love?"

The woman sighs. She knows the answer.

All lies hurt.

But now the girl knows about her father.

She knows the truth.

Well . . . most of it.

Chapter 18

CATHARIA'S SHARP TALONS WERE SURPRISINGLY GENTLE AS SHE gripped me beneath my arms. The sand whirled around us as she beat her powerful wings, and for the second time that night, my feet were lifted from the ground.

The Cove became a small anthill below as we flew higher into the sky, an anthill whose dark outer walls crawled with dozens of prowling shadows.

Wolves, I thought, happy to be high above them.

Something whipped past my face and I shrieked in alarm. "What was that?!"

It passed again, a single gust of wind like an arrow through the night.

On the third pass, the little gust slowed beside us; it was Fantom, the sleek falcon, cutting through the sky. His body was designed for speed, and he barely needed to beat his wings to keep up with us as he flew beneath Catharia's wing. We circled the Cove once, waiting as Felinia and Vulpeera climbed to the top of the black wall, then nodded to let us know they were ready.

As we set off inland, I noticed one tree near the Cove with a particularly dense pack of wolves beneath it. There must have been twenty or thirty of them, and the ones nearest the trunk stood on their hind legs, looking up into the branches. The top of the tree was bowed like a fishing rod, and on a thin branch near the top sat a fat raccoon.

"Proctin!" I yelled. "Catharia, turn around! That tree over there, the one surrounded by wolves—do you see it? Proctin needs our help!"

Catharia continued flying as if she hadn't heard me.

"Catharia! Please! My friend is in trouble!"

Catharia still didn't respond.

"Fantom," I said, appealing anxiously to the smaller bird. "Please, Fantom—can you go help him? He lives with me. We're practically family."

When it looked as if Fantom wasn't going to help, either, I tried a different tactic.

"I thought Guardians were sworn to protect *all* Terra Creatura!" I said.

The falcon looked back at Proctin and then up at Catharia. Catharia must have nodded, because Fantom turned and disappeared behind us. Before I'd even had the chance to see where he'd gone, he was back, Proctin squirming in his talons as he hung by the scruff of his neck.

"Let me go, you dirty pigeon," Proctin wailed, unsuccessfully trying to smack Fantom with his short arms.

"Good Terra, this thing must weigh as much as a walrus. And did he just call me a pigeon? Some thanks for rescuing him."

"Rescuing me?" Proctin cried, indignant. "Who said anything about needing rescuing? I'll have you know I was preparing a frontal assault on those drooling fleabags when you came along."

"A frontal assault?" Fantom laughed. "Looked more like hiding in a tree."

"I was breaking them down mentally, birdbrain. Something you wouldn't understand."

"The only thing breaking was that branch. You must be the fattest creature in all of Terra Creatura. Are you sure you're a raccoon?"

"Of course I'm a raccoon, you imbecile. Now, unhand me."

Fantom let go with one talon, and Proctin shrieked. "No, no, no, not up here! Not up here! I don't fly well!"

"Proctin," I called, "over here! I asked Fantom to help you."

Proctin lifted his head and looked at me. His giant belly hung down like a leaf filled with rain.

"Winter!" he cried. "Am I glad to see you!"

"And I'm glad you're still in one piece! Catharia and Fantom are taking us home. We'll be there soon!"

The word "home" had never sounded so sweet.

Proctin looked equally excited. "Oh, home!" he squealed. "I can smell my sweet, sweet garbage bin already! In that case, faster, birdbrain! Faster!"

Fantom didn't seem altogether pleased, but he grabbed Proctin with both talons and continued on, leading us away from the Cove.

I<small>T WAS A</small> relatively clear night, with only a few clouds scattered beneath the grey sky. Below us, the ground was a blur—partly because we were so high up, and partly because my eyes were starting to close.

You'd think it would be impossible to fall asleep dangling thirty metres above the ground in a condor's talons, but after the night I'd had, I could have fallen asleep in a rosebush. Between the rhythmic sound of beating wings and the rushing air, I closed my eyes and was asleep before I knew it.

When I awoke, the sun was rising, and green hills whizzed by below. I didn't know where we were, but I recognized the mountains to my left. They told me we were heading in the right direction. They told me we were heading home.

"It's not fat; it's storage!" a voice said behind me. Proctin and Fantom were twenty feet back, arguing.

"Storage for what?" Fantom asked.

"A famine."

"I wasn't under the impression there was a famine."

"Not now, birdbrain. In case there *is* a famine. It's called preparation. Look, there's a reason you're not the Sky Guardian of Wisdom, and I'm living with a human. Leave the thinking to me."

Fantom laughed. "You? As smart as a human? I bet you couldn't even tell me how many toes are on your feet."

"I can so!" Proctin scoffed.

"Alright then . . . ?"

Proctin hesitated. He lifted his feet to count his toes, but his belly was in the way. He lifted his belly, but couldn't stretch his toes far enough to see them. I couldn't help but laugh.

"Well?" Fantom prodded.

Proctin let go of his belly and concentrated. He concentrated so hard his whole face wrinkled and his eyes closed. For a moment, I thought he might pass out from concentrating so hard when suddenly, he did.

His body went limp and his head slumped forward. "I can't answer right now," he said. "I've fallen asleep."

Fantom looked down at him with a perplexed expression. "You've fallen asleep?"

"That's right," Proctin said, his head hanging. "Haven't you seen anyone sleep before? Now leave me alone."

"You don't look like you're asleep. And you're talking."

"It's called sleep-talking."

Fantom looked more confused than ever but didn't press it. For a while we flew on, Proctin doing a very poor job of pretending to be asleep, Fantom looking baffled, me enjoying the scenery.

It was a perfect day for flying. The sun was warm, the breeze gentle, and there wasn't a cloud in the sky. Well, at least not one nearby. A single, dark storm cloud hung over a distant mountain, but I paid it no mind. It was too far away to bother us and besides, I was enjoying the way our shadows danced over the hills and fields below.

I looked closer. One of the shadows had a funny way of moving very quickly, then stopping, waiting for the other shadow to catch up before moving on. That didn't make sense—Fantom and Catharia were flying at a steady pace.

I squinted. When the faster shadow stopped to wait for the other to catch up, I saw a distinct yellow sheen and realized the shadow was Felinia, the cheetah. She ran in spurts, then waited for Vulpeera to catch up. I smiled, watching the fox and cheetah prance over the foothills and fields and . . .

"Catharia, what's that?" I asked.

Vulpeera and Felinia had stopped in front of a wide path of dirt—like a scar across the landscape. It reminded me of a riverbed without water, but far more regular in shape.

Catharia made a noise not unlike a grunt. "You should know," she said. "It's your kind's creation."

I thought about this for a moment. Why would we make a path of dirt in the middle of nowhere? Why clear all the trees and rocks? It appeared to be heading straight toward the mountains.

"The roadway!" I exclaimed, the answer dawning on me. "They're extending the roadway! The Society is building a giant path called a road. It's for cars to drive on. They've connected almost all the major cities of Nacadia, and it's made travelling much easier."

"Easier!" Catharia scoffed. "Perhaps for your species! For the rest of us it, has made travelling decidedly more difficult. Homes have been destroyed, migratory paths cut off, animals have been killed trying to cross your so-called roadway. It's an ugly gash through Terra and not one I'd take pride in." She shook her powerful head and I felt myself shrink inside.

An awkward silence ensued before Fantom flew up beside us and whispered in an urgent tone, "They're tracking us."

Catharia nodded in agreement.

I followed Fantom's gaze to the mountains. The storm cloud I'd seen earlier had tripled in size and appeared to be much closer. Not only that, it seemed to be growing, a large spout of black smoke pouring from the mountain like a chimney.

Smoke. No, not smoke. Smoke didn't move like that . . .

Smoke didn't follow people.

Chapter 19

THE DARK CLOUD'S SHAPE SHIFTED AS IT MOVED TOWARD US.

"I don't think we can outfly them with this load, and we can't use our talons to fight them off, either," Fantom said. "I could jettison some weight and try to head them off."

Proctin yelped, but Catharia shook her head.

"It won't do any good," she said. "There are thousands of them. Head for the Red Woods—the trees will provide shelter for the girl."

The ground below had changed from grassy fields to a grey, gravelly dirt leading toward a large forest. The trees grew thick and dark, but the trunks glowed red in the morning sun.

Catharia and Fantom's wings beat faster as they sped toward the forest, but even with our increased speed, the cloud continued to gain. A shrill cawing sound grew louder as it neared, reminding me of the seagulls on Pitchi. I craned my neck for a better look. The cloud was no more than a hundred metres behind—it wasn't smoke, but an enormous murder of crows. Thousands, Catharia had estimated, and she was probably right.

"Why are the crows after us?" I asked, panicked.

"They follow the Dark Queen," Catharia said.

"The Dark Queen?"

"It's the name Lupora has given herself. The Red Woods are her domain and she has long hated the Guardians."

"Why?"

"Call it something of a grudge against Terra," Catharia said. "Lupora wants only one thing—power—and she resents that the wolves do not have a throne in the Cove. There are many that now side with her against the Guardians. They call themselves the dark creatures."

"But why would they side against us? Don't we protect all of Terra Creatura?"

"Yes, we do, but Terra Creatura is fractured. There is a growing distrust of the Guardians, and it's not hard to see why. We have weakened, and have been without a leader for years. Combine this with the fact that you humans have a throne in the Cove, and you have their reasons for doubting our goodwill."

Our conversation was growing difficult. The growing sound of cawing and fluttering wings drowned out our voices.

"Dive," Catharia said, and she and Fantom dropped lower as the first of the crows nipped at my heels.

It worked for a moment; the crows were slow to respond, but soon they moved above us like a giant thunderhead. We were trapped.

I looked up just as the birds dropped, surrounding us like smog so all I could see was black feathers and beaks. I shielded my face with my hands, but it was no use—talons scraped at my arms and yanked at my hair. I tried to yell but got a mouthful of feathers instead.

Catharia thrashed wildly with her beak, grabbing crow after crow and tossing them aside to drop limply below. But it wasn't enough—every crow she crushed was replaced by another five.

"To the woods!" Fantom shouted as Proctin yelped.

We dropped again, now only twenty feet from the ground. I had a moment to breathe and see the forest ahead—it was close—but the crows descended quickly, blocking my view. I kicked and batted, but it was like running through a wall of stinging nettle. A feeling I recognized from the Cove formed in my chest—a deep, burning sensation.

Not now, I thought, *not with Catharia holding my arms.*

I tried to fight the sensation, to stop it from spreading into my arms and hands, but the heat grew despite my effort. It grew until I felt ready to burst. My hands glowed a faint yellow and I was certain they were going to erupt. I screamed, trying to fight it, when suddenly Catharia's talons released my arms. I dropped through the air and the heat left me as I fell.

I knocked against feathered bodies as I plummeted to the ground, hitting it sooner than expected and rolling between two large tree trunks. Catharia dropped beside me, closing her wings at the last second to fit between the trees, and disappearing into the woods beyond.

"In here," she called.

The flock hit the trees like a wall, but those that got between the trunks tore at my hair. I crawled backward into the woods, shielding myself.

The crows began to pull back, unwilling to follow us into the forest.

I heard a thump. Proctin somersaulted into the trees, followed closely by Fantom. The crows were behind them, but Fantom turned and snapped his beak. He was much bigger than the black birds, and they pulled away.

The squawking and cawing faded as the flock took to the sky. Through the open spaces between the trees, they rose—hovering, waiting, blocking our escape.

I exhaled and lay back, my head resting in the softness of the mossy forest floor.

I'm alive, I thought, *I can't believe I'm alive . . .*

Also, I hate *crows.*

Chapter 20

I must have lain with my eyes closed for nearly ten minutes. No one said a word. The only reason I knew we were still together was the familiar sound of Proctin's high-pitched breathing.

"That . . . was close." I finally said.

I sat up to investigate my wounds. My body was a mangled mess. Between the scabs from where I'd fallen on the rocks in the Cove and the thin gashes from the crows' talons, I looked like some sort of cutting board.

I moved my legs to make sure they weren't broken.

Assured I was still in one piece, I stood up and looked around. The forest was dark and dense. Thick trees surrounded us, their winding branches curled and crisscrossed overhead like a spider's web. Not a single beam of light passed through the canopy, yet somehow it was bright enough to see. I realized the light was coming from the trees themselves—dull red streaks ran up and down the trunks as if an animal had clawed the bark and caused it to bleed.

I walked over and touched one of the glowing streaks.

It was sticky.

Sap, I thought. *The sap is glowing.*

"What is this place?" I asked.

"The Red Woods," Proctin said, stomach dragging as he came up beside me. "We shouldn't be here. Me least of all. No, no, no—definitely not. This is a bad place. A very bad place for Proctin."

"Well, it can't be worse than up there," I said, pointing toward the sound of the crows still circling above.

"Much worse," Proctin said. "Here is much worse." He grabbed my hand and pulled me as if to leave.

Something caught my eye, something moving overhead in the branches. I was sure of it, yet when I looked directly at the spot, there was nothing.

"You've been here before?" I asked, letting go of Proctin's paw and moving further into the trees, trying to confirm if I had indeed seen something moving.

"I was born here," Proctin said, now pulling on my pant leg. "And left for a reason. Which is why we need to go—right now."

"Leave right now?" a voice said from somewhere in the blackness above. "Without saying hello to your family?" Proctin jumped at the sound of the voice and scurried between my legs. I followed the sound to a small set of eyes moving along a branch above. "To think, my very own brother, returned after all these years in exile, and he wishes to leave without so much as a hello."

The eyes moved down a trunk into the dull red glow of the sap, and behind them appeared the body of a raccoon. It was much smaller than Proctin, maybe half his size, and had none of Proctin's gentleness in its glaring eyes. It was grinning as it approached, showing a row of sharp teeth.

"The years have not been kind to you, brother," it continued. "Living with the humans has made you even fatter. Mother would be most unhappy. After all, it was your gluttony that brought shame to our family."

Proctin peered out from behind my leg. "Mother? Is she here?"

"You won't be seeing her," the raccoon snapped. "Never to return, that was the deal. I recall there was a punishment if you were ever to set foot here again. What was it, again?"

"I forget," Proctin said meekly.

"Oh, I doubt you do," the other raccoon retorted.

"No dinner for a week?" Proctin offered.

The raccoon cackled, and the forest around him laughed back. Hundreds of similar eyes appeared in the darkness above.

"No," the raccoon said, "though it would be entertaining to watch you try to go so long as a day without food. The punishment for returning was"—he looked around dramatically before turning back to Proctin—"*death*!"

He hissed this last word and the forest hissed back, a horrible, high-pitched noise that echoed in my ears.

"But, but, I'm hardly even *in* the Red Woods. Couldn't you just say I was never here?" Proctin whimpered.

"I don't think so," the raccoon said, smiling. "Rules are rules."

The raccoon was now on the ground, stalking closer to Proctin. I stepped forward and blocked its path.

"Wait a minute," I said. "Who do you think you are, saying all these nasty things to your brother? You should be ashamed of yourself." The raccoon looked at me fiercely. If I wasn't five times its size I might have been afraid.

"Who am I?" the raccoon said angrily. "Who am I?! I am Raycor, King of the Red Wood Raccoons, servant of Lupora, and you are in her domain. So, the question is—who are you?!"

Catharia hopped in front of me. "This is Winter," she said, "Land Guardian of Wisdom and newly elected Terra Protectorum. You would be wise to address her accordingly. We demand safe passage through these woods and are uninterested in your family quarrels."

"The Terra Protectorum?" Raycor said, his eyes fixing on mine. Hundreds of other raccoons slunk down the branches and tree trunks, filling the area. "Your demands mean nothing here, bird, this is Lupora's domain and we answer only to her. But I'm sure our queen would be more than pleased to meet your new little"—Raycor stopped mid-sentence, his eyes brightening—"no . . . it can't be." He crept closer. "Yes! It is! She has it! The amulet!"

"The amulet!" a chorus echoed from all around.

I grabbed the amulet and tucked it under my shirt.

"Get it!" he hissed, and the raccoons surrounded us. They moved like little zombies, their hands reaching up toward my chest.

The first raccoon grabbed my leg, and I shook it off.

"Stop that!" I yelled, but they kept coming.

Catharia fluttered her massive wings, sending a number of raccoons sprawling. She cried a piercing cry and grabbed the closest raccoon with her beak, whipping it aside.

Still the raccoons came.

On the ground, Fantom's and Catharia's talons were useless, and the dense canopy prevented them from taking to the sky. All they could do was snap their beaks and bat their wings, but there were too many raccoons.

Something grabbed at my hair from above. I ducked and tried to back away, stumbling over the sea of raccoons as I did. A raccoon fell from the branches and landed on my backpack. I grabbed it and flung it away, but another replaced it quickly. The raccoons scrabbled up my legs, and as much as I kicked and flailed, I couldn't stop them.

They grabbed at the amulet, pulling the chain so that it dug tightly into my neck. The weight of several raccoons on my back made me buckle to the ground, and little hands grabbed at every part of me. I was drowning in a sea of fur. The amulet slipped from my fingers as they pulled it over my head.

"Nooooo!" I yelled, but there was nothing I could do except watch as the raccoons passed the amulet overhead. It was nearly halfway up a tree when something leapt through the air and snatched it.

A cat-like cry roared through the woods, and raccoons flew in every direction. Suddenly afraid, the raccoons turned and scurried back up the trees, fleeing into the darkness. Felinia and Vulpeera worked quickly, their jaws gnashing at anything that moved. Raccoons flew left, right, and centre. One hit a tree next to me and dropped with a thump.

Two more followed—thump, thump.

The raccoons climbed desperately, but even those halfway up the trees were not safe. I had never seen anything as fast as Felinia. My eyes couldn't move quickly enough to follow her. There, then there, then there—all around, all at once.

It was over in less than a minute, and Felinia and Vulpeera stood panting in the small clearing.

"About time you arrived," Catharia grumbled, smoothing her ruffled feathers with her beak.

"Sorry," Vulpeera said, "we came as quickly as we could. Is everyone alright?" She approached me and dropped the amulet from around her neck to the ground. "Keep this safe," she said.

"Easier said than done," I said, picking up the amulet and putting it around my neck.

She nodded sympathetically and turned back to Catharia. "It would appear the sky is no longer an option. The crows are still circling, and the longer we wait, the more time we give the wolves to catch up. They saw us leaving the Cove and followed. If we are lucky, we should be able to pass through the Red Woods without much resistance, as most of the wolves were out on the hunt."

Catharia nodded.

"Felinia, can you carry Winter?" Vulpeera asked.

Felinia was still peering into the trees but turned around. "On my back?" she asked.

"Yes."

"But I just gave my coat a good cleaning this morning."

"Felinia!" Vulpeera barked, looking cross.

"Oh, fine," the cheetah grumbled, sitting down and licking her paws. "I suppose I could carry her."

"Good. Then we must leave at once. Felinia is fast—the fastest—but in the tight quarters of these woods she will be greatly hindered."

"I will fly ahead and tell Lillian you are coming," Catharia said. "Fantom, you return to the Cove and update the others on what has happened."

Fantom had been pacing back and forth on the spot, staring up into the sky anxiously. "Yes, back to the sky," he said. "I'll return to the Cove just as soon as I've had my fill of crow." He took off through the trees and was gone.

Catharia turned back to us. "Be careful," she said, "these woods are full of dark creatures."

"We will." Vulpeera nodded.

The condor hopped to the edge of the woods to spread her massive wings, and took off.

"Okay," Vulpeera said, "let's go."

I reached down and grabbed Proctin before walking over to Felinia. She looked at Proctin with disgust but said nothing as she bent down low, her belly near to the ground, allowing me to climb on.

"Hold tight," she said, before leaping forward like a geyser exploding from the ground.

Chapter 21

FELINIA MOVED SO QUICKLY THROUGH THE FOREST, THE TREES BE-came a reddish blur, both beautiful and dizzying. I held on tightly, Proctin tucked beneath my chest, trying to anticipate Felinia's sudden jumps left and right. It wasn't a comfortable ride by any measure; Felinia's body was designed for speed, not carrying passengers, and her lean muscles dug into my butt with every bump and bounce. My thighs ached from gripping, and there was no chance to speak over the rush of whipping air.

Once in a while I caught glimpses of Vulpeera beside us, a slim shadow darting in and out of the trees. I wondered how she could keep pace—nothing was as fast as a cheetah—but in the dense forest, Vulpeera's agility appeared to give her an advantage.

We carried on for what felt like hours. Occasionally a sticky cobweb hit my face and I'd wipe it off, praying that whatever spider had made it wasn't still sitting in the middle. I was fighting the urge to complain or ask for a break when I saw a light ahead.

Freedom! I thought.

We burst through the last of the trees into the warm sunlight and found ourselves not at the end of the forest, but in a large clearing.

Felinia stopped and lowered herself to the ground.

"This is a good place for a rest," she said, panting.

Vulpeera leapt from the trees a few seconds later.

"Why have we stopped?" she asked.

"A short break," Felinia said, "to let the girl stretch her legs."

Vulpeera looked nervous and scanned the surroundings. "We shouldn't stop for long."

"Easy for you to say," Felinia grumbled. "You're not the one carrying the raccoon."

Proctin had jumped from Felinia's back the moment we'd stopped, and sat against a small rock near the edge of the clearing with his head down.

I walked over and sat beside him, but he didn't look up.

"Is everything okay?" I asked.

He looked away, but not quickly enough for me to miss the tears sitting on the fur beneath his eyes. He looked miserable.

Comforting a raccoon was not something I'd had experience with, but I cleared my throat to give it a try.

"So, this place was your home?" I asked.

Proctin didn't turn around, but he nodded slightly. His hands rested on his belly, his back slumped against the rock as he stared off into the woods.

"And that raccoon, is he your older brother?"

"Younger brother," Proctin corrected, his voice a low mumble.

"I see." I tried to think of something else to say, something that would make him feel better. The way he was sitting reminded me of the times I'd get home from school after a bad day of teasing from Penny and the twins. When nothing helpful came to mind, I pulled off my backpack and reached inside. Most of the food was gone, but there were still a few pieces of dried meat.

"Hungry?" I asked. "Maybe eating something will make you feel better."

Proctin's little eyes locked onto the meat, and his mouth opened slightly.

"I'm not hungry," he said, but his tummy growled in disagreement.

"You sure?" I asked, dangling the meat in front of him. "Well, I guess I'll just have to eat it myself." I took a small nibble. Proctin drooled. We hadn't eaten anything all day.

"Maybe just a tiny bite," he said, snatching the meat from my hand so quickly I didn't have time to react. He swallowed it whole and moved toward the bag in my lap. His mood looked much improved. "Got anything else in there?"

I handed the backpack to him, and he dug through it.

I waited for him to sniff out a few crumbs that had fallen to the bottom before continuing. "So how many brothers and sisters do you have?"

"Lots," he said, his head inside the bag. "Lots and lots. Twelve, to be exact."

"Really? Wow, that is a lot. And are they all as nasty as . . . what did he say his name was? Raycor?"

"Oh no, the rest of them are not like Raycor. The rest are very nice. You'd love my sisters Prontora and Proctinita. We were littermates, and used to be as close as mud fleas. Only, I haven't heard from them since I left."

Proctin's voice dropped to a mumble again, and the bag around his head drooped low to the ground.

"I'm sure they've missed you," I said, rubbing his back. "Maybe we could come back someday and visit."

The bag shook left and right. "I'm not allowed."

"Oh, right," I said, feeling stupid. "I forgot."

Proctin pulled his head from the bag and dumped everything onto the ground. "It's fine," he said. "I never wanted to come back here, anyway. It's different now that Raycor has joined with the wolves. Father would not be happy."

"The raccoons weren't always friendly with the wolves?"

"Oh no! No, no, no! When Dad was around he used to tell us an angry wolf was one to be feared, but a friendly wolf was one to be feared more. We used to live only in the trees and avoided the wolves."

"So why the change?"

"Raycor," Proctin said.

"Ah, right. Did your brother become king and join with the wolves when your father died?"

Proctin sniffed along the ground, searching for any scrap of food he may have missed. "Yes and no. Technically, I was next in line to be king—what with me being the oldest male and all—but before the ceremony could happen, Raycor told the entire gaze I'd eaten all the food storages, so they kicked me out. I haven't been back since, but I've heard Raycor joined with Lupora the second he became king."

"Why would he do that?"

"Power. Most of us raccoons pride ourselves on intelligence, but Raycor has only ever cared about being the strongest. When Lupora promised him the power of the pack, he jumped at it. She made him her Dark Prince and told everyone they wouldn't have to fear the wolves anymore. Only, from what I've heard, raccoons still go missing all the time, and everyone suspects it's the wolves."

I shook my head. "That's terrible, Proctin—absolutely terrible. You're the rightful king, not him. We should do something about this."

Proctin looked perplexed. "I'm not the rightful king—I'm exiled."

"Only because Raycor lied about you."

"Ohh, yes, well, about that. It wasn't so much that Raycor *lied* about

113

me eating the food storages as it was that he . . . tattled. It was his idea. He said, 'Proctin, you are looking hungrier than ever,' and of course I was. He led me to a big, hollowed-out tree filled with nuts and berries and said 'eat to your heart's content.' I'd never seen the food storage before—I'm not sure why no one ever showed me—so I did what he said. It was the most wonderful night of my life. And when I awoke the next morning, there was Raycor with the whole gaze. You can't even imagine the disappointment on my mother's face. It's something I'll never forget."

"That's awful. Why didn't you just explain it to everyone? They'd have seen that Raycor tricked you. You should be the leader. You'd be a great leader."

"I don't know about that. Besides, I never wanted to be king. I like food, and that's a fact. I'm quite happy living with you and my wonderful silver bin."

"Then who should lead? Your brother sounds awful, and if things are as bad for the gaze as you say, shouldn't you want to do something about it?"

"Oh yes, yes, yes, I agree with that. And I do want to do something. As long as it's not being king."

"But then who?"

"That's the problem. The king has to be male, and we had an unfortunate string of litters without males. There were really only two options. Unless . . ." Proctin trailed off in thought before shaking his head.

"Unless what?"

"It doesn't matter; it's not possible."

"What's not possible?" I prodded.

"Well, if we changed the law to let a female lead, then the choice would be obvious."

"Who?"

"My mother." A large smile spread over Proctin's lips.

"Your mother would be a good leader?"

"Oh, yes! Mother basically ran the gaze while father was alive. He was more of a figurehead than anything. She's intelligent, strong, loving—everything a leader should be."

"Where is she now?"

There was a long pause, and Proctin's eyes misted over again. "I don't know," he said. "The last I saw of her was the day I left. Raycor didn't even let us talk. For a long time, I sat in the field outside the woods waiting for her to come and get me. I stayed for three days, but she never came. No one came—not my friends, not my sisters, not my mother. So, I left and vowed never to come back."

I moved closer to Proctin and wrapped my arms around him, hugging him.

"I'm sorry, Proctin," I said. "We'll figure something out, I promise. I'm the Terra Protectorum—it's in my job description to look after all the animals of the world."

Proctin's expression brightened as if this information were new to him. He was just about to say something when he lifted his nose and sniffed the air. His face turned dark.

I looked over at Vulpeera and Felinia. They were standing stone still, noses raised in the air.

"What is it?" I asked.

"Wolves," Vulpeera said. "We'd better—"

Her words were cut short when three large figures stepped from the trees behind her.

Chapter 22

WOLVES—THREE OF THEM—STOOD SIDE BY SIDE, GLARING AT US.

The one on the left looked much like those that had been chasing me—big and grey and hungry—while the one on the right was by far the largest. It was covered in charcoal-black fur except for three white paws, giving the impression it was missing a sock. The middle wolf looked shabbier, its coat thin, white, and scraggly; its ribs visible through its fur; its tail as bald and ugly as a rat's. One of its ears was nicked, and its jaws didn't quite align, making its tongue hang loose. But despite all those flaws, all those imperfections, it was obvious the white wolf was the leader. It was something in its eyes. While the other two glanced back and forth between Felinia and Vulpeera, the white wolf's gaze locked onto mine, and it was like being held by a thunderstorm. There was something immensely powerful in its glare. Something that made me feel unwelcome, something that told me I was in its domain.

"Now this is a pleasant surprise," the white wolf said, her voice rough and raspy. "When Raycor told me five Guardian trespassers had entered my woods, I hardly believed him. When he said one was the newly selected Terra Protectorum, I had to come see for myself." The wolf approached with a slight limp. "Smaller than I expected," she said, stopping a few metres away and eying me up and down. "It seems the Guardians have embraced the weak-leading-the-weak system." A crooked smile crept over her lips. "What a shame. Arctos would have made a fine Terra Protectorum—strong, vicious, powerful. Instead, Terra has selected a human, weak by nature."

Felinia stepped forward. "You are a fool, Lupora! The humans have many faults, but weakness is not one of them."

"Fool?" the wolf retorted with a snap. "Humans are a species plagued by weakness. They build machines to make up for their deficiencies and trick the rest of us into believing they are mighty. But put a human alone in a field with any other animal—bear, wolf, even the weak little fox—and they will run. Put them in cold weather without the skin of another animal wrapped around them, and they will freeze. Put them in a race against a lowly dog, and they will lose. Put them in the middle of the ocean and they will drown. Drop them from the sky, and they will fall. They are the frailest of all species, yet we stand by and let them rule the world as if they are gods. But all this is talk . . ." She crouched low, ready to pounce. "Let me show you how weak they truly are."

"You, of all animals, know that strength comes in many forms," Vulpeera said, stepping between the wolf and me. "You are the leader of the Wolves of the Red Woods yet you were born with a lame foot—proof that strength is not always physical. Now please, sister, we have no quarrel with you. We wish only to pass through the Red Woods and be on our way."

Lupora's eyes moved to Vulpeera, and her lips retracted into a snarl. "How many times have I told you not to call me sister?" she growled. "You are right; strength can be earned. Not all of us are born into a life of privilege, like you. As for passing through, you are in my domain, and this one"—she pointed a paw in my direction—"has something I desire. Give me the amulet and I may spare the girl's life."

"Never," hissed Felinia, readying herself for a fight.

"Good," the white wolf sneered, "I'd rather just take it."

Chapter 23

Lupora moved fast for someone so sickly looking. She leapt at Vulpeera with her twisted jaw open, but the fox danced aside gracefully. The large grey wolf pounced, but a yellow blur shot through the air and caught the wolf in the side, sending it sprawling toward the trees.

The black wolf attacked next, but Vulpeera avoided this one as easily as the first. It appeared no more difficult than breathing, as if her body moved without thought. The wolves would have had more success catching a leaf in a windstorm. In and out, up and down, the wolves chased Vulpeera, while Felinia dashed back and forth across the clearing, a streak of yellow light that struck the wolves with a crack of thunder.

More wolves appeared from the trees, and I backed away.

"Proctin," I said, "stay close."

His soft fur wrapped around my ankle as a wolf came out of the woods directly behind Vulpeera.

"Vulpeera, watch out!" I yelled, but it wasn't necessary. She must have felt its presence, jumping out of the way at exactly the right moment.

I was so engrossed in the fight, I didn't notice the wolves behind me. If it weren't for Proctin's tiny squeal, I wouldn't have ducked in time to avoid the one that came sailing over my head, its teeth grazing the ends of my hair.

I turned around to find five wolves waiting.

We were surrounded.

"Vulpeera!" I cried, turning frantically back to the fox. She stopped and looked at me, eyes wide with concern. And in that fraction of a second, that brief moment where she took her attention away from her fight and thought only of me, the white wolf pounced and sank her teeth into Vulpeera's side, lifting her off the ground.

My scream stuck in my throat. All I could do was watch as Lupora shook her head violently back and forth, whipping Vulpeera like a rag doll before throwing her limp body across the clearing. She landed with a dull smack against a rock and didn't move.

Something broke inside me—some sort of dam that sent heat flowing through my veins. It grew to a burning sear, like kindling caught in a forest fire. As my anger grew, so did the heat, yet I felt no pain—only rage.

I screamed so loudly it paralyzed the clearing. The wolves, Felinia, Proctin—they all froze. The wind picked up, and the trees began to shake; the ground rumbled and the grass shuddered, and when the scream ended, I was encased in bright yellow flames.

The flames flickered white and orange before my eyes yet somehow, they didn't hurt. The only pain I felt was somewhere deep inside my heart.

"You!" I roared, pointing a finger at Lupora. From my extended arm a burst of flame leapt at the wolf, narrowly missing her and striking the trees behind.

I spun around to find the other wolves backing away, cowering with their tails between their legs. "And you!" Fire erupted from my hand and struck the closest wolf, throwing it backward against a tree. It landed with a yelp and wasted no time getting back to its feet and scampering away. The other wolves didn't wait for me to turn on them—they followed the first as fast as their paws would carry them, disappearing into the woods and not looking back.

All around the clearing, the wolves fled.

All but one.

Lupora stood her ground, staring at me with loathing and disgust.

Behind her the flames grew, jumping from branch to branch, circling the clearing as thick smoke rose to the sky.

"Look what you have done, oh protector of Terra," Lupora taunted. "The Red Woods burn—by *your* hands. A war has begun and it will not end until you and any who stand with you are dead. I will not stop until it is so."

Lupora leapt through the flames and was gone.

I stared at the spot where she had disappeared, my mind lost in a pit of anger, until I remembered where I was, and worse, what had happened to Vulpeera. The flames that had engulfed me fizzled away as my anger subsided.

I ran to the rock where Vulpeera lay, her eyes closed.

"Vulpeera," I said, falling to my knees and putting my hand under her head, lifting it slightly.

She winced, and a small part of my fear evaporated—Vulpeera was alive.

Her ruddy fur was soaked with dark blood, and she struggled to breathe.

"Felinia, what should we do?" I choked, tears forming in my eyes.

The cheetah looked around the forest; it was clear that if we didn't act soon, there would be no way out.

"We must get out of here. If we can make it back to Lillian, there is still hope. Quickly, lift her and climb on my back."

I did as I was told, picking up the surprisingly light fox and laying her across Felinia's back. I climbed on, and Proctin jumped on behind me.

"Hold on, old friend," Felinia said, rising to her feet and looking around.

The woods were ablaze—a wall of fire around us. Felinia ran toward a small gap where the flames were weakest.

"Cover your eyes," she yelled, as she jumped over a burning log that had fallen between two trees. The heat rose momentarily but disappeared once we had left the burning part of the forest behind. We travelled quickly through the trees, not saying a word. Occasionally Vulpeera let out a pained gasp that broke my heart, but reassured me she was alive.

The ride was rougher than before. Felinia travelled as quickly as she could between the crowded trees. I gripped hard with my legs while cradling Vulpeera in front of me.

"Stay with us, Vulpeera," I whispered.

It wasn't long before I saw light ahead. I prayed it wasn't yet another clearing.

As we neared the light, eyes appeared above us—raccoon eyes. I figured they must live near the edges of the forest, as we hadn't seen any in the deeper parts.

"Almost through," Felinia called.

Something grabbed at my hair and I ducked. Ahead, I saw tiny hands hanging down, reaching for us as we made our final push through the woods.

Felinia leapt through the last of the trees, and just as she did I heard a shrill cry behind us. I turned to see Proctin being yanked up into the canopy, his tail disappearing into the thick branches as we left the Red Woods behind.

Chapter 24

"Felinia, stop!" I wailed. "They've taken Proctin!"

Felinia looked back but didn't break stride.

"We have to go back and help him!" But even as I said the words, I knew it wasn't possible. We didn't have time. Vulpeera didn't have time. The Red Woods disappeared behind us, a pall of black smoke hovering ominously above. Lupora's words echoed in my head—*the Red Woods burn by* your *hands.* I looked away, ashamed.

Out in the open, Felinia could stretch her legs, and we flew across fields and rivers and valleys. The wind stung my eyes, and everything became a blur. I shut them tightly, feeling the force of the wind pulling me backward, my grip slipping.

"Felinia, can you slooow ... dooown ... a biiit?" I yelled.

The cheetah obliged, but instead of slowing down she stopped all at once, nearly throwing me off the front. I opened my eyes expecting more fields, but instead found the familiar trees of our orange grove. We were in my backyard, but there was no time for relief or joy or pleasant reunions, because Vulpeera was lying limply in my arms.

I jumped off Felinia, clutching the fox against my chest, and rushed up the stairs of our back porch.

"Granny!" I yelled, but she was already waiting in the kitchen, Catharia by her side.

"The couch," she said, pointing toward the living room.

I lay Vulpeera on the couch atop a grey towel, and Granny went to work.

Vulpeera's fur was matted and glossy, her eyes shut and her breathing sharp and pained. Granny wiped the fox's side with a cloth, then dipped it into a washbasin beside her. The water turned from clear to dark red as the blood leached from the fabric. Beside me, Felinia and Catharia watched anxiously, while high in the corner of the room hung Pteron.

"Will she be alright?" I asked, but Granny didn't answer.

She seemed to be in a trance, rhythmically moving her hands round and round, kneading an invisible ball of air. At first nothing happened, but then slowly her hands began to glow: a dull pink at first, before growing to a deep red that brightened to a sun-yellow. Granny clasped her hands together, cupping the air between them, and the brightness grew. It looked as if she were holding a light bulb, and when she opened her hands, a small, flickering flame danced above her palm, burning without a wick.

"Imperia," Granny said, "a powerful gift granted to the Land Guardian of Wisdom."

Granny passed the flame between her hands, pouring it like water.

"Tell me, Winter, what did you learn in school about fire?"

"In school?" I asked. Vulpeera was dying on the couch, and Granny wanted to know what I'd learned in physics?

"Yes," Granny said. "As the Land Guardian of Wisdom, it is important you understand your power."

I tried to think back. I vaguely recalled something about chemicals and oxygen and—"Energy," I said. "Fire is energy."

"Yes," Granny agreed, "fire is energy—or at least, a form of it. Terra's energy moves through everything, both living and dead. It is in the rocks and rivers and wind, it is the burning fire and blooming flowers, it is the very thing that brings us life. The creatures of this world are mere condensations of Terra's energy, and only the Land Guardian of Wisdom can manipulate that energy. That is why your gift is so powerful. It is also why you must be very careful." Granny turned toward me, the long scars on her face like two eyes looking at me. "You are aware that fire can destroy. It can sear and burn and incinerate. It is fierce and dangerous."

I looked nervously around the room. Could Granny already know about the Red Woods?

"But fire can also be good. It can cleanse and cauterize and heal."

The flame in Granny's hand flickered as if blown by a draft through a window. Beads of sweat formed on her forehead, and her face grew strained. As she concentrated, the flame changed from yellow, to green, to blue. When it was a beautiful sapphire colour, she lowered her hands to Vulpeera, and it washed over the fox's side like vapor. It swirled and formed small funnels around her open wounds before disappearing with a puff. When I leaned forward for a better look, I saw that the wounds had healed.

Granny ran her hand over Vulpeera's side, then stood up slowly. She looked pale and drained.

"Vulpeera needs to rest," she said, "and so do I. It takes much of my own energy to restore Vulpeera's." Granny looked ready to fall over, and I took her arm. "Tomorrow you will begin your training. Terra has asked much of you—to learn the other powers when you are still discovering your own. But Terra only asks for what She knows can be done. She sees great things in your future. As do we all. So long as you can hone your power so that further accidents do not occur."

I felt my face flush; she did know about the Red Woods.

As I GRATEFULLY crawled between my soft, cool sheets that night, I expected to be asleep in minutes. I was exhausted. The back of a turtle and a condor's talons hadn't exactly been refreshing places to rest. But when I closed my eyes, I couldn't find sleep. There were too many thoughts racing around in my head.

I thought about Proctin and the Red Woods, the flames and smoke I had left behind, and all the creatures that had called the forest their home; I thought about Arctos and Cano and their hatred of me; I thought about my father and all the unanswered questions that remained. I hadn't had the chance to ask Granny anything about my father, but the following day I would demand answers. I couldn't go on not knowing, especially when everyone else did. Especially with what had been said about him.

I did what I always did when I couldn't sleep; I turned on the light and wrote in my journal. I wrote about everything that had happened, names and places and events—details about details. I didn't stop until there was nothing left to write. When I finally laid down my pen and closed the journal, my eyes closed along with it, and I fell into a deep, dreamless sleep.

Chapter 25

THE NEXT MORNING, GRANNY STAYED IN BED MUCH LATER THAN usual. Pteron said it would be a day or two before she recovered fully, but that my training had to begin nonetheless. So instead of asking Granny about my father, I found myself sitting in our backyard, facing Pteron as he hung upside-down from a low branch in our elm tree. Behind me was a wooden table covered with a black sheet. Beneath that sheet was an unknown object Pteron had hidden.

"Today," Pteron said, "you begin your training as the Terra Protectorum. By giving you the amulet, Terra has granted you access to all the Guardian powers. First, I will teach you mine—Aminoculus, the power of the Sky Guardian of Wisdom."

He opened his long wings and gestured for me to come closer. I stood and walked toward him, noticing the thin veins in the webbing of his wings and the dusty gold of his fur. When I was in front of him, he reached out a long claw and touched the amulet around my neck. A sudden jolt of electricity ran through me, like the one I'd felt the first time I touched the amulet. The carved symbol of the bat glowed a dark green.

"Good, now go back to the chair," he said.

I did as he asked, and the green glow from the stone faded until the familiar gold etching returned to normal. When I was sitting, Pteron fell from the branch, parachuted himself into the air, and circled the yard.

"Without turning around," he instructed, "I want you to tell me what object is on the table behind you."

He swooped past, clutching the black sheet from the table.

"Without turning around?" I asked, looking for some sort of mirror or reflection I could use to see behind me. "How can I do that?"

"Aminoculus," he said, "the gift of the Sky Guardian of Wisdom."

"Your ability is to see behind you?" I laughed. "That, um . . . doesn't seem very useful."

"Not only behind," Pteron said, "all around. Aminoculus will allow you to see without seeing, to use your inner eye to visualize Terra's energy so that even in the dark, the world is clear. As Lillian told you, this energy runs through everything—the soil, the animals, the trees, the rocks, even the air. It is a river of vitality, connecting us all. That river is made up of tiny particles too small to detect with our eyes. You humans have a name for them. What is it you call them?"

"Atoms?" I suggested.

"Yes, atoms," Pteron replied with a nod. "I do not claim to be as smart as you humans so I take a simpler approach. I think of them as the particles of life—constantly in motion, constantly energized. Just as you might feel the wind on your skin or the change of temperature, you must teach yourself to feel this energy."

"And when I can feel the energy I will have this power—Aminoculus?"

"No, that is only the beginning. Many animals can feel Terra's energy. It is how the birds fly south and the whales navigate thousands of kilometres back to their breeding grounds. It is how a dog barks, minutes before an earthquake. Aminoculus is far greater than that. Aminoculus is the ability to see the energy, to visualize an object around you by the energy it gives off."

"But how can I see it if I can't look at it?" I asked. "Shouldn't I be facing the table?"

Pteron shook his head. "Your eyes are crude instruments for seeing light. To see Terra's energy, you must use something deeper. Something inactive locked inside us all. Relax, concentrate, close your eyes—*see* from within."

I closed my eyes as Pteron had instructed, and concentrated. Only, I had no idea what I was supposed to be concentrating on. "I still don't understand what I'm supposed to be doing."

"Begin by opening your senses—smell the air, hear the birds, taste the pollen, feel the wind. Return to Terra. Only then will Aminoculus come to you. Only then will you open your mind's eye. Feel the energy first—*then* see it."

I did what Pteron said. I tried to focus on everything around me.

"What do you feel?" Pteron asked.

"I feel the sun on my arms—warm and gentle."

"Good. Keep going. Tell me about your other senses."

"I smell the orange trees and the grass, and the garbage by the porch. I hear a swallow overhead, up there." I pointed to where I'd heard the noise. "And another, returning its call, over there."

"Good," Pteron said. "Now, tell me what is sitting on the table behind you."

I concentrated hard, gripping my hands on my knees and straining the muscles in my forehead, but nothing came. There was only blackness. I didn't even know where the image was supposed to appear—on the backs of my eyelids? In my head?

"I don't see anything," I said. "This is ridiculous."

"It's not ridiculous, it just takes time. You need to be patient and relax," Pteron said. "Don't force it; let it come to you. Let your body melt into your surroundings. Become one with the air and the earth."

I sighed and tried again. This time, I didn't tighten my hands on my knees or wrinkle my forehead. I relaxed and tried to let things come to me. I waited—five minutes, ten minutes, twenty minutes—but nothing came.

"This isn't working," I finally said, opening my eyes and standing up. "Who says I can even do this? Maybe all you other animals have some sort of inner eye, but as far as I know, there's never been a human who can see something with their eyes closed."

"Ah, but you are wrong. It takes time, but I assure you, it can and has been done—even by humans."

"It has?" I said. "By who?"

Pteron's small, thin mouth turned up in a smile. "There have been many people over the course of time. Most lived long ago, in places that no longer exist. Some were called shamans or witch doctors. But there is one in particular that you know well." He regarded me with a sly look in his eye. "Lillian has perhaps the keenest mind's eye of any animal."

"Granny?" I exclaimed. I thought back to all the times I had wondered how Granny could find her way around the house when her eyes had been shut for years. The adeptness of her movements, the knowingness of her step—there was no shuffling around chairs or feeling for things in the cupboards. She just knew. And now, it made sense.

"But if Granny can use her mind's eye, and she's a human, that means she was—"

"The Terra Protectorum," Pteron said.

My heart quickened. I'd just got used to the idea of her being the

Land Guardian of Wisdom, and now this!

"But if she was the Terra Protectorum, why isn't she still?"

Pteron closed his eyes and shook his head. "That answer must come from her," he said, before reopening his eyes. "Now, let us try again. Sit back down, open your senses, and focus."

I wanted to press Pteron into telling me more about Granny but at the same time I didn't want to keep disappointing him. I liked the bat, so I sat back in the chair and closed my eyes.

Initially I continued to think about Granny. What had it been like for her when she was learning the skills? Had she been as lost? As confused by everything that was asked of her?

As my mind gradually settled, I felt my body melting into the chair. Again, I noticed the sun on my skin, the grass beneath my feet, and the wind rushing through the orange trees.

There was a sense of release from my thoughts.

Things began to change.

I can't really explain how or where I saw it, but something came to me. Not an image—at least, not exactly—but a shadowy static that materialized into a vague outline. I saw the orchard and Pteron; I saw the ground and the chair where I sat. They weren't solid like normal images, but misty—moving and flowing. I concentrated on the object behind me. The table was there, shifting in and out of focus, and on it was . . . was . . . something tall and slender.

I focused harder, trying to bring the image into view, but the more I concentrated, the further it faded. It was like staring at an object in the dark—easier to see when I wasn't looking directly at it. Even after ten minutes of trying everything I could to relax my mind, I couldn't figure out what the object was. I grew frustrated and opened my eyes. "I give up," I groaned. "I can't do this. I'm sorry, Pteron. Maybe Granny can use her mind's eye, but I can't."

I got up and ran toward the house, briefly glimpsing the object on the table out of the corner of my eye. It was a marble statue that normally stood on Granny's dresser—a bear standing upright on its hind legs.

Tall and slender, just as the mist had shown me.

Chapter 26

I LAY ON MY BED, FACE IN MY PILLOW. THE DOOR TO MY ROOM opened and closed, and footsteps approached. I looked up to see Granny, her face only a few shades darker than her white nightgown, walking with a hunched back toward the bed.

I shifted over, making room for her to sit, and put my face back in the pillow. The bed moved only slightly beneath her weight, and she sighed long and hard. We sat in silence for a while, the only sound in the room our breathing as Granny ran her fingers through my hair.

Finally, she broke the silence. "Don't be disheartened," she said, her voice frail.

"I can't do it," I groaned. "I can't see what Pteron wants me to see. I can't use my Aminoculus."

Granny made a soft tut-tutting noise. "It took months before I could see even the grainiest of images with my Aminoculus. It is not an easy skill. Give it time."

"Months?" I said, looking up at her. "Really? I thought I was starting to see *something*."

"I don't doubt it. From what I've heard, you won't have any trouble learning your abilities. Pteron says your Imperia nearly knocked Arctos over."

"Nearly?" I grinned. "It did knock him over!"

Granny chuckled. "As I said, the skills will come easily to you. It's in your blood."

There was a sudden awkwardness in the room, as if Granny had said something she didn't mean to.

"Granny," I said, swallowing, "what exactly did Father do? Cano called him a murderer—is it true?"

Granny's lips tightened and she took her hand away from my hair, folding it in her lap. If she could see, I would have said she was staring at the wall. I worried the conversation was over, another dead-end talk, when she said, "I should have told you long ago—I just, well, I thought I was protecting you. Now I realize I was only protecting myself. Call it a mother's pride, but it's hard to talk about, even now."

Her face looked sad, and her shoulders slumped further. This obviously wasn't an easy conversation for her, and she was still recovering her strength, but I needed her to go on. I needed to know the truth.

"Your father wasn't a bad person," she said. "Rash, yes, quick-tempered, sometimes, but not a bad person. He was passionate about being a Guardian and loved Terra, but ultimately his passion and love consumed him."

"What do you mean, 'consumed him'?"

"Malum, the animals call it," Granny said. "The great evil. A sickness that cannot be cured. We do not have the same word in our language, but I suppose it is similar to what we call grief. Or at least, the emotion that comes from grief. You see, your father was a powerful Guardian, quick to learn his Imperia, a firm believer in the power of Terra, a lover of all creatures. He wanted to be the Terra Protectorum so he could heal our ailing planet, and he probably would have, if not for a great tragedy."

"My mother's death?" I whispered.

Granny nodded.

"She died during childbirth. The pregnancy was . . . complicated. Your mother's death was hard on everyone. But for your father, it broke him. Your mother was the kindest, gentlest soul that ever lived, and she tempered your father. She was his calming force, his voice of reason. When she died, so did he. I'm convinced that on that day, your father died right along with your mother, and all that was left . . . was Malum."

"What happened after Mother died? What did Father do?"

Granny paled and wrapped her arms around herself. Selfishly, I urged her to continue. "Granny, please, I need to know."

She sat up a little straighter and I put my hand on her shoulder. "When your mother died," she said, "your father was consumed by one thought: getting her back. He begged Orcavion to use his power as the Terra Protectorum to resurrect her. He thought the amulet could bring her back, but Orcavion said it could not be done. Your father didn't believe him. He grew irate. He felt cheated. He was angry with Terra, angry with Orcavion, angry with the world. He hired a fleet of whalers to hunt down Orcavion and take the amulet."

"It's true? He killed Orcavion—Cano's father?"

Granny nodded.

"And then what? The Guardians killed Father?"

Granny shook her head. "It wasn't their plan, but your father was too consumed by Malum at that point. He travelled to Mount Skire—the Guardians' most sacred place—and swore to destroy it. He wanted to destroy Terra completely, but Arctos was waiting. He demanded your father return the amulet—that he abandon his Guardianship forever and never return to their midst. Though he would not forgive your father, he would at least offer him an out. But your father refused. He fought with Arctos, and Arctos defeated him."

Everything in the room began to spin. I felt like I was going to throw up. My whole life, I had fallen asleep to images of a perfect family flitting through my head. I had pictured my parents as gentle and kind. I had imagined them tucking me into bed at night, holding me when I was sick, laughing at my jokes. Never had I imagined either of them even raising their voices. And now, my new reality: My father killed Orcavion. Arctos killing my father. It was one more reason to hate that stupid bear.

Granny put her hand on my knee. "I'm sorry, Winter. I imagine it is as difficult to hear as it is to tell."

Chapter 27

AFTER DINNER THAT EVENING, I SAT WRITING IN MY JOURNAL, trying to make sense of everything. I had hoped that by putting it on paper it would make the truth easier, perhaps give it some clarity. But it didn't. The truth was the truth—my father *was* a murderer.

No wonder Cano and Arctos hated me.

I looked down at the amulet hanging from my neck. It was like a thorn, stinging at my conscience. I took it off and threw it to the floor, where it landed with a heavy thud.

I was done being the Terra Protectorum. How could I continue when I knew the truth? What if Cano and Arctos were right? What if one day I was consumed by Malum and tried to destroy the earth? If being a Guardian was in my blood, then maybe so was being a murderer.

The door to my room creaked open, and I sat up like a shot, scanning the room.

"Hello?"

"Down here," came a pained voice from beside the bed. I looked over the edge to find Vulpeera, standing on four wobbling legs.

"Vulpeera!" I cried, reaching down and scooping her up.

"Careful," she winced, "my body is still healing."

"Sorry."

I put her down gently beside me on the bed.

"It's alright. I'm much better than I should be, thanks to your grand-mother."

The gloominess returned. "But no thanks to me. If I hadn't called out to you in the clearing, Lupora would never have caught you."

Vulpeera shook her head. "It is not your fault. I should never have been caught. It is a sign of the Weakening."

"The Weakening?"

"All of our powers are connected to Terra's energy," Vulpeera said. "As our Mother grows weaker, so do our gifts. We have all felt it. I have fought with Lupora many times before, but never has she come close to catching me, distractions or not."

"But the world is weakening because of the humans. Arctos said it himself. So, either way, it's my fault."

Vulpeera opened her mouth as if to argue but closed it when it appeared she had no response. Instead we sat in silence until another question came to me.

"In the forest, you called Lupora your sister. Why?"

"Because she is," Vulpeera replied.

"Your sister? How?"

"The same way as all sisters—our parents are the same."

"But you're a fox and she's a wolf."

Vulpeera smiled. "There are many types of families. In ours, two mothers: one a fox, the other a wolf. Love is love, no matter the animal. When our mothers met, Lupora and I were young pups, so it was the only family we ever knew."

"Okay, but if you and Lupora are sisters, why does she hate you so much?"

Vulpeera sighed—a long, drawn-out sigh. "Lupora is angry," she said.

"Why?"

"Because I am a Guardian and she is not, among other things. You

138

see, Lupora was born lame, or as she would say, jinxed by Terra. I never saw it that way. I tried not to draw attention to her paw, but there were things I could do as a cub that she could not. And when I was made a Guardian, Lupora saw this as a further spurn from Terra. She stopped thinking of our parents as being a unit. She started to see them as a fox and a wolf—different. She saw *us* as different. Why should a fox sit on a throne when a wolf could not? She grew angry. She swore to become more powerful than the Guardians. And in many ways, she has. Though her power comes from a place of anger."

"It sounds like I'm not the only one with a dark family past."

Vulpeera nuzzled her nose under my arm. "What happened to your mother and father was a terrible tragedy. It is wrong of Arctos and Cano to judge you based on your father's actions."

"But how could they not? My father killed Cano's father."

"Yes," Vulpeera said, "that is true. But you are not your father."

"But what if I grow up to be? What if one day I'm consumed by Malum? Who can say that won't happen?"

"You can," Vulpeera said. "Terra has given you the chance to prove that your bloodline is not full of hate and destruction. Your father did many good things before he was taken by Malum, but creatures tend to remember what happened last. And Lillian was one of the greatest Terra Protectora we have ever known. It is up to you to remind everyone of that. It is up to you to prove that your bloodline should remain."

I considered this. "So if I succeed, in a way, it would help make up for what happened with my father?"

Vulpeera nodded. "Not just your father, but all humans. There is a shadow hanging over your species that you can help lift. Show the rest of the Guardians that the humans are not a plague—that they care about more than themselves. Show them that they care about Terra."

I thought back to the miles of land stripped for the roadway. "Sort of a steep task to try and correct all the wrongs of an entire species, isn't it?"

"A very steep task," Vulpeera agreed. "But Terra has given you the power to do it. She made you the Terra Protectorum for a reason."

I nodded. "Okay," I said, "I'll do it. I'll prove Cano and Arctos are wrong about my family. I'll make up for what my father did. And if I have to make up for the rest of humanity at the same time—then that's what I'll do."

Chapter 28

FOR THE NEXT FEW DAYS, I WORKED HARD ON MY TRAINING, FOcusing on what Pteron was trying to teach me, no matter how strange the task. And believe me, some of the tasks were *very* strange.

Like the entire morning I spent blindfolded in the grove while he threw oranges at me.

"*See* the oranges with your mind's eye," he commanded.

The only thing I saw was a bunch of bruises the following day.

Next, he had me jumping through an obstacle course in the basement with the lights off. While I didn't find my inner eye there, either, I did find that we had a lot of breakable things in the basement.

On the third day, there were no more games, only the expectation that I wouldn't use my eyes the *entire day*. Breakfast, lunch, dinner— eyes closed. Up and down the stairs, getting dressed, showering—eyes closed. Going to the washroom (awkward, by the way)—eyes closed.

Every time I tried to cheat for even the tiniest fraction of a second, Pteron somehow knew.

"Eyes closed!" he'd bellow from the other room. Which was especially creepy while I was peeing.

But not all the training was in vain. I definitely wasn't Granny—I couldn't get from point A to point B in the house without knocking my shins on at least one footstool (Pteron kept moving the furniture to make things more challenging), but I was starting to see *something*. Hazy, faded, unclear somethings—but somethings nonetheless.

At night, Granny would sit with me in bed and teach me to use my Imperia. There were many forms of energy, she said, but fire was a good place to start. So, we sat and practiced calling the flames.

By the second night, I recreated the tingling sensation in my hands. And by the third night, I got my hands to glow a dull yellow. It wasn't until Granny had left my room on the fourth night that I was finally able to get a tiny spark to ignite. I was very excited until I dropped it on the sheets and singed a black hole in them.

Oops! All in the name of saving the world, I suppose.

Although my training was progressing well, there was still an air of concern hanging over the house. Felinia and Catharia had left shortly after our arrival, saying they were going back to reassess the damage in the Red Woods. I'd made them promise they would bring back Proctin, rescuing him from his horrible brother, but after four days they still hadn't returned. Even Granny and Pteron looked worried—though neither would admit it.

On the fifth day, it rained, which meant we couldn't train outside. Even Granny and Pteron had trouble using their Aminoculus in the rain, their minds' eyes muddled by the surplus of energy in the air. So instead we sat inside, and I practiced conjuring my Imperia.

It was nearly noon when the back door flung open and two sopping-wet Guardians entered.

Felinia shivered, her skinny legs quaking beneath her as she muttered something about her beautiful coat. Catharia appeared unfazed by her wetness, looking as regal as ever. I jumped up and grabbed a blanket from the couch for Felinia.

"What news do you bring of Lupora and the Red Woods?" Vulpeera asked when we were all gathered in the living room.

Felinia and Catharia exchanged nervous looks. "The Red Woods are gone—every last tree burned to the ground," said the condor.

Granny and Vulpeera looked stunned. I wanted to slip between the boards in the living room floor and disappear. If only there were a power to make myself invisible.

"The wood was dry, and the flames spread quickly. It was all we could do to get the animals out," Catharia continued. "If this rain had come a few days earlier it might have saved us a lot of trouble."

"And what of Lupora?" Vulpeera asked.

"She has moved her pack to the woods by Grander's Bay. She would not hear our plea, and I fear there is no point trying to reason with her right now. She has sworn vengeance on the girl and is amassing an army of sympathizers as we speak."

"With so many animals calling the Red Woods their home, she will not have trouble finding them," Felinia added.

"What about Arctos?" Vulpeera asked. "Lupora has always listened to him."

"Arctos is back at Mount Skire. The humans are making another push to blast their path through the mountains and are closing in on Mount Skire. Even if he wasn't angry right now, his paws are full."

"And Proctin?" I asked.

"The least of our worries," grumbled Catharia.

"He's being held in a small prison by the water of Grander's Bay," Felinia said. "Too far for us to make any attempt at a rescue."

"This isn't good," Vulpeera said, shaking her head. She was getting stronger every day, but she still spent most of her time lying on the living room couch. "It will take time to round up the Guardians and our supporters—Lupora could be here by then."

She looked up at Pteron, who seemed to be pondering everything from the corner of the room.

"We will need to take Winter somewhere safe to continue her training," he said. "Allow time for Lupora's temper to cool, and then we will see if we can reason with her. A lapse in Winter's training at this point would be detrimental, especially with the progress she is making."

"Where could we take her?" Vulpeera asked. "Back to the Cove? Lupora will have blocked the path."

"Not the Cove," Granny said. "There's a better place—one where the wolves won't be able to reach her." The animals' ears perked. "To the island of Pitchi," she said, "with her uncle and cousin."

"I can't go to Pitchi!" I protested. "Not without Proctin! We can't just leave him. You saw what his brother was like!"

I looked from Felinia to Catharia.

"Perhaps we can talk with Cheelion," Felinia said. "He is heading to Grander's Bay to keep watch on Lupora from the water. The prison is near the shore. With luck, he may be able to free your raccoon friend."

"Thank you, Felinia."

Granny clapped her hands together and stood. "Then it's settled. You will go to Pitchi to stay with your uncle and continue your training. If we hurry, we can get you out of here before Lupora's crows have eyes on the house."

"Yes, it is a good plan," Pteron said, nodding. "Winter, war was on the horizon long before the Red Woods burned. The dark creatures are disgruntled, and without a united Guardianship, they have grown stronger. It is up to us to remind them of the strength and guidance of Terra. To do so, we will need a leader. A strong leader. You can be that leader—I have no doubt. With patience and practice, you will learn the powers of the Guardians and become a skillful and formidable Terra Protectorum."

He stared at me with his dark eyes. "With patience and practice," he repeated, with a stern smile.

PART 3: THE ISLAND

It is night, and the forest around Grander's Bay is dark and cool. The waves lapping on the rocks and the gentle breeze through the pines are the only other sounds as two creatures talk quietly.

"How could you have missed her?" the first creature snaps. "She's had no training, for Terra's sake!"

"She wasn't alone," growls the second creature. "Your own Guardians were there, protecting her."

"Never mind," scoffs the Guardian, "we missed an opportunity, but there will be others. She is young and untrained, but if we don't act quickly she will grow stronger by the day."

The second creature steps forward into a narrow moonbeam cutting through the canopy. Its pale white fur catches the silvery light. "Young," it scoffs. "She is a child! As I have said all along, Terra is a fool."

The Guardian stiffens at the comment. "Terra is no fool," it retorts.

"Her judgment is simply clouded. A dark fog has shrouded her view. That cloud walks on two legs and claims to be ruler of Terra Creatura. We must remove that cloud. We must remove the humans."

The wolf runs her sharp claws over a dead log on the forest floor, tearing long gashes in its side. "The girl has destroyed my home," she says. "I want nothing more than to kill her myself."

The Guardian nods. "It will be easier if you do it."

A twig snaps nearby, and the creatures turn to look in the direction of the sound.

"What was that?" the wolf hisses. "Are there more of you lurking about?"

"No," the Guardian says, "it was nothing, a squirrel. I am alone. Now listen closely—the girl is at this moment heading for an island off the northern coast. She will stay with her uncle while she trains. Take your army there, surround the island, cut off all routes of escape, and prepare. I will think of a way to bring her to you."

Chapter 29

IF YOU EVER GET THE OPPORTUNITY TO VISIT OLPORT, THE CAPI-
tal city of Nacadia, I highly recommend that you don't. Once a fur-
trading post, the city grew considerably with each passing year. Every
summer I returned, there were more people, more cars, more smog. The
water was a little murkier, with more garbage floating in the foam, the
smell a little more pungent. It wasn't surprising. Most of the Society's
factories operated in Olport, and a steady stream of smoke poured from
their chimneys.

The only reason I went to Olport was to get to Pitchi, a tiny island
across the channel where I spent all my school holidays. The island was
shaped like a teeter-totter, sloping upward from the west to the east,
where it ended in high cliffs. Atop those cliffs stood a lighthouse, warn-
ing incoming ships of danger. My uncle and cousin maintained that
lighthouse year-round, living in the small cabin at its base. They were
the only people who lived on the island, likely because of the rocky ter-
rain and relentless wind, but when I wasn't being pestered by my cousin, it was a nice enough spot to spend my vacations.

As I sat on the docks waiting for my uncle, I watched the people bus-
tling about the wharf. It was market day, and blue-tarped stalls lined the
docks, selling everything from local produce to otter-pelt hats, a common fashion in the city. I must have been daydreaming, because my
uncle's boat was nearly at the docks before I noticed him approaching.
Uncle Farlin stood behind the wheel, waving and smiling like a lunatic,

and I couldn't help but smile back.

My uncle didn't even tie up the boat before leaping onto the dock and running toward me. He picked me up in a giant bear hug that squeezed the air from my lungs and the nervousness from my heart. I'd missed him. Even the smell of fish guts on his overalls was oddly comforting.

When he finally put me down, he took a step back and looked me over.

"You've grown," he said.

"It's been three months." I laughed. "I haven't grown."

"Then I'm shrinking."

Uncle Farlin was a tall man with wide shoulders and a shirt that was always dirty. His face always bore stubble, and you could count on there being some sort of fish guts splattered over his rubber boots and overalls. When he wasn't working on the lighthouse, he was out on the fishing rig. Either he never changed, or he owned ten pairs of identical overalls. When I was younger, I used to wish Uncle Farlin was my father. He was funny and kind and had big, gentle eyes that sparkled in the sun. I wanted eyes like that. Instead I was stuck with my weird cat-eyes, just like my cousin, Alectus.

A boy, strikingly similar to my cousin, climbed from the boat. He had the same dark hair, same elfish face, same green feline eyes, but it couldn't be Alectus . . . could it? Why was his hair slicked back and combed? Why was he wearing a clean white button-up shirt and a pair of dress pants? And most importantly, why had he just gotten off the boat?

My cousin never went on the boat. He had a desperate fear of water from an incident when he was very young. The story went that Alectus had been swimming alongside my uncle's fishing boat—not a smart idea, with all the dead fish in the water—when he was attacked by a shark. The men on board rescued him, but there was no saving his lower leg. He'd had a prosthetic foot ever since. I'd only seen him on the boat a handful of times, and when he was aboard, he always looked ill. Because of this, he was essentially trapped on the island.

And he *hated* the island.

There was nothing for him to do, so when I was around, he occupied his time tormenting me. When we were little, it was minor pranks—dead fish in my bed, beetle larvae in my soup, clothes hanging from the treetops in the morning. As we'd gotten older, his pranks had gotten nastier. The summer before, he'd tied me to a tree with a fishing net. This would have been harmless had he come back and untied me, but instead I'd spent the night alone in the forest. When Uncle Farlin had found me the next morning, he'd been as close to furious as I'd ever seen him. Which was not very angry at all.

That was part of the problem.

Uncle Farlin was too nice to get angry, so Alectus had no boundaries. He was like a feral animal with free reign over the island. Most of the time he looked so unkempt you would have thought he was raised by wolves.

So the clean-cut boy getting off the boat couldn't be my cousin.

"Winter," the boy said, approaching. "It's so nice to see you!"

He had the same limp as Alectus, but when he wrapped his arms around me, I smelled cologne.

Cologne?

No one my age wore cologne. Alectus and I were supposed to be in the same grade, but he'd dropped out of school because he wouldn't cross the channel. He was homeschooled by Uncle Farlin, meaning I'd never seen him open a book. And my cousin would never say, "it's so nice to see you." A punch to the arm and a sneer, with a "what the heck are you doing here?" maybe, but not "it's so nice to see you." That wasn't Alectus.

After an awkward embrace, the boy stepped back. "Here," he said, "let me get that for you."

I was too stunned to stop him from taking my bag. He turned and walked back to the boat.

"Betcha weren't expecting this?" my uncle said, nudging me and pointing after the boy.

"Alectus?" I asked.

Uncle Farlin nodded. "There have been a few changes around here. Come on, I think you'll like them."

I followed my uncle to the boat and was surprised when neither he nor my cousin went to set up the sails. Instead, Uncle Farlin sat beside me while Alectus went to the back of the boat, toward a large metal object that was fastened to the stern.

"What's that?" I asked.

"It's called an outboard motor," Alectus said. "It runs on petrol. There are only ten boats in the harbor with them. They're one of the latest inventions of the Society."

"A motor?" I asked. "Like a car?"

"Yep." Alectus nodded. "Like a car. They make travelling over water much faster."

"How on earth did you afford that?"

Uncle Farlin smiled proudly. "Your cousin has made some helpful connections."

Connections? I thought, *with the Society?*

"How did you—"

I was cut short by a deafening roar as Alectus pulled a cord to start the motor.

Chapter 30

THE ONLY WAY TO ACCESS PITCHI WAS FROM THE LOWER END OF the island—the western end. In other words, the end *furthest* from the lighthouse. This meant a long, slogging, uphill walk to the cliff tops every time I arrived.

The lower half was covered in dense forest, accessible by a small dock, and there was a narrow path cut through the trees, leading up to the lighthouse. I knew Pitchi well—every nook, cranny, and trail—and as we got off the boat and started walking, I knew exactly where each intersecting path went. The first led to one of my favourite spots on the island, a small pond hidden in the trees where I had spent many lazy days watching dragonflies and reading. The next two paths went to the north and south ends of the island, where Uncle Farlin liked to fish.

"So," I said, as we walked, "what's been happening around here?"

Uncle Farlin smiled. "You didn't even recognize him, did ya?"

"Honestly, no. What's with the new getup, Alectus? You look . . . civilized."

"It's part of my uniform," Alectus said, walking a few steps ahead.

"Uniform for what?"

"He's got himself a job," Uncle Farlin interjected, beaming with pride. "He works for the Society now. A real big shot."

"You work for the Society?" I asked in disbelief. "That outfit's a little fancy for working in a factory, isn't it?"

Alectus scoffed. "I don't work in a factory."

"You don't?"

Alectus shook his head. "I work in Sir Maychin's manor."

"Sir Maychin's manor? You mean the big white castle at the centre of the city?" I had never been to the building but I could see its three white towers pointing high above the city.

Alectus nodded.

"But isn't that where Sir Maychin lives and works? I've heard he has an office there and won't leave for weeks at a time."

"He sure does," Uncle Farlin said, "and guess who cleans that office?"

"I do more than clean the office," Alectus huffed.

"Like what?" I asked.

"All sorts of things—stacking books in the library, clearing the dining room, making sure guests know where they're going. I've already got a promotion. Now I'm serving tea in the sitting room. It doesn't sound like much, but it's an important job. I get to hear lots of private conversations. Plus, I've made some helpful connections with a few high-ranking members."

"I'm impressed," I said, hopping over a tree root to keep up. "What kinds of things have you overheard?"

Alectus turned to me, his eyes bright. "Technically, I'm not allowed to say. It's all very hush-hush. But I'll tell you this—the Society is planning to build a road right through the mountains. Sir Maychin is heading the operation himself, and they've already started blasting. He thinks that by early next year, they'll break through. He plans to lead a team to explore the Forgotten Lands, and he said if I'm still in good standing, I could potentially be picked for that expedition."

"Really?" I said, staring at Alectus in disbelief. "I'd heard rumors about that at school but didn't think it was true. Why would anyone want to explore the Forgotten Lands?"

Alectus rolled his eyes. "Why not? There's got to be something over there."

"Desert and toxic air—that's what everyone says."

"Sir Maychin believes those are just myths. He thinks there are people living on the other side. Whole tribes of primitive people. Anyway, he plans to be the first person to explore and return alive. I want to be a part of that."

It didn't surprise me that a boy who'd spent his whole life trapped on an island wanted to explore, but anything about the Society made me suspicious. The cars, the roads, the factories—these were all things the Guardians talked about. These were the things destroying Terra.

I was about to voice these concerns when I noticed something strange. We had come to a new intersecting trail—one I'd never seen before. It was a shorter path, only fifty metres to the end, where a small wooden hut stood nestled in the trees.

"What's that?" I asked, stopping and pointing down the trail.

"Your cousin's workshop," Uncle Farlin said. "He built it himself. When he's not off working at the Society, he's down here tinkering."

"Tinkering with what?"

"All kinds of different things. I don't get to look inside, but I do get to see the finished products. I'm sure Alectus would be happy to show you a few of them up at the house. Right, Alectus?"

"A master never shows his creations until they're finished," Alectus said. "But yes, I can show Winter some of the things I've built. It's like the Society says—'the Future is Forward.' I may not be able to build cars or motors yet, but I've got some of the basics down."

Alectus and Uncle Farlin continued to walk up the trail, while I stood behind. Something about the hut made me uneasy. Something didn't feel right. Or maybe it was something about the whole island that felt different. Was it too quiet? Too dark? Was I being watched? I couldn't put my finger on it. But I didn't want to be alone when I found out what it was, so I ran after my uncle and cousin.

The path climbed as we made our way toward the cliff top. The soft dirt turned to rough rock beneath our feet, and the wind began to howl. Once we were above the tree line, I looked back toward Olport across the channel, the ever-present smog hanging above the city like a cloud. The Society's castle stood in the centre—the three white spires reaching up like a pitchfork.

Alectus worked there? How had things changed so much in three months?

My uncle's house was a small wooden cabin tucked on the windward side of the lighthouse, that rattled and shook with the wind. The ground floor was a combined kitchen and living space, while three small bedrooms occupied the upstairs.

"Why don't you put your stuff in your room," Uncle Farlin suggested as we entered the cabin. "Haven't touched a thing since you left. Then we'll have supper—soup's already on the stove."

Alectus took my bag upstairs, so I followed. Uncle Farlin was right; my room looked exactly as I'd left it. Even the Dandy Boys book I'd been reading was still open on the bedside table. At least some things on the island hadn't changed.

Alectus dropped my bag in the middle of the room and turned to me, smiling. I didn't know what to say. After years of being tormented, it was hard to take this new Alectus seriously. I kept waiting for him to smack me in the side of the head.

"See you downstairs for dinner," he said. "Fish soup again—never gets old." He grimaced and pointed a finger into his open mouth.

I grinned, imagining how many times Alectus ate fish soup throughout the year.

He started to leave but stopped, giving me a curious look.

"What's that?" he asked, gesturing toward my chest. The amulet had come free from beneath my shirt.

Before I could tuck it back in, Alectus reached out and touched it.

"Ouch!" he yelled, wrenching his hand away and looking surprised.

When I looked down, the engraving of the human was glowing a dark green.

Chapter 31

ALECTUS STARED AT THE GLOWING AMULET, EYES NARROWED.

"What is that thing?" he asked, rubbing his hand where he had touched the stone.

I backed away, tucking the necklace beneath my shirt.

"It's nothing," I said.

"It's not nothing," Alectus countered. "Give it here, I want to see it. Does it use electricity?"

He reached for the amulet, but I slapped his hand away.

Anger flared in his eyes. For a brief instant, I saw the old Alectus, the one that would have grabbed my hair, wrestled me to the floor, and taken the amulet. The Alectus I feared.

"You shouldn't have done that," he snarled.

"Hurry up, you two!" Uncle Farlin called from downstairs. "Soup's getting cold!"

Alectus's face softened as he glanced at the door.

"Come on now!" Uncle Farlin called again.

Alectus took one more look at my chest—the green glow shining through my shirt—before turning and leaving the room.

I let out a long sigh of relief and leaned back against the wall.

Close call, I thought.

I hid the amulet in the spot I always used for anything precious when I visited my uncle, beneath a loose floorboard in the corner of my room.

When I got downstairs, Alectus stared at me suspiciously.

"What's for dinner?" I asked, sitting down and grabbing my spoon, trying not to make eye contact.

The question was meant to divert attention; I already knew the answer. We had the same soup for dinner every night with Uncle Farlin. "Whitefish special," he called it. My uncle wasn't much of a cook, to put it politely—the soup tasted like fish bathed in salt water. The only time I ate a good meal while visiting Uncle Farlin was on the odd occasion when we went to the Captain's Pub for breakfast.

"So," Alectus said, "I hear you got yourself into some trouble at school?"

There was a snootiness to his voice that annoyed me. "No," I said, "school's fine, thank you very much."

"That's not what Granny said."

It dawned on me that Granny had probably told Uncle Farlin I'd gotten into trouble at school as an excuse for me coming to Pitchi. Why else would I leave school before the holidays?

"I mean, things aren't perfect," I said, backtracking. "I've had some trouble with . . . um . . . bullies."

Alectus nodded. "You never could stand up for yourself, could you?"

A part of me wanted to kick him under the table but I resisted. The whole time, Uncle Farlin smiled, as if this were just friendly banter between two kids who hadn't seen each other in a while.

When dinner was over, Uncle Farlin suggested Alectus show me some of the things he'd been working on. The whole living room looked like a museum of gadgets and thingamabobs.

"Certainly," Alectus said, standing up and gesturing for me to follow him across the room.

Certainly? Alectus must be mimicking the language he overheard while serving tea. I couldn't tell if he was trying to impress me, or just being condescending.

He stopped in front of the first shelf of gadgets. "As I'm sure you're aware, the Society prides itself on innovation. Progress comes through invention, that's what Sir Maychin says. Just look at what he's accomplished so far—making travel easier with motorized cars and boats, powering houses with electricity, mass-producing books. So, I started working on a few things of my own. I figured it might help me get promoted faster, and it's turned out to be a fun hobby. I don't have the money or materials for big things, so I've borrowed stuff from work and I've got access to all the books I need in the library. Plus, I found a few really old books in Sir Maychin's office, full of invention ideas. I looked through them while I was cleaning."

Alectus pointed to a large metal object next to the shelf. "Here's a car engine from one of the Dorf Model Bs," he said. "I've taken the whole thing apart and put it back together. I didn't have room to keep it in my workshop, so I brought it up here." It looked like a spiderweb of pipes to me. Next, he moved over to the bookshelf and picked up a wooden box. "I made this from a piece of driftwood. Try to open it."

The top of the box had the Society's symbol engraved on it—a circle with an X through it—and though it had a lid, I couldn't open it. I fiddled for a few minutes before giving it back.

Alectus grinned. "It's got two secret levers," he said. "You need to press them both at the same time." Alectus pushed two pieces of wood on opposite sides of the box, and it opened.

"That's impressive," I said, taking the box back and examining it more closely.

Alectus turned and reached for the next object on the shelf. "This one is a model I, um . . . borrowed from one of the offices. It's called an airplane. One day, the Society claims people will be able to fly with these." He held up an object that looked like a car with wings.

"Fly?" I said, laughing. "With that? It's barely bigger than my hand."

Alectus scowled. "It's a prototype," he snapped. "The real one will be as big as our boat, maybe bigger."

"And we'll be able to fly in that?" I said. "Like some sort of bird?" I tried not to giggle at the idea.

Alectus put the model back on the shelf, clearly irritated. "You'll see. People like you laughed ten years ago when Sir Maychin told them he could make a car go faster than a horse. Now look around. There are hundreds of cars on the roads. The world is improving every day because of the imagination and innovation of people like Sir Maychin. He calls it a revolution—an industrial revolution. Who knows what the world will look like in another ten years!"

"Yeah, who knows," I agreed. "Just look at the smog over Olport and the garbage floating in the channel. At this rate, the world might not look like much in another ten years."

"Don't be so negative," Alectus spat. "You're focusing on the bad. Look at my foot." He pulled up the leg of his pants to reveal a metal rod where he'd once had a wooden stump. "This thing is spring-loaded and stronger than rock. You probably noticed I don't limp as much. Without the Society, I'd still be hobbling around here without direction. I owe a lot to the Society. They've put me back on my feet, in more ways than one."

Alectus walked over to the furthest shelf and picked up another object, this one made of wood, wire, and metal.

"Here's something I'm really proud of," he said. "I designed it myself."

"What is it?" I asked.

"A crossbow," he said, peering down the top. "The Society has improved the design of guns, but those need gunpowder, which is expensive and hard to come by. This thing is so powerful it can shoot an arrow straight through a tree branch."

Alectus turned the crossbow and aimed it at me, the wildness back in his eyes. I felt the heat rise in my chest immediately.

"Not in the house," Uncle Farlin said, stepping between us and pushing the front of the crossbow down.

Alectus grinned, pleased with my reaction. "It's not loaded," he said, "but if you come out back I'll show you how good a shot I've become. With minor adjustments to each new model, I've gotten it to shoot farther and straighter. I've even built one for the back of the boat. I call it a harpoon gun."

"I'm not a big fan of them," Uncle Farlin said, "but they've got their uses. The one on the boat has almost got your cousin over his fear of the water."

"Great," I said, feeling a little nauseous. "Glad to hear that, but I think I'll pass on going out back. I'm worn out from travelling and I should probably go to bed."

Standing around and watching Alectus shoot a crossbow was high on the list of things I never wanted to do. There was a good chance I'd end up getting shot. Besides, I really was tired. And if the other Guardians were anything like Pteron, they'd have me going through all sorts of exhausting exercises. I needed to rest and get ready for my training.

Chapter 32

I DIDN'T SLEEP WELL THAT NIGHT. BETWEEN THE BANGING SHUT-ters and the whistling wind, it seemed Terra Herself was trying to keep me awake.

I must have drifted off while writing in my journal, because I awoke with a thin stream of light shining between the shutters, the book lying open on my chest.

Alectus and Uncle Farlin were getting ready to leave when I went downstairs.

"Sorry to run like this," Uncle Farlin said, "but I have to be at the docks in an hour and I'm dropping Alectus off in Olport for work. We won't be back until this evening, but there are eggs for breakfast and fish for lunch."

Alectus waited by the door, holding it open. He wore another fresh pair of black dress pants and a white button-up shirt. On his head was a large otter-pelt hat.

"Thanks, Uncle Farlin," I said. "I'll be fine."

After they left, I ate a quick breakfast before setting out to search the island for Vulpeera and the rest of the Guardians. The island was small, but it would take a while to search all the places they could be. I stopped briefly at the top of the cliffs to admire the view, watching the waves crashing against the rocks far below, with Olport in the distance. My uncle's boat was halfway across the channel, a large, tarp-covered object standing at the back.

Alectus's harpoon gun, I thought with a shudder.

When the boat was out of view, I took off down the hill and into the woods. I followed the path until I came to the turnoff that led to Alectus's workshop. Across the door, a new sign read "Keep Out" in red paint. As I was the only one on the island, I knew the sign was directed at me. Not that I needed it. I had no interest in seeing what other death contraptions Alectus was dreaming up.

I hurried along to the last intersecting trail and veered to the right. A hundred paces brought me to my favourite spot on the island, a small pond the size of Granny's living room, shallow enough to walk across, with algae-covered rocks poking through the surface. I was searching for the frogs and turtles I often saw there when I heard a voice behind me.

"Not a bad place to learn Sensium," it said, and I turned to find Vulpeera. I dropped to my knees and wrapped my arms around her neck.

"You look much better!" I exclaimed.

"I feel better every day," Vulpeera said.

A large shadow passed overhead, and I looked up to see Catharia, slowly circling down toward us.

"Yes," the large condor said, "this place will do. At least until the wolves figure out a way to cross the channel."

"It's a long swim," I heard Pteron's voice say. I hadn't noticed him hanging from a branch in the nearby woods. "But we need to be careful. Just this morning, the wolves were spotted leaving Grander's Bay and heading in this direction."

"Already?" Vulpeera asked. "But we were so careful to get Winter out without being seen. Perhaps a crow spotted her?"

Pteron shook his head. "I have other suspicions," he said. "Crows don't fly that quickly."

"What suspicions?" I asked.

Vulpeera stepped forward. "Enough worrying. If we don't start training soon, there will be more to worry about."

"Right, sorry, Vulpeera," I said. "Am I going to learn your skill today?"

She nodded. "Sensium—the gift of the Land Guardian of Agility. Do you have the amulet?"

I had grabbed the amulet from under the floorboard before leaving the cabin. I pulled it from beneath my shirt and held it out while Vulpeera touched it with her nose. A familiar jolt shot through me and the symbol of the fox glowed green.

Vulpeera gave a nod and began pacing. "So far, the skills you have learned are skills of wisdom—abilities centred around Terra's energy. With Aminoculus, you learned to use your inner eye to see Terra's energy. With Imperia, you learned to manipulate Her energy. Today, you will learn something completely different. As a Guardian of agility, my ability centres around Terra's fluidity, not her energy."

"Fluidity?"

"Yes, fluidity. In other words, Terra's changes. Terra exists in a dynamic state—She is not static or unmoving as one might think. She is always adapting, altering, evolving. We call that ever-changing state fluidity. The mountains grow and crumble, the rivers flow and dry up, even Her creatures are changing. As the Land Guardian of Agility, I can control the changes to Terra Creatura. I shape Terra's beings so they may better interact with their Mother. Lillian once called these changes 'evolution.' I like that name."

Vulpeera stopped pacing and sat in front of me. "Tell me, Winter, have you learned about the ways in which we interact with our Mother? Can you name all of the senses She has given us?"

I thought for a moment. "In school we learned there are five senses—hearing, touch, taste, smell, and sight."

"That's all? Five?" Vulpeera asked skeptically.

I shrugged. "That's all we were taught."

"I'm beginning to doubt this so-called school of yours. There are more than five senses—many more. There are inner senses, the abilities that allow us to perceive when we are hungry or thirsty. And you have not even touched on two of the most important senses—balance and proprioception."

"Proprio—what?"

"It is a complicated name for a simple idea. Proprioception is our body's sense of itself in space. For example, if you close your eyes and raise your hand in front of your face, you will still know exactly where your hand is. You do not need to open your eyes or touch it with your other hand to know."

I tried it, and it was true. Anywhere I moved my hand, I knew exactly where it was.

"With Sensium, the ability of the Land Guardian of Agility, all of your senses will be heightened. You will see farther, smell stronger, but most importantly, learn to move to your body's fullest capacity."

"So, it's basically like having superhuman senses?"

Vulpeera laughed. "Superhuman? To a human, a bear's sense of smell is super. What I'm talking about are super-animal senses. But like all of Terra's gifts, you must learn to use it. You must hone your senses so that you become aware of them. By doing so, you will learn to move through Terra's physical domain in ways unknown to your species. You will become as agile as a river and as evasive as a windswept dandelion seed. Nothing more than a fleeting glint in a predator's periphery. But first, you must—"

Vulpeera stopped and looked back at me. I had been following as she walked around the pond.

"Is that truly how you walk?" she asked, looking at my feet.

I looked down at my shoes.

"Um, yes?"

"You sound like a horse walking on acorns. Stealth and swiftness go hand in hand, and right now I would hear you walking on moss a mile away. How do you place your feet when you step?"

"How do I place my feet?" I asked. "What do you mean?"

"Show me."

I walked to the far edge of the pond and back, my shoes clomping over the rock despite my efforts to walk quietly.

Vulpeera shook her head. "This won't be easy."

I rolled my eyes. "You weigh a tenth of what I weigh and have padded paws, not shoes."

"It is not about weight or padded feet. It's about being careful. A hoofed deer can run soundlessly over dried leaves. You must walk with care—each step planned. Start by placing the outside of your foot and rolling it toward the middle. This will dampen the sound."

I did as she instructed and was amazed to find an immediate difference.

"That's a start," Vulpeera said, sounding less impressed. "As you practice, it will become easier. Do it enough and it will become natural. Silence will become your friend." She continued walking around the pond. "But silence is only one piece of Sensium—next comes agility. You must learn to move the rest of your body in the same way. You must get close to Terra, feel Her rawness and energy, move as if you are one with Her. And for Terra's sake, use all the limbs She has given you. No more of this awkward two-legged bumbling."

"You want me to walk on all fours?" I asked. "I can tell you right now that won't make me look more natural. Humans aren't designed for walking on all fours."

"Says who?"

"Says science. I don't know, someone. Look, it's just obvious. The only humans who can walk on their hands are in the circus."

"Then join this circus. I'm not saying you must walk on four limbs everywhere—but when you're being chased up a tree or bounding over rocks, it's helpful if you can plant and spring and swing using more than just those two gripless posts you call legs. If you've got four limbs, why use only two?" Vulpeera turned and pointed with her nose toward the pond. "You see those rocks sticking up from the water?"

"Yes."

"Starting from this side, I want you to cross the pond using only those rocks. No swimming allowed."

"That's not possible," I griped. "I couldn't even jump to the first rock."

"To the first rock? It's only the distance of your height. Are you telling me you can't jump as far as you are tall?"

"Probably not. My legs aren't that strong."

"Jumping has little to do with strength. A cat can jump five times its own height, and I assure you, your legs are stronger. Jumping is about using your body effectively. It is about your arms and legs working to-

168

gether to maximize your propulsion. With the gift of Sensium, this will be easier, but it will still require practice."

"You want me to start from that end of the pond and jump to the other side using only the slippery, algae-covered rocks?"

Vulpeera nodded. "Reach with your hands, not your feet. It will make it easier with the algae."

"So, you mean I'm trying to move like you?"

Vulpeera grinned. "I want you to jump and land with your hands, not with your feet. I want you to capture that rock, brace your body onto your arms until you can bring your feet to meet them, then push off for the next. In essence—yes—I want you to move like me."

I stared at Vulpeera, trying to judge whether she was joking. When she didn't laugh, I walked toward the far end of the pond.

"I already know how this is going to end," I said. "But for you, I'll give it a try." When I was twenty feet from the pond—a good distance for a running start—I called, "Okay, here goes nothing!" and took off toward the edge.

I immediately noticed something different. The air stung at my face like needles and I felt, painlessly, every rock through the soles of my shoes as if I were running barefoot. The smell of the water was more pungent than I could remember, and I could see each individual strand of algae on the rocks.

What was happening?

I was so focused on my newfound senses that I forgot what Vulpeera had said about reaching with my hands, not my feet. I took off from the edge of the pond and soared across the water. I was like a skimming dragonfly. Never had my legs and arms and body felt more in sync.

The rock ahead rushed up quickly. I was in danger of overshooting it so I put out my foot to land, but the algae was wet and slick and my foot slipped off the far side, sending me backward into a flip. I landed in the pond headfirst, water filling my nose and mouth. When I stood, a long piece of wilting algae draped across my face. I spat out a mouthful of water and cleared my eyes to find Vulpeera laughing. Even the condor looked amused.

"I'm glad you enjoyed that," I said, tilting my head sideways to drain the water from my ear.

"I'm sorry," Vulpeera said, covering her snout with a paw. "It was good—your body looked fluid and natural."

"Yes," Catharia agreed. "Your landing needs work but I daresay the gift of the sky might come easily to you."

"The gift of the sky?" I asked. "Will I learn to fly?"

"I don't see why not," Catharia said. "Once you own the wind, you own the sky."

Vulpeera shook her head, smirking. "First, learn to fly over land, then think about joining the creatures of the sky. I assure you, there's nothing as stable as having all feet on solid ground."

"Sorry, Vulpeera," I said, "I didn't mean any disrespect. I'm excited to learn Sensium. I felt something different when I jumped."

She smiled. "I don't doubt that you did. The skill comes naturally to you. But we have much training to do. Crossing a pond is one thing, but contending with an army of wolves is another. These next few weeks will be difficult, but your body will change quickly, and you will grow stronger. Now, back to the edge of the pond. Try again. Only this time—hands, not feet."

Chapter 33

It had been two weeks, and as Vulpeera predicted, my body had changed. I sat high in a tree, overlooking the forest. The branch beneath my feet was damp with morning dew as I plotted my route. I had to make a split-second decision—time was wasting—trees or ground?

The forest floor was covered in thick vines, no doubt placed by Pteron. With my enhanced eyesight, I could make out sharp thorns on the vines.

Looked like it would have to be the trees.

I leapt from the branch toward the nearest tree. It was a long way off—at least ten feet—but my jumping distance had improved as I'd learned to engage more of my muscles. I soared through the air, tucking my arms by my sides to reduce the drag, grabbing the next branch as I fell. I swung myself around and used my momentum to launch myself toward the next tree.

I continued flinging myself from tree to tree, making excellent time through the course Vulpeera had set, when a rock came hurtling toward my head. It came from behind; I saw it as a glint of movement in my mind's eye and shifted my body in midair to avoid it. But the disruption set me off course for the next branch, and suddenly I was falling. My heart rate spiked, but I forced myself not to panic. "Panic is pointless," Pteron had said.

I looked down and spotted a branch approaching within arm's reach. I managed to grab it with the tips of my fingers and swung myself up and around, landing on top in a crouched position.

Darn it, Pteron, I thought. That rock was going to cost me a lot of time. Why did he always have to make things more difficult?

At least my Aminoculus was improving. Outlines of objects were grainy but perceptible in my mind's eye, although they were less clear when I was in motion. A few short weeks before, I would have gotten plunked in the back of the head.

I took off again. The next tree was thin and weak, so I spun my body and pressed my feet against the trunk. It bowed beneath my weight and snapped back, sending me flying in a new direction. I catapulted until I came to a larger trunk with no bend or branches. With no time to think (gravity is impatient), I wrapped my legs around the trunk and slid down it like a fire pole.

I landed hard but was happy to find no thorny vines below.

There wasn't a second to think before something shot through the trees toward me. I ducked as Pteron narrowly missed my head with a stick. I knew he would be back shortly for another pass, so I took off running.

Up ahead I saw a clearing—the finish line—but there was a thick wall of vines blocking my way.

Almost there.

I cartwheeled to avoid Pteron's next pass and slid beneath a third. He was doing everything possible to slow me down.

When I was ten steps away from the wall of vines, I called upon my Imperia, which was getting better, but only slowly without a teacher to guide me. I felt the heat grow in my chest, and my hands began to tingle, but there wouldn't be enough time to summon the flames on my own before I made my jump. I bit my tongue—a little trick I'd discovered that sent an instant surge of pain and heat through my body. The pain concentrated in my hands and they glowed a bright yellow. I aimed them ahead and released an enormous ball of fire that incinerated the wall of vines.

Perfect, I thought, as I dove headfirst through the flames and somersaulted on the opposite side. I stood up in front of Vulpeera, who was sitting on a rock in the middle of the clearing.

"Time!" I yelled.

Vulpeera smiled but Pteron swooped down and landed beside her, a scowl on his face.

"What?" I asked, panting.

He peered over my shoulder at the vines I had rolled through. "I thought after what happened in the Red Woods you would be a little more careful."

I turned. The flames had already fizzled out, but a thin wisp of smoke rose from the hole I'd blasted.

"It was the easiest—"

"Easiest is not always best," Pteron interjected. "A problem you humans have struggled with since the beginning of time. You must respect Terra. Always."

I opened my mouth to argue but let the air pass slowly from my lungs. Pteron was right. I knew he was right. "Sorry, Pteron," I said. "I'll try to be more respectful."

His scowl faded. "Good. Otherwise, excellent job. Your fastest time yet."

Vulpeera nodded enthusiastically, beaming with pride. "Yes, very good. Your coordination is improving remarkably, and you're using your hands more and more. There's no doubt you're a fast learner."

I grinned. "Well, I have good teachers."

It was true. Vulpeera and Pteron had dedicated countless hours over the past two weeks to training me. Every day we'd start early, beginning as soon as Alectus and Uncle Farlin had left for the day, and stopping only when we heard the roar of the boat engine returning.

I had climbed trees until my hands blistered, run until my feet bled, lifted rocks until every muscle in my body screamed. In the evenings, Alectus would make snarky comments about how lazy I was. "It must get boring doing nothing all day," he'd say, being sure to point out how many hours he'd worked. I wanted to show him my hands and feet, expose the blisters and bruises I kept hidden.

Instead I'd put my head down and mumble, "Yeah," before retiring to my room to continue my mental training. At night, Pteron would hang in the corner of my room, and we'd talk quietly of how to control my thoughts. I learned to focus on what needed to be focused on, compartmentalizing so I could call on whichever power was required. By the end of each day as I recorded my progress in my journal, I'd feel as if I'd been hit by a Dorf Model B, but the following morning I'd wake up feeling stronger and fresher than ever.

A bird circled around the clearing and landed next to Pteron on a stone.

"Fantom," Pteron said, "any news of the wolves?"

Fantom had been keeping close tabs on Lupora and her army. "No news of the wolves. They are amassing in the woods on the mainland but have no way to cross the channel."

Pteron nodded thoughtfully.

"But I bring other news," Fantom said, turning toward me. "It appears you have a visitor."

Chapter 34

THE FOG OVER THE WATER WAS SO THICK THAT DAY THAT ONLY A faint silhouette could be seen approaching. It moved slowly, a raft with a single passenger on board.

"Who is it?" I asked Vulpeera, but she only smiled and kept watching.

When the craft finally came into view, I gave an embarrassing squeal. It was Cheelion, but more importantly, he had Proctin on his back.

I nearly crushed Proctin in my arms when he stepped ashore.

"I missed you!" I screeched.

"Can't . . . breathe." Proctin gasped.

"Sorry," I said, letting him go. I put Proctin down and looked at him. He appeared more or less the same as when I'd last seen him.

"Thank you, Cheelion, for rescuing him," I said, turning to the turtle.

Cheelion gave a slow turtle nod. "It wasn't easy. They had him in a cave on the beach, and I had to wait days for the wolves to let their guard down long enough to break him out."

"Well, I'm glad he's back unharmed," I said.

"Unharmed?!" Proctin cried. "Look at me!"

Catharia and Vulpeera exchanged confused looks as Proctin lifted his arms and spun around.

"Er, look at what?" Vulpeera asked.

"Look how much weight I've lost! I've practically wasted away! They were the worst weeks of my life. They tortured me! They kept me locked in a tiny cell and starved me half to death!"

"That's awful," I said, sitting down next to Proctin and running my hand gently over his back.

Little tears trickled down his furry cheeks. "They only fed me three times a day," he sobbed.

A confused silence fell over the beach.

"How many meals do you normally eat?" Fantom asked.

"Well," Proctin said, thinking about this, "more than three. That's for certain. I mean, okay, sure, once or twice my sisters came and snuck me some extra food, but at most I had four meals a day. And they weren't large. A few handfuls of nuts or berries. It was horribly, terribly, uncomfortably difficult."

"You're here now, and that's all that matters," I said. "Come on up to my uncle's cabin—he keeps the kitchen stocked with fish."

Proctin's eyes lit up, and his tongue dropped from his mouth. I carried him up to the house, where he ate half the contents of the icebox. That evening, he crawled into bed with me, and even with his wheezy snore, I slept better than I had since arriving on Pitchi.

The following morning, Proctin stayed in bed while I headed down to the pond to train. It was Sunday, and Alectus had left for a meeting at the Society, while Uncle Farlin had gone to Olport for breakfast. It was his routine every Sunday to go to the Captain's Pub, and normally I would have joined him—he begged me enough—but I said I wasn't feeling well and that I'd join him next time. I hated lying to Uncle Farlin, but the Guardians had insisted it wasn't safe to leave Pitchi.

I sat by the pond waiting for Vulpeera, but after ten minutes she still hadn't shown. It was odd—she was usually the one waiting for me.

I entertained myself by practicing my Imperia, swirling my hands until the flames built between them, strong enough to hold their shape.

I threw the fireball into the pond where it landed with a splash, sending a hiss of steam into the air. I practiced making one-handed fireballs and tossing them two at a time.

Splash, hiss, splash, hiss.

Vulpeera's voice made me jump. "Winter," she said.

I turned to find her standing at the edge of the forest, a worried expression on her face.

"What is it?"

"Follow me; we have something to show you."

I didn't have time to ask where we were going before she leapt into the woods. I ran to catch up, then kept pace until we burst through the other side of the trees.

"Here?" I asked nervously.

We were standing in front of Alectus's workshop. Catharia waited by the open door.

I glanced behind me, half expecting to find Alectus.

It's okay, I told myself, *he's at his meeting*. He wouldn't be back for another few hours.

"What would I want to see in my cousin's workshop?"

I walked to the entrance and the answer hit me in the face with so much force, I nearly fell backward. I grabbed hold of the doorframe to steady myself.

The smell from the hut made my eyes sting and my lungs clench tight in my chest. I gagged and fought down the urge to vomit. It was horrible—like a mixture of rotting flesh and mildew. I wished I could turn down my Sensium as I covered my mouth and nose, trying to block out the stench.

"What is that?" I asked, my eyes watering.

"See for yourself," Catharia said, ushering me inside.

I pulled up my shirt collar to cover my nose and went into the hut. It was dark, but I could see a worktable in the centre covered with scraps of wood, tools, and a small lamp.

"Light the lamp," Vulpeera said from outside the hut.

I walked over, concentrating the heat into my hands until a small flame flickered to life. I opened the door of the lantern and guided the flame inside. The wick took and light gleamed through the hut.

What I saw made the very bones in my legs go soft. I stumbled backward, trying to get away from it, but I couldn't—it was everywhere, all around.

Death.

Hundreds of eyes looked down at me from the walls—hundreds of lifeless eyes.

The inside of the hut was covered with plaques carved from wood, and in the centre of each plaque was an animal.

Seagulls, turtles, frogs, squirrels, snakes, moles—they were all pinned to the plaques with thick metal bolts through their wings or feet or paws. I recognized the bolts from Alectus's crossbow.

"Winter!" I vaguely heard Vulpeera say from behind. "We need to leave! Quickly!"

Her words were like background noise in my jumbled mind. I heard them, but they had no meaning. Instead, my thoughts went to the day I'd arrived on Pitchi. I had wondered why it felt so quiet and assumed it was because of the time of year, but I had been wrong. The animals weren't staying away from the island—Alectus was killing them.

"Why?" I whispered. "Why would he do this, Vulpeera? Why would he kill them?"

I turned around expecting to see the fox, but instead found another figure lurking in the doorway.

My heart seemed to stop in my chest.

It was Alectus.

Chapter 35

"WHAT ARE YOU DOING IN MY WORKSHOP?" ALECTUS GROWLED, slamming the door behind him. "And who were you talking to?" He was wearing the same black dress pants and white button-up shirt he'd had on that morning when he left for his meeting. A crossbow was loaded and aimed at my chest. As he approached, he swung his crossbow left and right, scanning the room.

When he was a few feet away, he looked at me, eyes enraged. "I asked you a question! Who were you talking to? Who's Vulpeera!"

I choked out a few words. "I-I don't know. I wasn't talking to anyone."

"Yes, you were," he spat. "I heard two voices as I was walking down the path."

I tried to come up with an excuse. "No, it was just me. I sometimes talk to myself."

It was a weak attempt, and Alectus didn't seem convinced. He walked around the worktable, checking the corners of the hut closely. When he had finished searching, he came back to me.

"Can you not read? The sign on the door says keep out! I don't go rooting through your stuff, do I?"

"I'm sorry. I was just . . ." I couldn't think of a logical explanation.

Alectus raised an eyebrow. "Just what?"

"Just . . . curious. You know, because I'm bored and have nothing to do all day."

Alectus lifted his crossbow to rest on his shoulder. "Well then," he said, lips curling into a thin smile as he gestured proudly around the room. "What do you think?"

My words finally came to me, flowing from my mouth like lava. "What do I think?" I snarled. "I think this is disgusting! I think it's the sickest thing I've ever seen! I think you're sick! Why would you kill all these animals?"

Alectus's smile faded. "Why?" he said. "Why not? It's good practice for my crossbow, and anyway, who cares? They're pests!"

"Pests!" I raged. "These are not pests! These are living creatures with thoughts and feelings!"

"Thoughts and feelings?" Alectus laughed. "You sound completely insane. Why do you care so much?"

"I care because I should. Because we need to look out for those that are smaller and weaker than us. All of Terra Creatura has a place."

"Terra Creatura? What are you talking about? Winter, these are ANIMALS!"

"So are we!"

"Oh, come on, you can't seriously be comparing us to them?"

"Why not?"

"Because, well, look at them. They steal food and use the whole world as a toilet. They squawk and squeak all night while we're trying to sleep. They don't think. They don't evolve or invent. They don't have feelings."

"How do you know that?"

"How do I know?!" he yelled, his eyes taking on a whole new level of scary. "I'll show you how I know." He yanked up his pant leg to reveal the steel rod beneath. "Do you think that big fish felt bad when it did this to me? Do you think it cared that it was ruining my life? That because of it, I would be trapped on this island, afraid of the water that surrounds me twenty-four hours a day?"

"Alectus, I'm sorry." I reached out to touch his shoulder, but he batted my hand away.

"I've always hated them," he said. "Ever since the day that whale took my leg, I've hated them all."

"Wait, whale? Did you just say whale? Not shark?"

"Whale. Shark. What does it matter? All I know is that a big black fish followed our boat for days. The crew said it was attracted to the fish we threw overboard, but I saw its eyes, watching me. It didn't want the fish; it wanted me. And that day I sat there with my legs hanging over the side of the boat, just eating my lunch, it tried to take me under. It tried to kill me! And it would have if I hadn't been anchored to the boat."

"Cano," I said, the word falling from my lips as an image of the black whale flashed through my mind.

"What?" Alectus asked.

I shook my head, clearing the image. "Nothing. It's just that—well, that's not the story I heard. I thought it was a shark."

"I've never told you the story. And my father didn't see it happen. Besides, I try to forget that day. That was back then, and this is now. The point is, these are animals. They don't care about us, so we shouldn't care about them. It's a food chain and we're at the top. With the help of our inventions, that's where we'll stay."

A bang at the door of the hut caused both Alectus and me to jump. Before I could stop him, Alectus rushed to the door and flung it open.

"Who's out here!" he yelled, wildly waving his crossbow around as he stepped outside.

I followed closely behind, scanning the area, happy to find no sign of the Guardians.

Alectus turned to me.

"There's something funny going on around here," he said. "You stay away from my hut, you hear me? If I catch you so much as ten feet from it, I'll make you sorry."

He turned and slammed the door shut behind us before taking off toward the cabin, mumbling something about getting a lock.

Chapter 36

"Was it him?" I asked, looking around the circle of Guardians. "Did Cano attack Alectus?"

It was dusk, and we sat in a small clearing by the water. We talked quietly—Alectus and Uncle Farlin were up the hill in the cabin.

"Yes," Pteron said, hanging upside down from a branch. "Cano attacked your cousin. Your cousin was an easy target that day on the water."

"But why Alectus?"

The other Guardians looked at Pteron as he continued. "Cano wants to end your bloodline. You, Lillian, Alectus, Uncle Farlin—he seeks vengeance on everyone in your family. Until recently, we assumed he had given up his quest for retribution."

"You mean until the day he attacked me on Cheelion's shell?"

Pteron nodded. "Yes, until that day."

A part of me didn't blame Cano. And a part of me also felt sorry for Alectus. But the images of the dead animals in Alectus's hut eclipsed any feelings of sympathy for my cousin.

"The hut . . ." I said, fighting back tears, on the verge of breaking down after a rough afternoon.

"Your cousin is unwell," Vulpeera said, resting her head on my leg. "He, too, has been touched by Malum." Proctin was curled up on my other side, and it was nice having them both close.

"Malum?" I said. "But I thought that only happens when someone dies."

Vulpeera shook her head. "Malum can be caused by all manner of loss. Your father lost his life-mate, an injustice he blamed on Terra. Your cousin lost his leg and his independence, and for this he blames all of Terra Creatura. Malum is the anger and misguidance that comes from believing an injustice has occurred. It is the belief that because you were wronged, you have the right to wrong others. It is a dark and powerful force with the ability to destroy not only individuals, but Terra Herself."

Fantom had been pacing back and forth on a branch above and hopped down beside Vulpeera. "It's not safe here," he said, fluttering his wings. "We need to get Winter away. What if the boy's sickness grows?"

"There is nowhere else for her to go, and her training is progressing well here," Pteron said. "We have no choice but to stay. We will need to be more vigilant. The boy is obviously more troubled than we thought. I will stay in Winter's room at night and keep watch. During the day, we must monitor the boat. Catharia and Fantom can take turns watching from the sky to see when he returns."

A low moon was beginning to crest above the trees, and silver light bathed our clearing. Something else had been bothering me. Something Alectus had said.

"Vulpeera," I said, "Alectus mentioned he'd heard two voices talking in the hut. How is it that he could hear you?"

Cheelion had been sitting quietly in the surf. "Humans have long forgotten the common tongue of the animals," he said. "He may have heard sounds, but he would not be able to understand Vulpeera."

"But how can I understand?"

"Before the humans invented their own words for things, everyone spoke the same tongue. When Terra selects a human as a Guardian, She needs only to remind them of what they once knew. It was the same for

Lillian and your father—once they were selected as Guardians, some-how, they remembered."

"But I'm sure Alectus said two voices."

Cheelion shook his head. "You must be mistaken."

IN THE END, we decided I would stay on Pitchi and continue my training, but from then on, I worried constantly about Alectus. At night, I slept poorly—fearing every slam of the shutters was another break-in, every whistle of the wind another crossbow bolt whizzing past my head. When I'd sit up quickly in bed, Pteron would reassure me it was just another nightmare, but the haunting eyes of the animals in the hut never left me, even when I slept.

Thankfully, the island was now empty of any creature Alectus could harm, and those that might have come in the past—the seagulls and otters and seals—stayed far away.

During the day, I threw myself into my training, working hard to hone my skills and forget everything else. I tried not to think about Alectus or Cano or Arctos or Lupora, but the truth was, they were al-ways there, buried in the back of my mind, spurring me to train harder.

I took no days off. Even when Alectus and Uncle Farlin were home, I locked myself in my room and practiced my Aminoculus and Imperia. I remained focused, determined . . . obsessed. In the mornings, I'd wait for Alectus and Uncle Farlin to leave and then spring from my bed to begin my daily routine.

My Sensium improved in leaps and bounds. My body grew stronger, while my limbs grew nimbler. I could cover the length of the island in minutes, running silently over rock and swinging effortlessly through the trees. We practiced vigilance, constant awareness, never taking a moment off. I learned to fade into the shadows wherever I walked and to control my breathing so that even in complete silence, I was the quietest thing. At times, I'd walk up behind Uncle Farlin to get something from the cupboard only to have him jump with fright. "Holy codfish and crackers, Winter! I didn't even know you were there," he'd yell.

While Vulpeera shaped my body, Pteron continued to shape my mind. My Aminoculus sharpened to the point where Terra's energy formed distinct images that remained even when I jumped or swung or ran. Even my Imperia improved. I grew faster at calling the flame and relied less on biting my tongue. But for all this improvement, all the progress I was making with my abilities, there was one thing that eluded me:

The blue flame.

The healing flame.

In the evenings, I'd try to summon it to heal my scrapes and cuts, but no matter what I tried, no matter how much I mimicked what I'd seen Granny do, I couldn't replicate it.

And this worried me.

For what sort of Guardian could only use their power to destroy and not heal?

I could think of just one person.

And I didn't want to be like my father.

Chapter 37

THE GUARDIANS WEREN'T PLEASED WHEN I TOLD THEM I WAS leaving Pitchi for a morning.

"The wolves have gathered in the woods surrounding Olport," Catharia said. "It wouldn't be safe."

"But they're not *in* the city," I pleaded. "I'm just going to a small pub, right on the waterfront."

Pteron shook his head slowly, but Vulpeera seemed to be thinking it through.

I looked at her with pleading eyes. "Please, Vulpeera? Uncle Farlin has done so much for me. It would mean a lot to him if I went. It's only breakfast."

Vulpeera looked guiltily at the ground. "Well," she said, "I don't see much of an issue if it's just for the morning."

"It is! I promise!"

Cheelion nodded his agreement. "It is unlikely Lupora would take her wolves into the city. And Fantom can keep watch from above, in case there is any movement from her camp. I see no problem with it, either."

Despite Pteron's continued concern, it was decided that I could go with Uncle Farlin that Sunday morning to the Captain's Pub for breakfast. There were a number of factors that made me want to go. First, I couldn't stand the look on my uncle's face every time I said no. Second, Alectus hadn't so much as lifted a finger against me since that day in the hut. Third, and perhaps most importantly, I desperately needed a good meal. Something other than fish soup.

I awoke early that day, washed the dirt from my face, put on nice clothes, hid the amulet safely beneath the floorboard in my room, and went downstairs to join Uncle Farlin.

The Captain's Pub was a dingy restaurant right on the main wharf of Olport, always packed with fishermen and sailors. The food was good, but the crowd was a little rough around the edges. Still, I liked going. It was a chance to spend time with my uncle, and I liked the way he showed me off to the other fishermen like some sort of trophy fish he'd pulled from the water.

I ate an enormous feast that morning of bacon, potatoes, omelet, and pancakes while Uncle Farlin and I talked about life on the island. He told me about his fishing, and about the new roof he planned to put on the lighthouse. Briefly, we talked about Alectus.

"He's doing better," Uncle Farlin said. "The Society has helped him a lot—I'll say that much."

I had trouble agreeing as I pictured the animals in the hut, and it must have showed on my face.

"Oh, he's not perfect," Uncle Farlin continued. "I know that. He's given you grief over the years, and for that I'm sorry. But you must understand that living on the island hasn't been easy on him. His inventions have helped, but he still lives in fear. I see it in his eyes every time we're out on the water." Uncle Farlin crumpled a napkin between his hands as he spoke, looking down at the table. "The other day, we were crossing the channel early in the morning when a little dolphin swam up beside the boat. You'd have thought it was a great white shark the way Alectus looked at it. He fired his harpoon gun straight at the poor thing. Missed—thank goodness—but by the time we got to shore, I had to carry your cousin off the boat. He was shaking and sobbing and pale as a ghost." Uncle Farlin scratched his chin and cleared his throat. "Heck, that kind of fear would wear anyone down over time. He's not perfect, but he's trying."

"I know," I said. And I did. I truly did understand that life hadn't been easy for Alectus. It was just hard to forgive him for everything he'd done.

Uncle Farlin smiled softly and stood, grabbing his wallet from the table. As I got up to follow, my ears caught a conversation behind me. "Wolves!" someone said. "The woods were full of them. Bigger than any dog you've ever seen."

"Wolves?" a croaky voice replied. "I've lived here fifty years and never seen a wolf this close to Olport."

I turned my head slightly to see who was talking. Behind us was a table of four fishermen.

"You'd probably had too much to drink," the third sailor chuckled.

"No! I swear! It was first thing in the morning, and I hadn't drunk a drop! They were all just standing around waiting, as if something was about to happen. I couldn't leave my property, there were so many of them."

The other two voices laughed. "You? Not a drop? Now we know you're lying."

I wanted to keep listening, but Uncle Farlin stood by the door, waving for me to follow. It was time to go.

"Let's get going," he said as I walked toward him, "I've got a little surprise for you."

"A surprise?" I said, squinting as I stepped into the glaring sun.

"This way," he said, and I followed eagerly as he led me along the wharf, away from the boats.

The surprise turned out to be a beautiful dress. Uncle Farlin had spotted it in the window of a fancy store downtown a few days before, and had already bought it. I wasn't sure where I would wear it, but I oohed and aahed and twirled in front of the mirror as the seamstress pinned and hemmed it.

On the way back to the boat, we got ice cream, and laughed about the time Uncle Farlin had tried to make his own. Cod Cream, he'd called it, and it had positively been the worst thing either of us had ever eaten.

It was nearly noon when we got back to Pitchi, and I felt lighter and happier than I had in a long time. It was nice to spend a morning doing normal things.

"I've got some errands to run," Uncle Farlin said, as he pulled up to the dock, "but I'll be back for dinner."

I thanked him again, jumped off the boat, waved goodbye, and ran up toward the cabin, eager to give Proctin the bacon I still had tucked inside a napkin in my pocket.

Halfway up the hill, I realized something was wrong.

There was a loud banging noise coming from the cabin—the door, opening and closing in the wind. Someone had forgotten to close it, and it hadn't been me.

As I got closer, I saw something stuck to the door.

My journal.

It was nailed to the door with a crossbow bolt. Across a blank page was written a single word in red:

"CANO!!!"

Chapter 38

I TORE DOWN THE JOURNAL AND BURST THROUGH THE FRONT door, flying up the stairs to my room. Inside, everything was in complete disarray. The pillows and blankets had been thrown on the floor, the mattress was upturned against the wall, the lamp knocked over, the drawers opened and emptied, my clothes scattered everywhere.

I rushed to the corner. The floorboard was loose, and I felt beneath it with my hand. There was nothing there. The amulet was gone.

"Proctin? Pteron?" I called.

They had both been in my room when I'd left.

I searched under the bed for Proctin, but the space was empty. When I looked up into the rafters where Pteron had been sleeping, I found a single red streak dripping from the wood. I looked at the ground by my feet to find a few small red droplets. I touched them with my finger.

Blood.

My mind raced as I put the pieces together: the diary, the amulet, Pteron, Proctin . . . It all pointed to Alectus.

Where was he?

It took me all of one second to come up with the answer.

My feet moved before I'd thought anything through. I ran down the hill toward the woods, toward Alectus's workshop.

The door was open when I arrived, but there was no light coming from within.

"Pteron?!" I cried. "Proctin?!"

I ran inside and tried to use my Aminoculus to scan the dark room, but my mind was too distraught to focus.

"Pteron?" I called again.

Something moved beside me, but before I could duck, a hand grabbed my hair, wrenching me sideways. My head hit the wooden doorframe hard, and everything went black.

WHEN I WOKE up, I knew by the stench I was still in the hut. I was sitting in a chair, and my head hurt, but when I tried to reach up and touch it, I found my hands were tied behind my back with thick rope.

Someone had lit the lantern on the nearby table, and as I looked around I saw the familiar plaques on the walls.

Was I dreaming? Was it a nightmare?

My chair was only a few feet from the wall where a new plaque was mounted. On it was a giant bat, its wings splayed wide with two cross-bow bolts holding them in place.

Pteron . . .

The weight of his body pulled on his wings, ripping the fragile webbing. His head hung low and his eyes were closed.

"Pteron!" I cried, but he didn't move. He was as still as the air in the hut. He looked no different from the other animals mounted to the boards around him, except for a wet patch on his stomach that was still fresh.

"Pteron!" I tried again, my throat tight. "Pteron, please wake up."

He's dead, I told myself. *It's too late. Alectus killed him.*

But then his head moved—ever so slightly.

"Pteron, wake up!"

He raised his head and looked at me with half-opened eyes.

"You're alive!" I shouted. "Thank goodness you're alive! I'm going to help you, hang on." I pulled at the restraints around my wrists, trying to free myself.

Pteron looked as if he was trying to say something.

"What is it, Pteron?" I asked.

"Proctin," he mumbled.

"Proctin? Where is he? Is he alright?" I scanned the room for anything resembling a raccoon, but my Aminoculus was still muddled.

"Alectus," Pteron continued.

"Alectus? Did he do this? Where is he?"

Pteron's breathing was uneven and raspy.

"Traitor."

"What do you mean? Where's Proctin, Pteron? Does Alectus have Proctin?"

"Proctin ... Guardian ... Wisdom ... you ... careful ... the ... amu-let ... traitor ..."

Pteron mumbled nonsensical words, his eyes closing.

"It's okay, Pteron," I said, trying to sound calmer than I felt. "I'm go-ing to get you out of here. Just hold on."

I was still struggling with the ropes around my wrists when the door behind me swung open with a bang. A gust of fresh air blew in before the door closed again, and I heard Alectus breathing quickly.

"Darn fox," he muttered under his breath.

A scratching noise came from the other side of the door, followed by a weak thump. Vulpeera was trying to get inside the hut.

"Alectus, let me go!" I yelled, struggling against the ropes. "Look what you're doing! Pteron is dying! Take him down!"

Alectus came up beside me and calmly set his crossbow on the table. His pant leg was torn, a gash bleeding beneath it.

"You should have told me," he said, his voice eerily quiet. "You knew it was him who attacked me. I read your diary."

"Alectus. Yes, I did know it was Cano, but not until recently. I'm sorry. I should have told you, but I knew you'd be angry."

"OF COURSE I'M ANGRY!" Alectus screamed, smashing his fist on the table. "You don't think I have the right to be angry?"

"I do. You have every right to be angry. But hurting Pteron isn't the answer. He's not to blame."

"They're all to blame. They protected that whale after what he did. Even this so-called god you worship, this Terra, She's to blame, too. She selected him as a Guardian after what he did. It's all there, in your own handwriting."

"If you read my journal, then you also know my father killed Cano's father. Cano was rightfully angry. That doesn't mean he should have attacked you, but he was . . . he was consumed by Malum."

"Malum?"

"It's what the animals call grief. The anger and misjudgment that comes from grief. I don't blame you for being angry, but you shouldn't take this out on the Guardians. They're not at fault."

Alectus walked toward the wall, standing a few feet away from Pteron. He reached out and touched Pteron's fur, and the bat flinched.

"These creatures," he said, "these Guardians you've joined. They're a cult. They've brainwashed you into believing what they say." Alectus walked back to the table and grabbed his crossbow. "But they need to learn their place."

"Alectus, no! Please, don't do this!"

"You, of all people, should want me to destroy them."

"Destroy? They're like family to me!"

"THEY KILLED YOUR FAMILY!" Alectus screamed. "They may only have taken my leg, but they took your father's life! Have you forgotten that? The bear killed your father. And yet you stand beside him and the others, acting as their so-called leader. You're a disgrace to your family and to your father's name." Alectus leaned in closer to me. "But it doesn't have to be that way," he whispered. "You have the power to change things—to finish what your father started and avenge him. I can help you. Together we can destroy them, Winter."

"Never!" I said. "I would never do that!"

Alectus stood and raised his crossbow, aiming it at Pteron's heart.

"I'm doing this for you, Winter. And for me. And for your father."

And with that, his finger tightened on the trigger.

Chapter 39

THE THOUGHT OF AN ARROW PIERCING PTERON'S HEART SENT A surge of heat through my chest and down into my hands. Within a fraction of a second, it concentrated to a scorch and the ropes disintegrated.

I grabbed Alectus's shoulder just as he pulled the trigger.

A loud twang echoed through the hut, followed by a thud as the bolt hit the wood two inches from Pteron.

Alectus growled angrily and swung the butt of his crossbow at me. I instinctively ducked out of the way, a reaction ingrained from my training.

"Alectus, please, I don't want to fight you," I said, raising my hands and backing away. He charged at me, but I sidestepped him easily.

"You're angry," I said, moving to the far side of the table and putting it between us, "but fighting with me isn't going to help. Maybe you should speak with Cano. I can probably arrange that."

A guttural sound came from the back of Alectus's throat like a snarl. "Why would I want to talk to that whale?!" he spat, picking up a piece of wood from the table and throwing it at me. I ducked and continued to walk around the table to keep it between us.

"You could hear each other out. You've both been wronged. It might make you feel better."

"I'll feel better when he's dead!" Alectus said.

His eyes fell on a spare crossbow bolt in the centre of the table. We looked at each other and then back at the bolt. Alectus dove first, but I swung my legs up onto the table and kicked the bolt out of his reach.

He grabbed my pant leg, and before I could wriggle free he pulled me to the floor.

We landed hard, wrestling for position. He was slower but stronger, and while he couldn't pin me down, he had a firm hold on my wrist that I couldn't break. I managed to stand, but he grabbed my hair from behind, pushing me into the wall. My face pressed up against something cold and furry.

"Stop this!" I screamed.

He pushed my face harder into the dead carcass on the wall. "What's wrong?" He laughed. "I thought these animals were your family."

I kicked and flailed and managed to turn around, freeing my face from the animal, but Alectus grabbed my wrists and pinned me to the wall. We were inches apart, his eyes staring into mine.

His eyes.

Those dark, cat-like eyes.

My eyes.

"You move like that fox," he said, "but you're still weak."

"Let me go, Alectus! Pteron is going to die!" I tried to squirm free, but it was no use. I looked over at Pteron. Two pools of blood were forming beneath his wings. He wasn't moving.

"It doesn't take long," Alectus said, following my gaze. "They bleed quickly. He'll be dead soon, and the process will have begun. I'll rid my island of every one of them. And then, I'll find that whale."

The image of Pteron triggered something inside me, like that day in the Red Woods. I felt something snap. I couldn't control my Imperia as the heat rose inside me like a forest fire untamed. It was the heat of anger, and it burst through my skin, encasing me in hot white flames.

Alectus roared, and let go of my wrists, but it was too late. His hands were on fire, and he waved them back and forth frantically. With each scream, the flames seemed to climb higher into the air.

I rushed to Pteron and wrapped my arms around his soft torso, lifting him from the bolts.

"Pteron, are you alive?" I asked, eyes brimming with tears. He didn't move in my arms.

Behind me, Alectus continued to scream.

"Hold on, Pteron, I'm getting you out of here."

I turned to the door, smoke filling the air and making it hard to see. In the centre of the room stood Alectus, his hands still on fire and raised in the air. He was no longer flailing them back and forth. He was no longer screaming. In my panic, I didn't notice how unusual that was.

I held Pteron's limp body to my chest and moved carefully around Alectus to the door. I had my hand on the knob when I heard another sound from behind. I turned to see my cousin standing in the centre of the hut, hands raised beside his head. The flames had spread down to his elbows and were burning high above his hands like two tall pillars that touched the roof. As he watched the flames, he was laughing.

Laughing?

Alectus turned his eyes to mine. The flames danced in their reflection. He smiled and gritted his teeth, and the flames grew.

I fumbled behind me for the lock and managed to pull it free, just as Alectus ran at me. I fell to the side and pulled the door open, narrowly missing a flaming fist.

A flash burst through the door and hit Alectus in the chest. He toppled over backward and the fire went out.

"Vulpeera!" I shouted. She stood on Alectus's chest, glaring down at him.

"Get Pteron out of here," she said.

My legs didn't respond. Instead I stood frozen in place. Alectus tried to grab Vulpeera, but she swiftly dodged his hand and bit his wrist.

"Ahh!" he yelled, "get this dog off me!"

He rolled back and forth as Vulpeera nipped at his legs and arms. Finally, Alectus stood, shielding his face. Vulpeera backed him toward the door.

"This isn't the end," he said, glancing at me, then back to Vulpeera. "I'll kill every last one of you!"

Vulpeera jumped forward and Alectus tripped over his own feet. He stumbled backward and screamed, raising his hands to his face. "Stay away from me!"

Vulpeera snarled and pushed him further out the door.

"I won't forget this, Winter!" he whimpered. "I won't forget what you've done."

Vulpeera lunged again, and Alectus toppled all the way through the door. He scrambled to his feet, shooting one last glare back at us before taking off down the path. He had only gone a few paces when his feet lifted from the ground, and he rose high into the air.

His screams echoed as Catharia carried him, kicking and flailing, across the channel.

Chapter 40

PTERON LAY SPLAYED OVER A ROCK NEAR THE WATER.

"Can you heal him?" Fantom asked.

We were gathered in a circle—Cheelion, Vulpeera, Catharia, Fantom, even little Proctin—and they all looked up at me, pleading with me to do something.

"I-I'll try," I said, kneeling beside Pteron. I didn't want to tell them there was no point—that I already knew I couldn't. Besides, I had to try. If I didn't, Pteron would die.

I moved my hands around and around, the way Granny had when she'd healed Vulpeera. I focused my energy, and the flames ignited. Granny's healing flames had turned blue—somehow, I needed to do that. But how?

I moved my hands faster, but nothing changed. I tried repeating the word "heal" in my mind, but still, nothing changed. Frustration began to build inside me.

There were wide gashes in the silky membrane of Pteron's wings, and a straight cut through the golden fur of his torso, now surrounded by dried blood. His eyes had remained closed since we'd pulled him from the burning hut. I wanted to cry. I wanted to break down and sob. My hands continued to circle, and the fire began to change. It wasn't blue, not quite, but there was a faint bluish hue. When I focused on it, the colour changed quickly back to yellow and white.

I tried to force my thoughts back to Pteron, but a vision of Alectus flashed through my head. His dark green eyes inches away from mine, the word "Cano" repeating from his lips. A jolt of pain shot through my head, and I dropped the fire.

"What is it?" Vulpeera asked, suddenly by my side.

The image vanished as quickly as it had come.

"Alectus," I cried, holding my head.

"He's gone," Catharia said, hopping forward, "and won't be back. I do my best not to harm other creatures of Terra, but I can't say the same for the wolves. I dropped Alectus in the woods on the far side of Olport among Lupora's army. Leave it to them to decide his fate."

I nodded. I didn't like the thought of the wolves hurting Alectus, but at least he was gone. I looked back down at Pteron, but my hands were shaking and I could barely sit up. "I-I don't think I can do what Granny does. I can't heal him."

Tears welled in my eyes. Vulpeera rubbed up against me like a cat.

"Don't worry," she said, "it will be alright. Fantom will carry him back to Lillian. With his speed, it shouldn't take long."

"I will fly my fastest," Fantom said, hopping forward. He grasped Pteron behind the neck and took off into the air, a flash through the paling sky. Behind us, the fire crackled as the hut continued to blaze. Soon it would be nothing more than ashes, and I would be happy for that.

The flames.

A thought occurred to me.

"Vulpeera, how was it that Alectus could hold the flames?"

Vulpeera looked at me blankly. "I don't know. I was wondering the same thing. And you were right—he speaks the common tongue. I'm not sure what to make of it, but then again, I am not a Guardian of Wisdom. Cheelion?"

Cheelion floated just beyond the rocks, his large shell bobbing slowly in the waves.

He thought for a moment, opened his beak, closed it, shook his head, opened it again. "I don't know. It is only the Land Guardian of Wisdom who can hold the flames. And the Terra Protectorum, if they have been taught. If what you say is true, if he can truly hold the flames and speak the common tongue, then we must go at once to speak with Terra."

"Maybe it's because he has the amulet," I said, thinking out loud. "Does that make sense?"

The Guardians all turned and looked at me in shock. I hadn't told anyone. There hadn't been time.

"He took it from my room," I said, guiltily.

"He took the amulet?!" Catharia blurted. "Then we must get it back at once!"

Cheelion nodded. "Yes, we must get it back. But it does not explain how he can hold the flames. The amulet is only a vessel to help pass the Guardian skills to the Terra Protectorum. It should do nothing for someone who is not the Terra Protectorum. We must go to Mount Skire and speak to Terra to find out what is going on."

"And who will retrieve the amulet?" Catharia asked.

"You take Vulpeera and get it back from the boy. I will take Winter and head south, to the mountains," Cheelion said.

"But I thought Lupora had cut off all the rivers and trails?" I said.

"Rivers, trails, forests—yes—but not the ocean," Cheelion said. "If we round the northwestern point, we can catch the southern current. It will take us to the west end of the mountains, where we will have access to Mount Skire."

"I should go with Winter," Vulpeera said, stepping forward.

Cheelion shook his head. "Catharia will need your help. Get the amulet and meet us at the mountains. We shouldn't have trouble getting there."

I could tell Vulpeera wanted to come, but she didn't argue.

"What about Cano and the orcas?" I asked.

"Cano is far away," Cheelion said. "You don't have to worry about him."

"How can you be sure?"

I remembered the horrible incident when I'd nearly been killed by the orca. Being trapped on Cheelion's shell again wasn't something I was keen to repeat.

"It is the Water Guardian of Wisdom's skill to feel Terra's energy. By doing so, I can sense the location of all Her creatures. Cano is far from here. His energy is miles away. There is no threat between us and the mountains."

I reached down and scooped up Proctin. "Okay, but we're taking Proctin," I said.

Proctin didn't seem very excited about coming and squirmed in my arms. I didn't blame him. He'd been there for the unfortunate incident with Cano. Still, I couldn't leave him on the island and I wanted his company, even if I was being a little selfish. "Don't worry," I whispered into his ear, "there'll be plenty of fish."

Even that didn't seem to perk him up. Something was bothering him.

Cheelion gave an irritated look toward Proctin, but agreed. "We'll take the raccoon. But we must leave soon. The winds are right and the current moves quickly. The longer we wait, the more opportunity there will be for Lupora to learn of our plan."

I took one last look around. Would it be the last time I would see Pitchi? And what of my uncle? I turned back to Cheelion with a sigh.

"Okay," I said. "Let's go ask Terra for some answers."

PART 4: THE BAY

Deep in the forests surrounding Olport, a boy stands alone. The woods are dark and quiet. The boy can hear nothing, yet he knows he is watched. He can feel their eyes.

"Come out!" he yells. "I know there's someone there!"

Nothing happens.

He waits.

Finally, like fireflies, glowing orbs materialize between the trees. They creep into the clearing and surround the boy. They are the eyes of large grey wolves.

If he were an ordinary boy, the wolves would already have attacked. They are hungry and the boy is alone. But it is fear they feast on, and the boy has none.

"Where is the one they call Lupora?" the boy yells, his eyes never leaving the largest of the wolves.

The wolves only watch, their bodies crouched low to the ground, ready to pounce.

Something moves behind them and they separate, allowing another to enter. It is a white wolf with ragged fur and a limp, yet the others bow out of her way like branches in the wind.

The two study each other—the dark-haired boy with the eyes of a cat, the white wolf with the eyes of the night.

The boy speaks first. "I understand we have a common interest," he says.

"What interest would I share with a human child?" the wolf growls.

"The girl you want—she is my cousin, but she runs with the animals that call themselves Guardians. I intend to destroy the Guardians."

The white wolf ponders this. "And why would you wish that?"

"They have crossed me. And they have crossed my family. I want to show them they are not as powerful as they believe. We can help each other."

The wolf licks its lips. The boy is speaking her language, but what can a boy offer an army of wolves? "You are but a child. How can you possibly help me? I seek power, and you have none."

A wolf beside the white wolf grins, and it offends the boy.

"Power?" he says. "Power comes in many forms."

The boy raises his hands, and with his eyes never faltering from the white wolf's, he tightens his lips and clenches his fists. His hands erupt into flames, and the wolves step backward. All but the white wolf.

The boy turns and hurls the flames at the wolf that grinned, and its fur ignites. It yelps and runs off into the woods, and the other wolves ready for a fight.

But the white wolf raises her front paw to stop them.

She smiles.

"Forgive my error," she says. "I have misjudged you."

The wolf turns and begins pacing, thinking.

"So," she says, "we destroy the girl."

The boy shakes his head. "My cousin is a pawn—a leaf in an overgrowth of weeds. Kill the leaf and another grows back. Kill the root, and we end the problem."

"The root?" the white wolf asks.

"Mount Skire," says the boy.

Chapter 41

WE HAD BEEN TRAVELLING FOR THREE DAYS, AND MY BODY yearned for exercise. After Vulpeera's rigorous training, sitting on a turtle shell was torture. I needed to run and swing; I needed to fly through the air and jump between trees. Instead I sat, watching endless waves roll past.

Proctin had barely spoken since we'd started the trip, and instead sat nervously eying the shoreline. No matter how many times I told him Cano wasn't coming, I couldn't reassure him. Maybe because I wasn't so reassured myself.

On the fourth day, driving rain caused the waves to grow so high they crashed over the carapace.

"Cheelion," I yelled over the wind, "we should head to the shore and wait out the storm."

"We'll be fine," he yelled back. "It's safer out here than on land."

"What if you roll and we're swept out to sea?"

"Hold on tight," he said. "I won't roll. I have swum through hundreds of storms. This is a tiny squall. It will pass soon."

Proctin and I clung to the shell as the waves continued to pound, but Cheelion was right—even with the thunderous power of the waves, he never rolled.

After the storm passed, we came to a place where the shoreline banked and headed south. Cheelion called it the northwestern point. In the distance, the outline of mountains came into view. In the centre stood two peaks taller than the rest, one pointed like a spire, the other flat at the top.

"Is that Mount Skire?" I asked. "The twin-peaked mountain in the middle?"

"Yes," Cheelion said.

"We have to travel all the way *there*?" I groaned, thinking about my already aching back.

"Once we enter the southern current we will move faster," Cheelion said, veering his course further out to sea. "But first we must cross the northern current, which runs closer to shore."

I felt a slight jerk as he said this, as if a line were attached to his tail, pulling us backward.

"Will this northern current not push us back as we try to cross it?" I asked.

Cheelion shook his head. "The currents are strong, but I am stronger. I could swim against the current if needed, although it would be slow going."

Once we were through the northern current and had entered the southern current, the trees on shore glided past, as if I were back on Uncle Farlin's motorized boat.

Uncle Farlin . . .

We had left so quickly I hadn't had time to leave a note. What would he think when he returned to the island to find the hut burned and Alectus and me gone? Thinking about it made me sick, so I occupied my mind by trying to get Proctin to talk.

"Hungry?" I asked.

His stomach growled, but he shook his head.

"Nervous?"

He shrugged.

"You haven't been the same since Pitchi. What's bothering you, Proctin?"

Proctin's little eyes looked back into mine, more sad than nervous.

"Are you mad at me?" I asked.

He didn't answer.

"Is it because I left you in the room and you saw what Alectus did? Did you see Pteron get hurt? Were you there?"

Proctin didn't answer, so I gave up yet again and went back to watching the waves. The sun was setting over the mountains, and I fell asleep to the rhythmic rocking of the shell. When I awoke, it was early morning and the sea looked unchanged. Proctin sat on the edge of the shell, staring off into the distance—had he slept?—and we moved gently through the water.

I'd had a terrible dream, and it was still vivid. I had been on Cheelion's shell, just as I was at that moment, except we were on the river heading toward the Cove, on my first day with the Guardians. Something about it left me uneasy.

Suddenly it hit me.

"Cheelion?" I said. The turtle gave a slow nod but did not turn his head to face me. "You said before that the northern current was strong, but not strong enough to push you backward?"

"That's right," Cheelion said. "We turtles are strong swimmers. Slow but strong."

"Would the current be as strong as, say—a river?"

"Stronger," Cheelion said.

I thought about this. *Then why wasn't he able to swim against the river when we drifted toward the wolves on the log?*

"And the waves of the storm, you said they could not flip you?"
Cheelion nodded.

Then why did he flip when Cano sent a wave over him?
My heart raced.

The pieces fell into place in my head—the river, the fight with Cano—it all added up. Cheelion had said his gift was to know the exact location of everyone on Terra, so why hadn't he told us Cano was coming before we were surrounded? Why hadn't he known the wolves would be on the log over the river before we'd rounded the bend?

Cheelion turned his head, and his lazy eyes locked on mine. My whole body grew tense. *Did he know that I knew?*

I looked away. How much farther were the mountains?

The mountains . . . I had a sudden, horrible realization. The mountains were no longer in front of us—they were behind us. We must have rounded a point while I was sleeping and were now heading east. Up ahead was a rocky shore, flanked by high cliffs on one side and a veil of forest on the other. We were in an unfamiliar bay.

"Cheelion," I said nervously, "why aren't the mountains ahead of us? Shouldn't we be heading south, toward them?"

"We're not going to the mountains," the turtle replied.

Chapter 42

THE RUSHING WIND CREATED SMALL WHITECAPS ON THE WATER as Cheelion swam toward the rocky beach.

"Cheelion," I said, "where are you taking me?"

He didn't answer, but continued swimming toward the shore. A welcoming party came into view on the rocks—a line of wolves watching us approach, while raccoons scattered the beach and trees behind. I suppose it wasn't that welcoming.

I realized where Cheelion had taken me—Grander's Bay, into the heart of Lupora's army.

"Cheelion," I stammered, "why?"

He swam without answering.

"Proctin, when we get to the shore, you run. I'll do my best to hold off the wolves long enough for you to escape."

Proctin glanced at me quickly before looking back down at the shell. I had a sudden, sinking realization: Proctin was a part of it.

"Proctin? You're . . . but I thought we were family?"

I pulled him toward me, but he wriggled free and went to the far side of the shell, not looking back.

I sat down and put my face in my hands. Cheelion was one thing—but Proctin? My heart felt as if it had been torn out and thrown overboard. This was what Pteron had tried to warn me about when he'd said something about a traitor.

Had Proctin been lying all along? Had he always been working for

Lupora? Could I really have been so blind?

"Ninety-two years," Cheelion said, interrupting my thoughts.

"What?"

"You asked me why, so I will tell you. I have served Terra for ninety-two years, seen four Terra Protectora come and go, patiently waiting my turn, only to be slighted again in favour of a human. When you were chosen as the Land Guardian of Wisdom, it was a mistake. Look at your bloodline—first Lillian, kind and powerful, but ultimately a failure. Then it was Gregor—your father—a plague like this planet has never seen before. From him came you—the youngest Terra Protectorum ever selected. I won't say your powers aren't impressive, and I have no quarrel with you directly, but your bloodline is tainted. Your whole species is tainted. Terra is rotting from the inside because of the humans. Do you think Vulpeera would ever have been caught by a creature as slow and ungainly as Lupora in the past? Do you think Pteron, the Sky Guardian of Wisdom, could have been maimed by a mere boy when Terra was healthy? It was not my intention for Pteron to get hurt, but sacrifices are sometimes necessary, and his pain serves as further proof that I am doing what is best for us all. Our powers come from our Mother's energy, and as She weakens, so do we all.

"And as this happens, Terra sits by and watches. Worse, She assists in her own demise. There is something about you humans that clouds Her judgment. Why She would select you as the Terra Protectorum is a mystery. Why would She continue to allow a human to sit on Her throne as your species drains the life from Her core? Her judgment is failing as She weakens. The time has come for me to do what I am sworn to do: to protect Terra, even if it means protecting Her from Herself. With you gone, She will name me Terra Protectorum, and I can begin healing our Mother."

Cheelion drifted up to the rocky beach, and the wolves formed a semicircle around us. The largest was the black wolf with three white paws I had seen in the Red Woods. He stepped into the circle, watching me with sharp black eyes. Behind him sat a familiar raccoon on a tall boulder with a crown of twisted twigs. It was Raycor, king of the raccoons and Proctin's hateful brother.

"I suppose the word of a Guardian is worth something after all," the black wolf sneered. "Lupora will be most pleased."

Cheelion pulled himself onto the rocks, and two wolves circled behind him, snapping at me until I was forced off Cheelion's shell and into the middle of their circle.

I clenched my fists and called the fire. My hands erupted into flames, and the circle of wolves stepped back in alarm. I spun around, waving my hands in an attempt to keep the wolves away. There was no chance I could beat them in a fight, but at the very least, I would try.

The wolves didn't seem interested in attacking. Instead they watched the black wolf, waiting for his command while he eyed me with a mixture of curiosity and contempt.

"Believe me," the black wolf said, "if it were up to me, I'd tear you apart. Everyone here called the Red Woods their home, and you have taken it from us." He raised his voice so that it carried over the beach, and anger flashed in the eyes of many of the wolves and raccoons. "But luckily for you, Lupora has claimed you for herself." His smile broadened to a grin. "Or maybe that's not so lucky."

"Tantum," Cheelion interrupted, and the black wolf turned to him. "I must leave before anyone sees me. Do what you like with the girl, just make sure she doesn't return." Cheelion turned toward the water, Proctin still sitting atop his shell.

"Not so fast," Tantum said. The wolves behind him snarled, not letting Cheelion pass. "The amulet. Where is it?"

Cheelion's expression hardened. "The deal was only for the girl. The amulet belongs to the Guardians."

"That's not how Lupora sees it," Tantum growled. "Where is it?"

"I don't have it," Cheelion said, but even I could tell he was lying.

Proctin crawled forward on Cheelion's shell and reached inside. From behind Cheelion's neck he pulled a familiar gold chain with a large white stone. He hopped off the shell and approached Tantum.

"Raycor promised I could see my mother if I—"

The black wolf snatched the amulet from Proctin's paws and snapped at him, causing him to jump in surprise and scurry toward the other raccoons.

"This was not the deal!" Cheelion bellowed. "Tantum, why is Lupora not here to speak for herself?"

"Lupora is away on important business," the black wolf snarled. "She's left me in charge. Now, you have been most helpful and we thank you for it, but I suggest you leave before we decide to have turtle for lunch."

The wolves behind Cheelion stepped aside while those in front snapped and snarled, forcing him back into the water, where he slowly submerged. His massive body disappeared beneath the dark waves until all that was left was the top of his head, his angry eyes glaring at Tantum a moment longer before they, too, disappeared.

Tantum turned away from the bay. "Put the girl in the cave and have the raccoons seal her in. I want two guards watching her day and night until Lupora returns. Be careful with her; she's more dangerous than she looks."

Chapter 43

Two wolves led me to a cave carved into the base of the high cliff. It wasn't very big—barely tall enough for me to stand, and only a few paces deep—and the bottom was covered with cold, damp rocks.

Once I was inside, four raccoons worked to seal the entrance with a fence made of sticks and vines, while two wolves paced back and forth. As horrible as I felt, I couldn't help but marvel over the craftsmanship of the raccoons. Their tiny paws worked nimbly to wind the loops of vine and close the gate. Proctin had been right—the raccoons were smarter creatures than we gave them credit for.

When they were finished, the black wolf, Tantum, came to inspect their work, and growled that the vine was too loose and the sticks too wide. The raccoons worked quickly to fix it, nervously glancing back at Tantum, as if at any moment he might gobble them up. Eventually, he scoffed that it was as good as could be expected from a bunch of inept raccoons. He sent them on their way and they scurried off into the woods.

Tantum turned and stared at me, an eerie look in his eyes as he licked his lips. I was too dejected to give him a piece of my mind, so I sat down and rested my head on my hands, trying not to think about my predicament.

When I looked up again, Tantum was gone. From the mouth of the cave, I could see out over the water, and in the distance the mountains stood in contrast against a silvery sky, the two middle peaks taller than the rest—Mount Skire, as Cheelion had pointed out. That's where I was supposed to be. Not in a dank cave in Grander's Bay.

A stiff breeze carried over the water and into the cave, whistling around and rustling my hair. I shivered in my sweatshirt and jeans; there was no way to hide from the wind and the rocks were still wet beneath me. I could not get comfortable. Sleep would not be easy, despite my exhaustion.

I rubbed my arms, trying to get warm, when I had an idea. Keeping my hands close to my chest, I focused and called my Imperia. I tried to keep the flame small and hidden, but the cave was too dark for it to go unnoticed. It had only just lit when one of the wolves stopped pacing and came to the bars.

"Put that out!" he growled.

The heat felt so nice, I considered ignoring him.

Instead I let the flame flicker and die in my hands. I couldn't fight all the wolves myself. My only hope was that the Guardians would learn I had been taken prisoner and come to my rescue. I had to survive long enough for that to happen. But how long would that be, and would they come before Lupora returned? That was the important question. Perhaps Cheelion would tell them I'd drowned or been swept out to sea, and they would never come at all. It was a terrible thought, but also the last one I had before inexplicably falling asleep.

The next morning, the beach was alive with raccoons, rushing around like ants on an anthill. All along the shore stood a line of them with sticks in their hands. The ends had been gnawed into sharp points to make spears, and periodically they'd lash out at the water, sometimes managing to stick a floundering fish. Others hurried back and forth between a large expanse of green brush on the far side of the bay, carrying fistfuls of what appeared to be berries to a flat rock, where they heaped them into a pile. From the woods came more raccoons, carrying pinecones and nuts.

All the while, six wolves lay watching from the beach, barking orders and grumbling over how slow the raccoons were.

"I'm starving," a smaller wolf with a brown collar of fur complained. "How can these raccoons expect us to protect them if they barely feed us?"

Another wolf, with grey fur and a white belly, nodded. "There are hundreds of them, yet it takes this long to gather fish? If there were hundreds of us, we would have had breakfast, lunch, and dinner by now."

I found that hard to believe, judging by how lazy the wolves seemed. Even if there were hundreds of them, it didn't appear anything would get done. They never lifted so much as a paw to help.

One raccoon caught a fish and ran over to the pack, holding it out to the wolves on his stick.

"That one's mine," said a larger wolf. "I've not had one in the longest time."

"But the fish you had was twice as big as the one I had," complained another. "I should get this one."

They snarled at each other, and for the first time looked like they might move, when Tantum strolled from the woods. He stopped and stretched, his jaw opening in a long yawn showing sharp yellow teeth, before approaching the pack. The other wolves stopped squabbling immediately.

"Boys, boys, boys," Tantum said, "you're bickering like cubs. If you're hungry and upset, take it out on the raccoons, not each other."

Another little raccoon had come toward Tantum carrying a small fish, but stopped a few feet short when it heard this, its look of excitement vanishing as Tantum stared down at it.

"What's that?" the black wolf asked, nodding toward the raccoon's catch.

The raccoon glanced down at its spear as if it had forgotten what it was carrying. "It-it's a fish, sir," the raccoon stuttered.

"A fish? Really? Pass it here then," Tantum said, and the raccoon nervously scuttled over to hold it out for him.

Tantum snapped and grabbed the raccoon by the scruff of its neck, and the little creature gave a shrill cry before dropping the spear. "You call that a fish?" Tantum growled through clenched teeth. "You insult me! Bring me another minnow like that and I'll eat you, instead." He tossed his head sideways and the raccoon flew through the air, landing with a thump on the rocks.

The poor thing sat up swaying, and rubbing its head, but before it could stand, another wolf sprang forward and grabbed it. Again, it was tossed into the air, this time even higher, and the little raccoon landed with a cry.

By now, all the raccoons had stopped what they were doing, and watched as the wolves took turns throwing their comrade in the air. It was like a horrible game of catch, only there was no catching involved.

The wolves howled with laughter, all six of them now playing.

Each time, the small raccoon was slower to its feet, and I knew that if the game went on much longer it wouldn't get up at all.

I fumed. Why was no one helping? Why were the other raccoons letting this happen?

The little raccoon landed with another crash near the trees, but when the next wolf went to pick it up, it stopped dead in its tracks. A different raccoon blocked the wolf's path and it didn't look like it was going to move anytime soon.

"Out of my way, old rat," the wolf growled.

The raccoon did look old, with greying black fur on its cheeks, and milky eyes. It made no effort to move, but instead stood fiercely glaring at the wolf.

"I said, out of my way," the wolf repeated, but there was no conviction in its voice.

The standoff continued until Tantum approached. "Don't be such a stiff, Procynia," he said. "We were only having a little fun. Come on, Zare, leave the raccoon be. I'm hungry and the less they work, the longer I have to wait."

When the wolves had gone, the old raccoon scooped up the little one and disappeared into the woods.

Shortly afterward, Raycor waltzed out of the very same woods, heading toward the cave. He was followed closely by Proctin, who waved a pine branch back and forth over his king's head as if fanning him from the heat, despite it being cool outside.

Raycor stopped in front of the cave and waved his hands at the wolves standing guard by the entrance, telling them to step aside. The wolves glanced at each other angrily but did as they were told.

"Look here, Proctin," Raycor said, stepping forward with a smug sneer on his face. "A good reminder, don't you think? A lesson to choose your friends wisely. You see, this is what happens when you don't have friends like Lupora to protect you."

Proctin nodded, but didn't look up at me. Instead he stared at the ground, still waving the pine branch.

"Yes, choose your friends wisely," I scoffed, nodding toward Proctin.

Raycor's sneer turned to a twisted smile. "Aww, you didn't really believe Proctin was your friend, did you?" He let out a squeaky laugh. "A so-called Guardian of Wisdom and you weren't smart enough to figure out Proctin would side with his own family?"

"If you were my family, I'd pretend to be an orphan," I said.

Raycor's eyes narrowed. "I suppose I can't fault you for that. After all, what do you know about family? If I'm not mistaken, it was your father who killed the last Terra Protectorum." My hands clenched and my fingers began to tingle. "No, Proctin is home now, and if you ask me, he's done quite well for himself. Official servant to the king is not bad for someone once banished from the gaze, wouldn't you agree, Proctin?"

Proctin nodded.

Anger grew inside me. If I looked at them much longer I might explode into flames. There were so many words I wanted to say—none of them very nice. After all those nights I'd stayed up worrying about Proctin, feeling sorry for him, hating Raycor for the way he'd treated him—only to find they'd been working together! All those years under my deck, had he been spying on me? And what about on Pitchi—had he watched Alectus shoot Pteron? Had he even tried to help? Or had he already made off with the amulet?

"Well, don't get too comfortable in there," Raycor said. "Lupora will be back soon, and we're all looking forward to your little reunion."

He grinned and left, Proctin following close behind.

Chapter 44

THAT NIGHT, AS I SAT AWAKE IN THE SHADOWS OF MY PRISON, THE two wolves on guard talked beneath a nearby tree. I crept to the edge of the cave, careful to keep myself hidden. With my heightened senses, their words reached me clearly.

"I swear," the first wolf said, "if that fur-ball king comes along and waves his hands at me one more time, I'll tear them off."

"The whole lot of them make me angry," the second wolf said. "They're useless. Why Lupora keeps them around is beyond me."

"I'm sure Lupora has her reasons. Best not to question her judgment."

"Oh no, no, I'm not questioning her judgment. But I wish I understood why she thinks having them as allies is better than having them for dinner. We're sitting in a forest of fresh meat, yet surviving on minnows."

"I hear you. Every time I look at the king's new servant, my mouth turns to a pool of saliva. That's five meals in one!"

"Mmm . . . thinking about him makes my stomach growl. I'm starving. Maybe we could pick off a little one tonight. Just a quick snack— no one will notice."

There was a short silence, as if the other wolf was contemplating the idea.

"Not tonight," it finally said. "Besides, it won't be long before Lupora returns. If she and the boy have done as they planned, the Guardians will be finished and we'll have no further need of the raccoons. We'll celebrate with a feast."

Boy? What boy? I wondered.

"I call dibs on the fat one."

"Then I claim the so-called king. I'm going to eat him slowly, then have the girl for dessert."

"Good luck with that. You'll have to fight Lupora for her."

The wolf shuddered. "Well, that's a pity. I've never tried human. They look so tasty, all pink and furless. I bet they're like warthog."

"But not as meaty. She's skin and bones. Which makes me wonder what all the fuss is about, keeping her locked up and guarded as if she's the next Arctos."

"Tantum claims she burned the Red Woods herself."

"A story to gain further support from the raccoons, I'm sure."

"No, he swears it."

"Well, either way, she'll be gone in a few days when Lupora returns."

"The sooner the better. I'm sick of this place."

The wolves stopped talking, and the night grew quiet. I lay down, resting my head on a flat rock, listening to the sound of my stomach growling.

I hadn't eaten all day.

What had the wolves meant by "the boy"? I couldn't shake the feeling they were talking about Alectus. Catharia had said she'd dropped him among the wolves. Had he and Lupora somehow teamed up? If they were together, it would be bad news for the Guardians.

Something moved outside the cave entrance—a shadow slinking across the rocks—and I jumped to my feet. I couldn't see anything through the bars except dark woods and the moonlit bay.

Something soft touched my leg, and my hands instinctively clenched, the heat forming in my chest.

"I'm sorry," a voice said. "I didn't mean to frighten you. I mean you no harm. Please, if the wolves hear you they will come for us."

Staring up at me was the old raccoon I'd seen earlier on the beach. Silver moonlight reflected off her milky eyes and white whiskers. Up close, she looked even older than before. She held a small fish in her paws.

"I thought you might be hungry," she said. "The wolves are stingy with what they give us, but I managed to steal this from their stores."

I hesitated. The raccoons were helping the wolves hold me captive. Could I trust this one? I'd made the mistake of trusting one before.

The ache in my stomach was too much. If I didn't eat, I'd die anyway.

"Thank you," I said, taking the fish. It was slimy and uncooked, so I closed it between my hands and focused my Imperia. I didn't let the flames come, but the searing heat was enough to cook the fish. A wisp of steam rose from my hands, and when I opened them, the fish was crispy and blackened.

"Amazing," the raccoon said, standing on her hind legs to watch.

I'd cooked the fish a little too much—it was charred and crunchy, but it felt better having something in my stomach.

"Now that I've learned to control it a little, it comes in handy," I said. "Unlike before when, well . . ."

The raccoon reached out a paw. "We don't blame you for what happened to the Red Woods, despite what the wolves would have you believe. You did what you had to. We know that. You have more support here than you think."

"I don't feel very supported," I said.

"No, I imagine not. Raycor has made sure of that. And while he sits on the throne, we are all slaves to the wolves."

"But why? I've seen how they treat you. This isn't an alliance. They're using you. Why not leave?"

The raccoon closed her eyes and shook her head. "It's not that simple. The raccoons have always followed their king. The gaze is not used to making decisions for itself."

"Then convince Raycor to leave the wolves. He must see the way they treat you."

Again, the old raccoon shook her head. "Raycor is blinded by power. He always has been. Even as a cub, he was desperate for control. Lupora gives him what he has always wanted, and he is too smitten to see it as a guise. The wolves respect him as much as they respect anyone—that is to say, not at all. In time, they will turn on him, too. Which is why I have come to ask for your help."

"Me? Help?"

"Yes," the raccoon said. "There is only one other besides Raycor the raccoons would listen to. The true heir to the throne, Raycor's older brother, Proctin."

The name made me bristle. "Why would I want to help him? You obviously don't know what he did to me."

"I do. But you must understand why. Proctin is not evil—far from it. If anything, he is too kind. That has always been his failing."

I rolled my eyes. "If you want to call betraying your friend kind, then sure, yeah, he's real kind."

The old raccoon looked saddened by this. "Don't blame him," she said. "He only betrayed you because of me."

"Because of you?"

"Yes. It's my fault. He betrayed you because he wanted to see me again."

"You're Proctin's mother!" I said, making the connection.

The raccoon nodded. "My name is Procynia."

"But Proctin said you never came back for him. He told me the story of when he was banished by Raycor for eating the food stores. He said he waited for you outside the Red Woods, but you never came. Why would he want to see you again?"

Procynia's back hunched further. "A decision that has not been easy to live with."

"Why didn't you go back for him?"

"Because I knew if I did, he would return to the gaze."

"You didn't want him to come back? But he's your son. And he was supposed to be king!"

"That is true," Procynia agreed. "He was supposed to be king. But Proctin is every bit his father—kind, caring, compassionate, and incapable of making decisions. I worried that, impressionable as he was, Raycor would change him if he returned. I thought it would be better for him if he left. It was never his desire to be king. He never longed for power the way Raycor did. Raycor, on the other hand, is nothing like his father. Sadly, he is more like me—proud and stubborn, and fearless to a fault. He resented Proctin for being firstborn. It was only a matter of time before he usurped the crown. And Proctin was only too pleased to let him have it. But without the crown, Proctin could not stay. The gaze would see him as a failure. They would never have looked at him the same way. So, I let him leave. A terrible thing to do—to watch your son walk away and not go after him—but I thought it was best for him. I could not have predicted what would come of it. I did not know the extent of Raycor's quest for control. And now we are here, the survival of our gaze in jeopardy, threatened with destruction by those that claim to be our allies."

I thought for a moment, processing everything Procynia had said. My anger toward Proctin dulled a little, but it was hard to forget how he had given me to the wolves. "There's something I don't understand. You said Proctin is exactly like his father. Was his father not a good king?"

"The gaze thrived under his father, yes, but only because I was there to back him. He was the good, I was the will."

"Then why can't you help Raycor in the same way?"

"Raycor listens to no one. Any suggestion I make, he does the opposite. He does things to spite me. He believes I still side with Proctin."

"Which you do."

Procynia smiled. "I will always have a soft spot for Proctin."

"It's hard not to," I agreed. "But what can I do to help? I'm in here. And even if I wasn't, why me?"

Procynia stood up straight, her white eyes looking directly into mine. "Because Proctin trusts you. Since coming here, he has not stopped talking about you and how he has thrown away the only true friendship he ever had. He is torn to pieces over what he has done. He would come down here himself, except that he can't bear to look at you. But if Proctin is to be king, he needs you. He needs someone strong behind him."

"What about you? Why can't you help him?"

"I am old and tired. But more importantly, I must be impartial. As much as I know Raycor is destroying our gaze, he is still my son. I can't bring myself to side against him. Just as I can't side against Proctin."

Procynia watched me closely as I paced back and forth in the cave.

"Well," she said, "will you help us?"

"Let me think about it."

I needed to be careful. Trusting too freely was what had got me in trouble in the first place.

Procynia nodded. "Of course. But know this—before Raycor, before Lupora, before everything that has happened, our kind were loyal to the Guardians. I hope you can help us return to the light of Terra. You are, after all, the Terra Protectorum."

She bowed low to the ground before disappearing back into the woods.

Chapter 45

GREY CLOUDS BLANKETED THE SKY, AND A HEAVY MIST SAT OVER the water the next morning when I awoke. It almost felt as if my conversation with Procynia had been a dream. I needed to speak with Proctin to straighten everything out, but there was only one animal standing by the bars of my prison that morning, and it wasn't a raccoon.

Tantum must have been watching me sleep, and judging by the thin string of drool hanging from the corner of his mouth, he hadn't been singing lullabies.

An idea came to me. I needed information, and this was my chance to get it. I stretched my arms over my head and yawned, looking lazily at Tantum. "You know," I said, "of all the creatures I've come across since becoming the Terra Protectorum, you might be the creepiest. I mean, threaten to kill me, sure. Growl, snarl, bite—okay. But watching me while I sleep? Even in the animal world, that has to be considered creepy."

Tantum didn't like my taunts and leapt at the bars of the prison, gnashing his teeth and snarling. "If I hadn't sworn to Lupora to keep you alive, I'd come in there right now and have myself a fine breakfast."

I stood up slowly, crossed one arm over my chest, and pulled it with the other, a stretch I'd learned in PE class. "Yeah, and I'd be shaking in my boots except for one thing—you're not exactly scary. I mean, what kind of wolf gets left behind from—what was it you called it?—very important business? Am I *really* threatened by the wolf that got left behind? You must not be popular with Lupora. Maybe she was worried you'd watch her sleep."

Tantum grew more agitated and paced quickly in front of the bars.

"Lupora didn't *leave* me here," he said, "she *chose* me to stay. She selected her twelve best wolves to guard you while she went with the boy to the mountains. I was asked to lead those twelve wolves. It was an honor."

Twelve wolves? Hmm . . .

"To the mountains, huh? With a boy? Does he have her on a leash?" Again, Tantum flung himself at the fence, bending the bars. I paused, nervous I was pushing him too far, but continued when he stepped back again. "That wasn't very nice of me, was it?" I shook my head in feigned remorse. "No, I shouldn't say that sort of thing. Anyway, I believe dogs should be allowed to run free. Get their exercise." I pretended to search the floor of the cave. "If you bring me a stick I'd be happy to throw it for you."

"We are not dogs!" Tantum spat. "Those sycophants you humans pull around on ropes, waiting on you like children, they are not our blood."

I shrugged. "You said yourself Lupora was off playing with some boy."

"Lupora is not chasing sticks or being pulled on a leash. At this very moment, she is destroying that which you are sworn to protect. She and the boy—your cousin, he claims—have taken the army to destroy Mount Skire. And with it, they will destroy the Guardians." He turned and looked across the bay. "I hope the mist doesn't hang around long— you should have a wonderful view from here."

There it was. The plan. I knew if I antagonized Tantum enough, he'd let it slip. This was bad news. Alectus and Lupora would be a devastating combination. Both hated the Guardians, both had a personal vendetta against me, both were smart and resourceful enough to make terrible things happen. I wasn't sure how they planned to destroy a mountain, but I didn't want to wait around to find out. I had to leave—and soon.

My mind went once again to my conversation with Procynia. I wouldn't have time to help the raccoons *and* get to the mountains. As soon as night came, I would have to leave. The raccoons would have to fend for themselves.

I spent the rest of the day planning my escape. I would wait until nightfall and hope that the wolves let their guard down. Getting out of the cave wouldn't be difficult—I could burn through the twine easily with my Imperia. Afterwards, I would travel along the beach toward the mountains. The idea of travelling through the trees had occurred to me, as I would be safe from the wolves, but the trees here were not like the trees on Pitchi. The pines had small, thin branches, spaced too far apart for me to jump. It would be faster and more direct to move along the beach to the mountains. With luck, I would be far enough away by the time the wolves realized I was gone.

NIGHT FELL AND I stood at the bars of my cave, looking up at the moon. It was half hidden beneath a thin veil of clouds, but with my enhanced sight, the light it shed was enough to make everything visible around the bay. Although my escape would not be easy.

Tonight, there were four wolves on guard instead of two. Luckily, they seemed occupied by something on the ground under a nearby tree. It must have been some sort of food, because they tore off pieces and chewed loudly. It wasn't ideal—they were close, but maybe they would be distracted long enough not to notice I was gone. Once they did, it wouldn't take long for them to catch me. Even with my training, they would be faster. Unfortunately, I didn't have time to wait around for a better opportunity. In my mind, this was the only way to escape. I'd just have to hope I was lucky.

I grabbed the knot of vine holding two of the prison poles together and focused the heat. A thin trickle of smoke rose in the air as the vine burned. I was nearly through the first rope when—

"STOP!" came a high-pitched squeal.

I let go of the vine and spun around.

The voice had come from behind me.

The voice had come from *inside* the cave.

Chapter 46

THE MOON CAST ENOUGH LIGHT FOR ME TO SEE ALL THE WAY TO the back of my prison—so why couldn't I see anyone? I walked around, scanning all the little nooks and crannies. Even an animal as small as a raccoon couldn't possibly go unnoticed. When I stopped to think for a moment, I heard a faint humming noise that wasn't there before.

"Is someone here? I heard you say something!" I called out softly.

"Of course I said something!" a squeaky voice replied. "You were about to break out of here with four wolves twenty feet away. They would have caught you in an instant. I just saved your life, that's what I did."

I was certain the voice had come from inside the cave. I scanned everywhere with my Aminoculus, but there was nothing. I took a chance and lit my Imperia, a quick spark, but again I saw nothing but rock walls surrounding me.

"Well, I appreciate you looking out for me," I said, "but I need to get out of here."

"Yes, yes," said the voice, "you need to leave—I agree—but there are better ways than getting yourself devoured by wolves."

I gave up trying to find the owner of the voice. "Well, I'm open to suggestions," I said, walking to the back of the cave. "Where are you, by the way?"

"Right in front of you," the voice replied. "Ten inches from your nose."

I squinted but still saw nothing.

"No, you're not," I said.

"Of course I am. Why would I lie?"

"But I can't see you," I said.

"Just because you can't see me doesn't mean I'm not here."

The voice appeared to be moving as it spoke, jumping from place to place, so that it had an echo-like quality.

"I guess that's true. I just—well—I'm not used to speaking to someone I can't see."

"And I'm not used to being seen," said the voice. "I have a little saying and it goes like this: When you're not hiding, your life's in danger."

"I see. And what exactly are you in danger of?" I asked.

"When you're my size, everything is dangerous. Predators are everywhere—wolves, coyotes, raccoons, large insects, humans."

"Humans?"

"Oh yes. I've heard of humans setting up bird eaters in their backyards to kill my kind."

"Are you sure you don't mean bird *feeders*?" I asked.

"Hmm."

"So, you're some sort of bird?"

"Yes, I'm a . . . well, I suppose it wouldn't hurt if I—"

A sudden shimmer appeared in front of me as if the moonlight were reflecting off the air, and it took me a moment to realize what I was focusing on. Hovering in front of my face was a tiny hummingbird, no bigger than my fist. Its wings were so fast, only its body was visible. It had a long, needle-like beak and a brilliant royal-blue breast that sparkled in the moonlight. The humming noise was coming from its wings.

"You're the Sky Guardian of Agility," I said, my hand instinctively going to my chest, where the amulet had been.

The hummingbird nodded its tiny head. "Aurora," it said. "Pleased to finally make your acquaintance."

I looked through the bars to be sure the wolves were still beneath the tree.

They were.

"Pleased to meet you, too," I said. "Am I ever glad you're here. I need to get out of here right now. Lupora has gone to Mount Sklre with my cousin, Alectus, and they're planning to destroy it. We need to warn the other Guardians before it's too late!"

Aurora shrieked and disappeared.

"Where did you go?"

"Don't say things like that," Aurora said. "You scared me."

"Sorry. I didn't mean to. But I'm telling the truth. We have to get out of here right now and warn everyone."

Aurora reappeared in a different spot, near the top of the cave.

"Yes, yes, get out of here right away. But there are wolves over there." Aurora moved with a flash to the entrance of the cave as if teleported. "If you leave right now, they will see you."

"Well, maybe between the two of us, we can fight them."

Aurora shrieked and disappeared again.

"Oh no, no, no," she said. "I'm a hider, not a fighter. When you're not hiding—"

"Your life is in danger. Yes, I heard that. But how can I get out of here?"

Aurora reappeared and tilted her head backward, looking up to the roof of the cave. Her small black eyes were half closed, as if she was thinking very hard about something. "Aha! I know! You could hide! Yes—that's it, you could hide in here and wait for the wolves to come check on you. Then, when they think you're not here, they'll go off to find you, and while they're gone, you escape. Simple!"

Aurora flitted around excitedly.

"Yes, simple, except for one little problem," I said. "There's nowhere in here to hide." I pointed around the cave to emphasize how small it was.

Aurora shook her head in disagreement. "Nowhere to hide? Nonsense. When you have Evanestium, everywhere is a hiding spot. Forest, field, land, water, day, night—none of that matters. You could be as small as a flea or as big as an elephant. With what I'm going to teach you, you could hide right in front of a predator. If you wanted to, you could spend your whole life hidden. Which, by the way, I highly recommend."

Aurora disappeared and reappeared several times around the cave, moving as if she were jumping in and out of reality. "Okay," she said, "bring out the amulet. Let's get started. Not a moment to lose."

My face went hot. "Um, that's another problem. I don't have it anymore."

Aurora reappeared, inches from my nose. "You don't have the amulet?!" she squealed. "What do you mean? You lost it?"

"The wolves took it when I first got here. Then they locked me in this cell, and I haven't seen it since. I don't know where they put it."

"This isn't good," Aurora said, suddenly a blur around the cave. "Not good at all. A Terra Protectorum without an amulet. What will we do?"

A twig snapped outside the cave and Aurora disappeared like a candle flame snuffed out. I spun around to find an unmistakable silhouette on the opposite side of the bars, looking up at me. Short, stocky, and as round as a watermelon—there was only one raccoon with a profile like that.

Proctin!

Chapter 47

Proctin and I stood looking at each other through the bars. I felt torn, my mind a mix of emotions. A part of me was angry—I could feel it inside like a small, hot ember. Another part of me understood what Procynia had said. When I had learned my father killed Orcavion, it didn't change how much I wished to have known him. It didn't change the fact that I would have done anything for a chance to speak to him or my mother. I guess there's something about family that's bigger than reason or logic.

Proctin hung his head and turned to leave, apparently taking my silence for anger. I grabbed him by the thick fur behind his neck and yanked him into the cave. His body barely fit between the bars, but he came through with a pop, and I hugged him so tightly he must have thought I was trying to suffocate him. He tried to squirm free until I whispered "I forgive you" into his ear and nuzzled my face into his fur.

"You do?" he said, turning around in my arms and looking up at me. I nodded.

His face lit up, and he flung his little arms around my neck.

When I finally put him down, he blurted out everything in a voice that made me worry the wolves might hear. "Raycor told me if I brought him the amulet he would forgive me, and that I could come back to the gaze and see my mother again, and that everything would be wonderful here with the wolves to look after us, but the wolves are awful and make us work all day long and don't let us eat anything!"

I put my finger to his lips, shushing him. "It's okay, Proctin," I whispered. "Procynia told me everything. I know why you did what you did, and I forgive you."

Proctin turned and pointed toward the wolves by the tree. "You see them over there?" He sniffled. "They're eating Protito."

"Protito?"

"My cousin!" he wailed, and I put my hand over his mouth to stifle the cry.

"You have to whisper," I cautioned.

Once he had calmed down again, I removed my hand. "The wolves aren't our friends at all," he continued. "Raycor is wrong. They're using us and planning to eat us when they're done. I tried to tell Raycor, but he got angry and told me I was being a coward."

I looked over at the wolves more closely. I still couldn't see what they were eating, but I didn't doubt Proctin. It made me furious. All day long the raccoons waited on them hand and foot, and at night, this was happening?

"Proctin, listen to me," I said, putting my hands on his shoulders and forcing him to look at me instead of the wolves. "You're right—the wolves are planning to turn on you after they destroy Mount Skire. I overheard them talking the past few nights. I need to leave Grander's Bay to stop Lupora, but—"

"You're leaving?!" Proctin said, so I put my finger over his mouth to shush him again.

"Just listen. Yes, I'm leaving first thing in the morning, but I'll take you with me. You and anyone else who wants to come."

Proctin beamed. "You will?"

I nodded. "I need you to go around tonight and spread the word.

Find anyone who wants to leave, and tell them to be ready at first light."

"You want me to round everyone up? B-but maybe Raycor should do that. He'd be better at it. They'd listen to him."

"No, Proctin, you've seen what Raycor is like. He won't want to leave. You're the only one who can help the gaze. Right now, I need you to be what you were always supposed to be—a leader, the true king of the raccoons. Just like your father."

Proctin's eyes flashed panic. "But my father always had my mother—"

"And you have me," I said.

He thought for a moment. "And you're the Terra Protectorum," he said.

I nodded in agreement.

"Okay, I'll do it!"

Just then, something whispered in my ear—a small, squeaky voice. I had forgotten Aurora was even there.

"The amulet, what about the amulet?" she asked.

"Oh right, I almost forgot. Proctin, do you know where Tantum is keeping the amulet?"

Proctin smiled broadly. He took his front paw, lifted one of the rolls of fat on his stomach, and reached in with his other paw. From his fat rolls he pulled out a long gold chain with its familiar white stone glinting in the moonlight.

"You little genius!" I said, hugging him again.

"Like I always say—it pays to have storage."

Chapter 48

"We haven't got long," Aurora said, shimmering blue in front of me. "But there are shortcuts we can use."

She landed softly on top of the amulet around my neck, and the expected jolt shot through me. The symbol of the hummingbird glowed dark green, and I covered it with my hand so the wolves wouldn't notice.

"Now," Aurora said, flying back up into the air and disappearing, "how much have you already learned about the Guardians of Agility and our powers?"

"Vulpeera taught me that the Guardians of Agility are the protectors of Terra's changes—fluidity, as she called it."

"That's right," Aurora said. "As the Land Guardian of Agility, Vulpeera governs the changes to Terra Creatura, while Tully, the Water Guardian of Agility, is tasked with maintaining the changes to the elements. My gift is far more subtle, but no less important. The changes I control are small, often imperceptible things, but they affect everything around us, all the time. One such aspect will be of importance to you now. We call it resonance."

"Resonance—all right, what's that?"

Aurora appeared in front of me. "Everything around you—the rocks, the water, the creatures—is vibrating. We refer to this vibration as the resonance of Terra."

"But I don't feel anything vibrating," I said, placing my hand on the wall of the cave.

"The vibration is too small to be detected," Aurora said. "My ability, Evanestium, is the ability to control that vibration."

"How will controlling something so small help me?"

"Not all important things are large," Aurora said, with a humph. "There are many undetectable things happening around us that are necessary parts of Terra. They are a part of the balance as much as the ones we see. And Evanestium has one particularly important use. It allows you to control your own vibration, and in doing so, it allows you to hide anywhere."

"Invisibility," I whispered. "I'll have the power of invisibility. I'm going to be able to disappear whenever I want, aren't I?" The prospect was exciting. Hiding from Penny at lunchtime would be a breeze.

Ugh, why was I still thinking about Penny with a pack of hungry wolves thirty feet away?!

"Not disappear—hide," Aurora corrected. "There's a difference. Evanestium will allow you to be unseen—a mere deception of the eyes—but in reality, you are still there, as much as you would be if you were visible. So, no, it will not allow you to disappear."

"Okay, I get it. I can make myself invisible. But how do I do it?"

"It would take hours and hours to teach you the true way to use the gift, but that's something we don't have. Luckily, there is an easier way. As you may already have learned, there are shortcuts with many of the Guardian powers that are often used when starting out."

"Like when I bite my tongue to help call my Imperia?" I asked.

"Yes," Aurora said, nodding, "but you must be careful. Shortcuts are the easy way, but they are not the right way. By biting your tongue, you cause pain. From pain comes anger, a powerful emotion that can trigger your Imperia. But anger and hatred and pain are emotions of Malum.

They are powerful but unruly. You must try to avoid using them, instead learning to draw your ability more naturally. Today, I will teach you Evanestium. It cannot be drawn from pain, but there is another shortcut. Look at my wings and tell me what you see."

Aurora hovered in front of my face. I could see all of her but her wings. They were moving so fast it was as if they weren't there, giving the illusion her body was hovering in midair.

"I can't see them," I said.

"Exactly. When something moves fast enough, it cannot be seen. That is what you will learn to do tonight."

"But how can I possibly move my whole body as fast as you move your wings? Even if I could run like Felinia, this cave is only six feet wide."

"Run? Who said anything about running? No, you will quiver, back and forth in one spot. Just like my wings."

"Quiver? How?"

"By controlling your own resonance, your own vibration. As I said, there isn't time to teach you the true skill—it takes great mental fortitude to control your own resonance. But there is a trick."

"What is it?"

"Start by taking off your sweatshirt."

"Take off my sweatshirt?" I blurted. "But it's the middle of the night, and it's cold! I'll freeze!"

"Precisely!"

Hesitantly, I pulled my sweatshirt over my head. "If you're going to ask me to take off my pants next, I'm finding another way out of this cave."

I threw my sweatshirt aside. I had only a tank top underneath, and the cool night air bit at my skin, pulling up goose bumps.

"Now what?" I said, rubbing my arms to warm them.

"What happens when you get cold?" Aurora asked.

"I g-g-get very irrrr-itable."

"Yes. Perfect. You shiver. And when you shiver, your body quivers at a rate you could not normally move. We will use this to our advantage. Later, when you learn the true Evanestium, you won't need the cold, but for now, it will take some of the thinking out of it. Watch."

Aurora moved back and forth slowly before steadily picking up her pace. Her body became a blur, then disappeared.

"You see?"

"You mean I *don't* see."

"Exactly. Now you try."

I shifted back and forth on the spot, transferring my weight from foot to foot, willing my body to move faster and faster. I must have looked as if I needed to pee, and I definitely wasn't disappearing—I didn't need a mirror to know that.

"No, no, no. You're thinking too much. Use the cold. Focus on how cold you are, not how fast you're moving. Let your subconscious do the moving."

I did as Aurora said, concentrating on how cold I was. That was easy. I was freezing. I crossed my arms and held my shoulders, shifting back and forth. For the briefest of moments, something happened—I stopped thinking about Aurora and what we were doing, and thought only about how cold I was, and the cave started to blur. It was only for a fraction of a second, until I noticed the change and everything went back to normal.

"Excellent!" Aurora exclaimed. "You're a fast learner. Now, this time, stay focused. We only have a few more hours before the sun rises, and you will need to hide for much longer than a second."

Chapter 49

THE SKY WAS BEGINNING TO BRIGHTEN AS I STOOD AT THE BACK OF the cave, waiting for Aurora's command. We had gone over the plan a number of times, but I was still worried. With each passing minute the sun rose higher, which meant the air was getting warmer. The colder it was, the easier it would be to remain focused. If I let my mind slip for even a second, the wolves would see me and everything would be lost.

"GONE?!" a voice bellowed from the woods. I recognized Tantum's gruff tone. "What do you mean, the amulet is gone?!"

"It was in the hole, right where I left it when I went to sleep, sir, and then, when I woke up, it was—"

"GONE!" Tantum yelled again. "You were supposed to be guarding the amulet, not sleeping!"

"Right, sir, I know, I—well, er . . . I dozed off, sir."

There was a thrashing sound, followed by a yelp.

"When Lupora hears about your incompetence, she'll have your liver for lunch. Tell the others to spread out and find the amulet. I want every raccoon questioned, starting with that lazy one who calls himself king."

"Yes, sir."

"And check the girl!"

"Yes, sir, right away, sir!"

Aurora suddenly appeared in front of me.

"Okay," she said, "they're coming. Time to hide."

I shifted quickly from foot to foot, trying to focus on the morning chill. My body gave a little shiver, but that was it. I was too nervous to stop thinking about everything else. I needed something more to help me. I imagined myself standing in the rain on a cold day, and the cave wall blurred slightly. I imagined myself swimming in the frigid water around Pitchi. The cave blurred further, as if I were spinning. The colder I felt, the more the colours smeared—greys melting into greys until everything went black.

The world had disappeared, but I could still hear voices. I had to force myself not to focus on them.

"Th—there's no one in here!" a nervous cry came from just outside the cave.

Focus on the cold, Winter, I told myself.

A few moments later, I heard Tantum's familiar growl. "Who was supposed to be watching her?"—a short pause—"Never mind. I'll deal with them later. Spread out, find her, NOW! If the girl isn't back by the time Lupora returns, we're all dead!"

I nearly lost my focus, and the cave wall reappeared momentarily before I recovered the grey blur.

"Hold it," Aurora whispered beside my head.

Wood snapped as the wolves tore open the gate. I sensed Tantum beside me, sniffing the air, pacing the cave. Could he smell me? *What would happen if he walked right into me*?

Again, the thought of something other than the cold made my focus slip. The wall of the cave reappeared. I was standing behind Tantum—he was only two feet away with his back to me. Two more wolves stood outside, but they were looking frantically around the bay, not into the cave. A small group of raccoons standing near the woods spotted me,

246

and their faces registered their shock.

Luckily, right then, Proctin burst through the trees.

"We've found her!" he cried. "She's making her way through the woods. She was travelling too fast for us to catch her."

"Of course *you* couldn't catch her," Tantum growled. "I can *smell* her. She's not far. Follow me!" Tantum took off into the woods, followed closely by the other two wolves, and I exhaled in relief and slumped backward against the cave wall.

Chapter 50

I waited a few minutes to be sure the coast was clear before coming out of the cave. Wisps of cloud sat over the mountains in the distance, and behind them the sky continued to brighten.

Proctin stared nervously into the woods. The howls of the wolves echoed off the trees, and they didn't sound very far off. We needed to get moving.

"How many raccoons are coming?" I asked.

Proctin waved his arms over his head, signaling toward the trees. From them came a slow stream of waddling black-and-grey creatures, like smoke flowing out over the beach. I don't know what I'd expected—ten? Twenty? Maybe thirty? But the stream kept coming until the whole beach was covered with raccoons. There were hundreds of them. Small, big, old, young, a few mothers with kits in tow.

A sudden heaviness filled my chest—the weight of responsibility. All those little faces staring up at me expectantly, hoping I could take them somewhere safe. Hoping I could get them away from the wolves.

"Okay," I said, steadying my voice, "let's go."

We set off down the rocky beach toward the mountains, the high wall of the escarpment on our left leaving only a narrow strip of beach. I felt claustrophobic. If the wolves returned, we'd be trapped. It would be a massacre. Our only hope was to be far enough away by the time they got wise and turned around.

"We should run," I said, looking down at Proctin as we followed the escarpment. By his side was Procynia, moving nimbly over the rocks and boulders despite her age.

"We could probably make better time if—" My words caught in my throat. We had rounded a corner and there, sitting on a large boulder, was a familiar raccoon, his arms crossed defiantly over his chest, twiggy crown sitting lopsided over his right ear, an unpleasant scowl splayed across his face.

"Raycor," Proctin groaned.

The last thing we needed was to be held up.

"Just where do you think you're going?" Raycor spat, his usual mocking tone replaced by something between hurt and anger.

"We're leaving," Proctin said meekly.

"Leaving!" Raycor yelled, his eyes twitching as he glared at the raccoons.

"Yes," continued Proctin, "we're going with Winter to the mountains. We're getting away from the wolves. Come with us."

"Since when did you start giving orders?" Raycor snarled. "I wear the crown." He pointed at the rim of twigs on his head. "I make the decisions. No one is leaving! Especially not with Lupora's prisoner."

Proctin stepped sideways to hide behind Procynia. "But Raycor, the wolves have been—"

"Shut up!" Raycor hissed, jumping down from the boulder and walking toward his brother, finger pointed like a dagger. "After all I've done for you. Bringing you back after you shamed our family, giving you a second chance, making you official servant to the king, and this is what I get in return? A mutiny against our allies? Aiding Lupora's prisoner to escape and manipulating the gaze to follow you? I should never have let you come back. You're a disgrace to our family, a disgrace to the gaze, a disgrace to every raccoon on the face of this planet. The only thing you're good at is eating."

Proctin's head slumped and he sat, defeated, behind Procynia.

"And you," Raycor said, lifting his finger and pointing it around the beach at the rest of the raccoons, "all of you—you should be ashamed of yourselves! After all the wolves have done for us, offering their protection and asking nothing in return."

"Raycor, the wolves—" Procynia started, but Raycor lifted his hand and struck his mother across the face with the back of his paw, sending her sprawling sideways over the rocks.

There was a collective gasp from around the beach. Proctin got to his feet and glared at Raycor.

Raycor, however, didn't notice. He stared down at Procynia, nostrils opening and closing, seething with rage. "How dare you even open your mouth?" he shot. "My own mother—leading the pack. It sickens me. But then, you've never loved me as you've loved Proctin or Father. I've always known that. It's been clear in your every gesture, your every criticism of my leadership. Look at what I've done. Look at what I've accomplished. Does it mean nothing to you? When Father was around, the gaze cowered from the wolves like rats in the trees, and now we walk among them as equals. I have raised us up and made us important in this world. I have given us power."

"The wolves are not our allies," Procynia said from the ground. "They have been picking us off one by one in the night, and they plan to finish us once Lupora returns."

"Lies!" Raycor spat. "Manipulative lies."

"It's the truth," came a voice from the middle of the crowd. Several raccoons stepped aside to show the speaker, a mother raccoon surrounded by several little ones. "Just last night they took one of my sons." The raccoon let out a loud sob, and the others moved to comfort her. There were murmurs of discontent.

"Even if that is true," Raycor said, waving his paw flippantly, "how many more of us would have died without their support? How many would have gone missing when the wolves were our enemies? No one of importance has been taken, and the wolves have made no threat to your king."

Proctin walked slowly toward Raycor, his fists clenching and unclenching at his sides, his back stiff, eyes narrowed—an expression I'd never seen on his usually gentle face.

He looked possessed.

"If we go back now, the wolves might be merciful. Perhaps Lupora won't need to learn of what happened." Raycor shook his head from side to side. "Nearly setting her prisoner free—the very prisoner that destroyed our homes, I should remind you. Yes, if we are lucky it can all be blamed on one fat raccoon and—"

Raycor stopped. He had finally noticed Proctin, two feet away, and fear flashed in his eyes.

He took a step backward.

"Now you look here—" he began, but Proctin cut him off.

"You. Hit. Mother!" he said through bared teeth.

"Well, I . . ."

Proctin continued to advance, pushing Raycor toward the water. "And you've known all along what the wolves have been doing—haven't you?"

Raycor stumbled over a loose rock, his hands raised in defense. "As I said, no one of importance—"

"*Everyone* in the gaze is important!" Proctin growled, his nose inches from Raycor's.

"Well, it's my decision!" Raycor said, his confidence returning as he held his ground, the two raccoons now in a face-off. "I'm the king! I wear the crown! I make the decisions! Your talents are for eating, not for leading. You passed up your chance to be king long ago."

Proctin wasn't backing down. He was much larger than Raycor—both in girth and height—and it looked as if it would take a hurricane or tsunami to stop him.

"Maybe I won't be a good leader!" Proctin yelled. "And maybe I'm better at eating than I am at leading. But you know what? It wouldn't take much to be better than you. And I'll have Mother and Winter to help me. I'm going to listen to their advice—unlike you."

Raycor was slowly sinking toward the ground under Proctin's downward glare. "B-b-but I wear the crown—" Raycor said feebly, touching his head as if to convince himself it was still there.

Proctin reached out and snatched the crown from Raycor's head, snapping it in two before tossing the pieces into his mouth.

Just like that, it was gone.

Impressive.

"That was mine!" Raycor cried, fear overcoming him. He stood and tried to claw at Proctin's face, but Proctin thrust out his large belly, which struck Raycor square in the chest like a heavy sack. I'd never seen a raccoon fly until that day, but up Raycor went, catapulting five, ten, fifteen feet through the air before landing with a splash in the cold water of the bay.

There was a collective cheer from around the beach.

"Hurray for Proctin!" called a raccoon from the back of the group.

"Our king has returned!" yelled another.

"King of the Red Woods!" called a third.

Proctin turned around and looked at the gaze, his angry expression evaporating and a nervous smile replacing it.

"Well, King Proctin," I said, loud enough for everyone to hear, "what do you say?"

Proctin looked at me, confused.

"What do you mean, what do I say?" he whispered out of the corner of his mouth.

I bent down. "Say something to the gaze."

"Like what?"

"Say . . . something inspiring. They want you to be King."

"Okay," Proctin said with a nod. He stood up straight, thrust out his chest (as much as he could) and yelled, "Something inspiring! They want you to be King!"

A silence fell over the gaze, and I put my hand over my face before leaning over and whispering, "Just say, I'd be glad to be your king. Follow me, and together we will find a new, safe home, away from the wolves."

Proctin repeated obediently. "I'd be glad to be your King! Follow me, and together we will find a new, safe home, away from the wolves!"

The raccoons cheered again.

"Now turn around and start walking," I prompted.

"Now turn around and start walking!" he bellowed.

"Not *them*, YOU! Ugh." I grabbed Proctin's little paw and marched down the beach with the raucous gaze of raccoons following closely behind.

Chapter 51

WITH SUCH A LARGE GROUP, IT WAS IMPOSSIBLE TO MOVE QUICK-
ly along the beach. We were only as fast as the slowest raccoon, and
with so many little ones in tow, I feared we wouldn't get more than a
kilometre before Tantum and his pack caught us. The high wall of the
escarpment loomed on our left, trapping us like pigs in a pen.

"Does this wall follow the beach all the way to the mountains?" I
asked.

Proctin and Procynia had been walking side by side, not saying a
word. Well, at least not to anyone else. Proctin had been muttering to
himself since we'd left Raycor. Things like, "King . . . King Proctin . . .
Proctin the King . . . need to be smart . . . need to be heroic . . . need to
be brave . . . don't think about lunch . . ." Other than that, everything
had been relatively quiet.

"Yes," a small, chirpy voice answered next to my head, "the escarpment follows the beach all the way around the bay."

I had nearly forgotten about Aurora. She hadn't shown herself since
we'd left the cave, and I had become accustomed to the low humming
sound she made.

I looked up at the wall: a sheer mass of grey rock. There were a few
cracks and ledges, but I doubted the smallest raccoons would be able to
climb that high.

"How will we get to the mountains?" I asked. "We won't be able to
climb this."

"There's a gorge up ahead that cuts through the cliff," Aurora said. "A river runs through it, but at this time of year, it should be low enough to pass. We can follow the gorge all the way to the mountains. There is a grove of trees at the foot of the mountains where the raccoons will be safe."

Proctin and Procynia were looking around as if they'd heard a ghost.

"It's Aurora," I said, as if that should make sense. "She prefers hiding."

"Prefers staying alive," Aurora retorted.

I laughed as Proctin batted at the air around his ears.

"Okay," I said, "let's get to this gorge before the wolves return."

As we continued to walk, our pace slowed further. The rocks on the beach got progressively bigger—first they were the size of oranges, then watermelons, until finally they became as large as hay bales, requiring us to climb and jump between them. They were slippery from the mist that showered us with each crashing wave, and there were sharp barnacles and slick seaweed on their surfaces. Even with my Sensium, I slipped on several occasions.

"How much farther?" I asked, after we'd been travelling for what felt like an hour.

"Less than a kilometre," Aurora said.

"Good," I said, grunting as I jumped from a large boulder down to a smaller one. I stopped and turned, helping the line of raccoons that followed.

I was beginning to think we might make it—there was still no sign of the wolves, and we had covered a lot of ground—when someone yelled, "LOOK OUT!"

My first thought was that the wolves were coming, until I saw movement with my Aminoculus and ducked my head. A large boulder sailed over top of me, narrowly missing my skull before landing with a splash among the rocks.

"Get down!" I yelled, as another boulder came sailing from the water.

I pressed my stomach to the rock and waited.

Another boulder flew toward me, and I rolled to the side. It was followed by an odd clicking noise from the water.

Cano, I thought. He was the only water creature large enough to throw rocks that size.

When the third rock came, I was forced to jump to another boulder, but my foot slipped and my shoe wedged between the rocks, trapping me.

I pulled hard to free my foot, but it wouldn't budge.

When the next rock came, all I could do was raise my hands in front of my face, although I knew it would do nothing to soften the blow.

The rock was enormous, twice as large as me, and I closed my eyes, bracing for the hit.

I expected to be knocked unconscious, or worse, but was instead hit by a giant wave of water. When I opened my eyes, my clothes were drenched and there was kelp hanging from my hair.

The noise returned, a mechanical click punctuated by short, high-pitched squeals.

I looked around to find the raccoons looking just as confused and startled as I was. I wriggled my foot free from the rocks and slunk over the boulders toward the water. When I got to the edge, I peered down.

At first, I saw nothing but waves, floating kelp, foam. Nothing out of the ordinary. Then I spotted them: two bright eyes looking up at me—two bright, innocent, adorable eyes. A sea otter lay on its back with its hands folded neatly over its chest, floating in the kelp. It had a dark brown coat with silver-grey speckles, and long whiskers coming from a pale face.

The squealing, clicking noise had stopped the moment I looked over the edge, and there didn't appear to be anyone else besides the otter.

"You didn't happen to hit me with a rock just now, did you?" I asked, removing a strand of kelp from my hair.

It seemed like a dumb question; the rock had been ten times the size of the otter.

"Me?" said the otter, looking hurt. "You think I would hit you with a rock?" It blinked its big eyes innocently.

"No, well, I didn't think so. I'm sorry, I didn't mean to offend you."

The otter smiled. "That's okay. Shall we play a game?"

"A game? I'm actually trying to figure out—"

"Great," said the otter, "let's play catch! I'll get the rocks."

Before I could answer, it flexed its body backward and disappeared beneath the waves. When it returned, it was holding a large stone on its chest.

"Catch!" it said, and threw the rock to me.

I reached out to grab it, but the second it hit my hands, it turned to water. It was as if it had melted on contact.

"You missed!" the otter said, spinning around and around and making the clicking, squealing noise I now saw to be laughter.

"It *was* you!" I said, pointing my finger at the otter.

"No," said the otter, "you asked if I hit you with a rock. And I didn't."

"Well, you threw a rock at me, didn't you?"

"Oh sure, I threw a rock, yes, but I thought you'd catch it."

"You thought I'd catch a boulder hurtling toward my head?"

The otter thought for a moment. "Yes," it said, nodding vigorously. "Now, let's play again!"

"I don't have time for games," I said, irritated. "I need to get to Mount Skire before it's destroyed."

"Destroyed? By what?"

I stood and began jumping from rock to rock as the otter swished its tail lazily, following along in the water.

"Lupora," I said. "She's taken her army and my cousin, Alectus, to destroy Mount Skire."

The otter scrunched up its face. "That doesn't sound like a very fun game."

Aurora flew up beside us. "Ah, I see you've met Tully," she said. "I figured he'd show up sooner or later. We're in his home, after all."

"Tully?" I said, looking at the otter.

"Water Guardian of Agility," the otter said with a nod of his head.

"More like Water Guardian of Mischief," Aurora said dismissively.

"Now, we'd better get going. I've just flown ahead, and it looks like the gorge will be passable. With luck, we should be there before lunch."

"I should probably come," Tully suggested, still following along in the water. "It sounds as if Lupora is not much fun. I bet I can change that. Does she like to play games?"

Aurora flew a few feet over the water and looked down at Tully. "No, that's alright, I'm sure we'll be fine without you. You can, um, stay here and guard these rocks."

Tully looked upset. "But I always guard these rocks. Why can't I come? I'm a Guardian, after all!"

"A very young Guardian," Aurora said. "I really think it's best if you stay here."

"But I've been a Guardian since I was just a pup and have never once got to do anything fun!"

"You were a Guardian when you were a pup?" I asked.

Tully nodded happily. "Youngest Guardian ever selected. So young I don't remember. But now I'm bigger and stronger and older and faster and smarter and—"

While Tully continued to list his attributes, I turned to Aurora.

"Why would Terra select a pup for a Guardian?" I whispered.

"There weren't any other options," Aurora said.

"No other options?"

"As I'm sure you're aware, there has been a sharp decline in the otter population around Olport. Tully's family has borne the brunt of that mass exodus."

I pictured Alectus's fashionable otter-pelt hat.

"That's awful," I said, looking at Tully swimming along, smiling and talking to himself. I felt bad for him. He probably wanted to play because he was lonely. "I think we should let him come," I said to Aurora.

Aurora shook her tiny head from side to side. "Tully is still young and learning, and well, frankly, he's a bit of a troublemaker. I really think—"

"I'm young and learning," I said, offended.

Tully heard this and stopped talking to himself. He nodded excitedly. "Yes! She's young! Let me come. We can play all sorts of games."

"You can come," I said. "It would be fun to have you along."

Tully squealed and spun around in rapid circles, so fast a whirlpool formed in the centre. He clapped his paws and chanted, "Fun, fun, fun, fun!"

Aurora let out a faint harrumph beside me. "Well, don't say I didn't warn you. He'll be your responsibility, not mine."

And with that, the hummingbird vanished.

Chapter 52

AS WE MADE OUR WAY OVER THE FINAL STRETCH OF BOULDERS toward the gorge, Tully swam beside us, occasionally picking up rocks and throwing them at unsuspecting raccoons, who groaned as they were showered with water.

"What exactly is your power?" I asked, hoping to distract Tully from bothering the raccoons.

"I can change the physical elements of Terra," Tully said. "Like water into rock and rock into water." He gave a powerful swish of his tail, shooting himself out of the surf and landing on top of the waves, where he began walking. It looked as if he were lighter than water, but when I looked closer I saw that the water had turned to stone. "Ta-dah!" he said, jumping back into the sea.

"Wow, that's amazing!" I said, and Tully chirped and clicked excitedly.

"And you must have super strength to be able to throw those boulders?" I guessed.

Tully flexed his arm muscles and nodded. He disappeared beneath the waves and resurfaced holding a rock the size of a shopping cart, covered with seaweed and barnacles.

"Super strength!" Tully said, in a singsong voice.

"Incredible!"

The rock suddenly lifted from Tully's paws and hovered above his head.

"Hey!" he said, as Aurora appeared above the rock.

The little hummingbird held the boulder by a strand of seaweed. "He doesn't have super strength," Aurora said with a scowl. "He hollows out the rocks so that they're nothing but empty shells. They're as light as a feather." She lifted the rock higher to show us the hole in the bottom.

The rock disappeared with a pop, and a shower of water rained down.

"Well, you're no fun," Tully pouted. He pulled a small stone from a pouch beneath his armpit and threw it at Aurora, but the hummingbird disappeared before it hit.

"Super strength or not, I still think it's impressive," I said, giving Tully a wink.

"Thank you!" he said, clapping his hands.

As we walked, Tully found new games to play. When he tired of throwing rocks, he invented a game he called, "Not that one!"

As I'd jump toward a boulder he'd turn it into water and yell, "Not that one!" then laugh hysterically as I landed awkwardly below.

This game was both irritating and dangerous, and by the time we neared the last of the boulders I was beginning to think Aurora had been right about leaving Tully behind.

"We're nearly there," Aurora said, appearing beside my ear. "You should be able to hear the waterfalls."

She was right. A low rumble sounded ahead. I climbed a high boulder and spotted a gap in the escarpment further down the beach, where a large river flowed into the ocean. The source of the rumbling wasn't the river, but two large waterfalls straddling the entrance of the gorge. They came from either side, landing at the base of the river and filling the air with a thick, white mist.

"The runoff from the mountains drains through the gorge," Aurora said. "The main river runs down from Mount Skire, but there are many others that join along the way. The waterfalls will be cold and unavoidable, but it's not far up the passage to the woods."

I nodded. Getting wet wouldn't be a big deal if it meant we could finally walk on flat ground. There were only about fifteen more metres of boulders to cross before the ground leveled out.

"We can have a race!" Tully suggested.

"I'm not going to race," Proctin said, waddling up beside me and looking at the gorge. He seemed to be growing particularly annoyed with Tully.

"Well of course *you're* not going to race," Tully said, jumping from the water and landing beside Proctin. "No one should race when they're pregnant. That would be dangerous for the babies."

Before I could stop him, Tully reached out and rubbed Proctin's belly.

"Pregnant!" Proctin shrieked, taking a swipe at Tully's head but missing as the otter ducked and leapt back into the water.

"Don't be mad," Tully said. "I just thought a race would be a fun way to get away from the wolves."

"Get away from what wolves?" I said, focused on climbing over the last few boulders.

"Those ones," Tully said, calmly pointing across the bay.

We turned to see a pack of wolves racing down the beach in our direction.

Chapter 53

"How far up the gorge is the forest?" I yelled as we scrambled down from the boulders, the sound of the waterfalls getting louder as we closed in on the gorge.

"Too far!" Aurora said. "We'll never make it before they get here."

The wolves had already cut the distance in half. What had taken us hours to walk would only take them minutes to run.

"We'd better think of a plan," I said, searching the beach for an idea. "How well can the gaze swim?"

"Not well," Procynia said. "The wolves would only have to wait a few minutes before we either drowned or were forced to return."

"And the wall, is it too high to climb?"

She looked up at the grey escarpment. It must have been thirty metres high, with hardly any ledges or cracks in the sheer stone. It would be next to impossible to scale.

"We are good climbers, so we could try," Procynia said. "It might be our best chance. But the mist from the waterfalls has made the rock wet, which will only add to the difficulty."

The waterfalls.

"I've got an idea," I said, looking at the opening of the passage between the falls. "Forget climbing. Get everyone into the gorge! Quickly! Through the waterfalls!"

Without asking questions, the gaze moved as I'd directed. It took longer than I would have liked—the raccoons had to shuffle single file behind the falling water, and by the time they were through, the wolves were halfway across the boulders. Procynia and I stood watching as they approached.

"What will we do?" she asked. "They will be here in a matter of minutes."

"Follow me," I said, turning and entering the mist.

Once inside, it was hard to see, and my Aminoculus was useless with all the water in the air. I put my hand on the wall to guide myself behind the waterfall. The sound was thunderous, and my clothes were drenched by the time I got to the other side.

I emerged in a long canyon with a wide river flowing through it. The walls were steep, and several smaller waterfalls fell from the sides into the river as it led up to the mountains. There was only a narrow riverbank, where the raccoons huddled in a line. Everyone looked frightened—especially Proctin. He stood knee-deep in the water, muttering, "The wolves are coming! The wolves are coming!" with a petrified look on his face.

Beside him swam Tully, clapping his hands and chanting, "The wolves are coming! The wolves are coming!" in an excited tone.

"Aurora?" I called, and a second later she appeared beside me. "Can you fly up and see how close the wolves are?"

She nodded and disappeared.

"Keep moving everyone further into the gorge," I said to Procynia. "Get them as far from the waterfalls as possible."

I took a few steps backward, surveying the entrance to the gorge, deciding on how best to carry out my plan.

Seconds later, Aurora returned. "They're already over the boulders!" she shrieked. "They'll be here any moment!"

"Already over the boulders!" cried Proctin, putting his hands over his face.

"Already over the boulders!" sang Tully, taking a mouthful of water and spitting it into the air like a fountain.

Darn, there wouldn't be time to explain.

"Tully, come here," I yelled, "I've got a game for you."

Tully's eyes lit up and he scampered over.

"A game? Oh, I love games! Is it tag, or—?"

I grabbed Tully by the shoulders and spun him around toward the mist. I held his hands from behind and aimed them up toward the tops of the waterfalls.

"The game is called 'raining rocks'!" I shouted over the thundering water.

"Ooh! That sounds like fun! How do we play?"

The first silhouette of a wolf appeared in the mist.

"Turn the waterfall into rocks, Tully!" I yelled. "NOW!"

His arms turned cool and his body stiffened as the water above changed. There was no longer a thick mist in the air, but pebbles and rocks of all different sizes. Where the waterfalls had been were now two towering rock cascades. Stones fell to the ground like cement and began filling the entrance to the gorge.

The wolves that had been underneath yelped and turned around. Only one made it through, but its tail was pinned by a large boulder before it could attack. The rocks continued to fall, piling higher and higher. Tully had turned both waterfalls into rockslides, and it didn't take long for the entire passage of the gorge to be sealed.

When it was over, the only sound was the low rumble of the smaller waterfalls behind. I turned to see hundreds of stunned faces.

"That *was* fun!" said Tully, breaking the silence and hopping around me in circles. "Can we do it again?"

Behind the otter, the lone wolf that had managed to get through the waterfall pulled its tail free from the rock pile and bounded toward us.

"Tully!" I yelled, as the wolf ran at him. "Watch out!"

Tully spun around just as the wolf prepared to pounce, but—it was weird—it was almost as if its feet and paws had been glued to the ground. The wolf's head lunged, but then snapped back when its body didn't follow. It just . . . stayed.

It let out a pained howl and looked down at its legs. There was now a slab of grey rock around its feet where the water had been, and Tully was clapping merrily. He had trapped the wolf.

Proctin came over to inspect.

"Genius," he mumbled, looking down at the stone. The wolf suddenly looked afraid.

"Woooo-eeeeeeeee!" came a shrill cry, and I looked up to see Tully sitting on the wolf's back, one hand gripping the fur behind its neck, the other waving in the air as if he were riding a bull. "Giddyup!"

Proctin snickered and climbed on behind the otter. "Yee-haw!" he yelled.

The wolf looked more like an injured dog than a wild beast. Its ears were flat to its head, its tail tucked between its legs. As I approached, it shied away, as if I were going to hit it.

"Get off!" I said, looking from Tully to Proctin. "You're hurting it!"

Tully slipped into the water and disappeared, while Proctin slowly climbed down.

"What's the matter?" he asked.

"Look at the poor wolf," I said.

"Poor wolf? It was about to eat us!"

"Eat us or not, look at him now. He's scared."

"So? He's a wolf."

The wolf stood hunched and trembling, its legs trapped in the block of stone. Proctin was right—it *was* a wolf. One of the same wolves that had thrown the little raccoon in the air over and over, one of the same wolves that had eaten the helpless creature the night before. Did it deserve to be left there? To rot in a stony prison? The thought made me nauseous. But why? Why not leave it? Then the answer occurred to me—

"I'm the Terra Protectorum," I said. "I'm sworn to help all of our Mother's creatures—wolves or not. He may have been trying to hurt us before, but he's part of a pack and he follows a leader. He was only doing what he was told. He won't hurt us now, will you?"

The wolf looked at me curiously. There was no viciousness—just the eyes of a scared, trapped animal.

It shook its head.

"Good," I said, "then Tully, please let him go."

Tully was standing in the shallow water and his mouth dropped open. "Let him go? I'm not sure that would be much fun."

"It will be no fun if we leave him here, trapped in the rock. He would starve in a few days."

Tully scratched his chin, thinking, then shrugged and pointed at the rock. The stone turned back to water and the wolf looked down in amazement.

"Now go," I said. "Go where you like. I suggest you leave Lupora and her pack, but if you want to return, that's up to you. I don't make your choices for you."

The wolf looked around once before taking off through the gorge. The raccoons pressed themselves against the rock as it passed, but the wolf made no move to hurt them.

Procynia looked at me and nodded approvingly.

"Good," I said, "now let's keep moving. There are much bigger problems ahead. Mount Skire awaits."

PART 5: THE MOUNTAIN

IT IS NEARLY DUSK, AND THE SUN HAS LONG SINCE SUNK BEHIND the tall twin-peaked mountain beneath which the men are working. Though their backs ache and their legs wobble, the men continue to carry their heavy loads up the winding trail to the summit.

They should stop. It is madness to keep going. But they don't stop.

If they stop, they will die.

The wolves will tear them apart piece by piece and gnaw on their bones. They have seen it happen.

So they walk, up and down, thinking about how this has happened. Thinking about the boy who came to them three nights ago, demanding their help.

They laughed at the boy. They told him to leave. They are not laughing now.

It happened in the evening. The men in charge of the camp were sitting in the large steel housing structure, playing cards and drinking rye. They had been working on the roadway and were finished for the day.

There came a knock at the door.

"Who's there?" they asked.

Behind the door stood a boy with the eyes of a cat.

"I need your help," the boy said.

"Help with what?" they asked.

"Destroying the mountain."

They laughed at the boy.

"If you don't help me willingly, I will make you," the boy demanded, his eyes hard and his face stern.

They laughed more. They were tired from a long day and in no mood for the antics of a boy.

"You'll make us?" said the largest of the men, standing up and approaching the boy. "You and what army?"

The boy merely smiled and raised his hand.

From the darkness behind came his army.

Chapter 54

THE SUN SANK IN THE DISTANCE AS WE FOLLOWED THE GORGE up toward Mount Skire. Everyone was tired and quiet after a long day of walking—even Tully—and we moved like a row of zombies up the sloping riverbank. The walls of the gorge became progressively lower until they disappeared altogether, and we found ourselves in front of a dense forest. The river carried on through the trees toward Mount Skire, and as much as I wanted to follow it, my body couldn't continue.

"We should rest here and leave first thing in the morning," Aurora said.

I nodded in agreement. The last of the sun's rays were gone, and the air had grown cold. It would be better to rest and leave early in the morning.

"Come on," Procynia said. "Up in the trees—it will be safer."

I pulled myself up a thick trunk and lay with my body sprawled between two branches, my arms dangling below. As soon as I settled on the branch, a number of warm, furry bodies curled around me, and I fell asleep quickly.

I AWOKE TO a wet black nose prodding my cheek. "Guess what?" Proctin said.

"Uhhh," I moaned, trying to push him away.

"The trees—they're oak trees!"

I cracked open my eyes, rubbing the sleep from the corners. It was still dark.

"Oak trees?" I mumbled.

"Yes! And guess what oak trees have?"

I wasn't in the mood for guessing games. "I dunno, what?"

"Acorns!" Proctin exclaimed, holding up his paws to show me a pile of nuts with pointed ends and small caps.

"Oh, great," I mumbled.

Proctin took an acorn and shoved it into his mouth, followed by another and another, until his cheeks bulged.

"They're delicious," he said, several acorns falling out in the process. "I've never had them. Mom says when she was a kit, her family lived near a forest full of oak trees and they ate acorns all the time!"

"I'm glad you found breakfast," I said. "What time is it, anyway?"

Proctin was too busy counting the acorns to answer, so I lifted him off my stomach and rolled out of the tree, landing softly on the ground below. All around, raccoons combed the ground for fallen nuts.

I found the river and was rinsing my face when a blast of cold water hit me. "Good morning, Tully," I said, wiping my eyes as he clicked and clapped in the river.

"Want to have a splash fight?" he asked.

"Not right now," I said. "We need to come up with a plan."

"Yes," Aurora said, a bodiless voice above me, "there'll be no games today. We need to move quickly. The very idea that Lupora and her army are at Mount Skire worries me."

I nodded in agreement. Lupora and her army worried me, and Alectus worried me more. Together they were as scary as a two-headed monster. I thought back to the Twin Terrors, Carly and Marly. They were nothing compared to what I was about to encounter.

"Where are the other Guardians?" I asked.

"I suspect they're already at Mount Skire," Aurora said. "News of Lupora's movement will have spread, and the Guardians will not stand for her being anywhere near their mountain. The battle may already have begun."

"Then I'd better get going."

"WAIT!" a voice called from behind. Proctin climbed down a tree, followed closely by his mother. "I'm coming with you!" he said, his cheeks still full of acorns.

I shook my head. "Proctin, you need to stay here with the gaze. They need you."

Proctin swallowed and scowled. "They don't need me."

"Of course they do, you're their king."

A small crowd of raccoons gathered.

"Right, well, I was thinking about the whole king thing last night." Proctin pulled his tail around in front of him and ran his paws over it nervously. "I-I'm not sure I'm cut out to be king."

The raccoons looked at one another, whispering amongst themselves.

"Proctin," Procynia said, "we need you. You're the only one who can lead the gaze."

"About that," Proctin said. "I have an idea. See, I'm the king now . . ." Procynia nodded.

"And if I'm king, then I get to make the rules, right?"

Procynia looked skeptical. "Well, yes, I suppose so. Why?"

"I've decided to change things. I'm making a new rule. From now on, anyone can be king—male or female. And therefore, I make you king."

He pointed at Procynia and she smiled. "Proctin, that's very nice, but—"

"But what? You basically were our king when Father wore the crown." There was a lot of nodding from the other raccoons. "If all I'm going to do is listen to everything you say and then do it, well, why not just do it yourself?"

The raccoons stared at Procynia. The group had grown, crowding the forest floor.

"Well . . ." Procynia said, apparently at a loss for words.

"Well?" Proctin prodded.

"Well, I suppose you can do whatever you like as king. And if you say females can lead, then I guess that's so."

"So, you'll be our new king?" Proctin asked, looking very excited.

"Queen," Procynia corrected.

"Oh yes, queen."

"If that's what you really want, then yes, I'll be queen. But only until we find a younger replacement. I'm getting too old for this."

Proctin hugged Procynia, and the crowd of raccoons screeched in approval.

I picked up Proctin and gave him a giant hug.

"You know," I whispered into his ear, "I think that may be the smartest thing you've ever done."

"As smart as a human?" he whispered back.

"Smarter," I said, laughing.

Chapter 55

By the time we had finished congratulating Procynia, the sky was a dull shade of grey, and daybreak was near.

"We should get going," Aurora said, echoing my thoughts.

I looked up at the twin peaks of Mount Skire, looming ominously above.

"Okay," I said, "let's go."

We set off, following the river through the woods, Proctin by my side while Tully swam along close to the riverbank.

"Aurora," I asked, attuned to the soft humming noise she made when she was nearby, "what exactly would happen if Alectus and Lupora destroyed Mount Skire?"

"I cannot be certain," she said, "but I imagine it would be nothing short of apocalyptic. Mount Skire is our most sacred place. It is the source of much of our Mother's energy."

"The source of Her energy?"

"As we get closer, you will notice Her presence more strongly. You will also find your abilities become easier to use."

My Aminoculus had seemed a little crisper that morning, though I'd thought it was due to a decent night's rest. Perhaps the reason Aurora's humming sounded louder was that my Sensium was working better, too. I tried using my Imperia and was surprised at how easily the flames came. I rolled the fire through my fingers for a moment before extinguishing it.

"Very nice," Aurora said.

"You're right," I said, "it is easier."

"It was once that easy everywhere," Aurora said, solemnly. "Our Mother's energy is weakening, and with it, our abilities. If Mount Skire were destroyed, I suspect it would be the beginning of the end."

"We won't let that happen," I said.

"No," Aurora agreed, "we won't."

The sky was growing lighter, and Mount Skire seemed to grow taller the nearer we got. Was Alectus already up there? Was he able to call the flames? He shouldn't be able to; he wasn't the Terra Protectorum. He wasn't even a Guardian. But I'd seen him hold the fire. Would Terra know why?

"Aurora," I said, "how exactly does Terra answer our questions? Does She speak?"

"In a way, yes, though not with words."

"Then how?"

"You see the taller of the two peaks?" Aurora said, appearing in front of me and pointing a wing at Mount Skire.

"You mean the pointed one?"

"Yes, the pointed one. At the top of that peak is a pool through which Terra shows us Her answers. It is said the pool goes straight down to the heart of Terra, and through it we see Her heart's desires. It is where Scanda goes to learn of the new Guardians, and where we go to ask our questions."

"Have you asked Her a question before?"

"No," Aurora said, "but others have."

"And they got answers?"

"So I've been told."

"Blah, blah, blah," Tully said, swimming up beside us. "I'm tired of all this talking. Can't we play a game?"

"Now is not the time for games," Aurora said irritably.

Tully lay on his back, scowling up at us as he pushed himself along with his tail.

"I've got an idea," I said. "Instead of a game, why don't you teach me how to use your ability?"

Tully's face lit up. "You mean Petraquim?"

"Is that what it's called?"

Tully nodded vigorously. "Ooh, that sounds like fun! Then we could play splash catch together! How do I teach you?"

I pulled the amulet from beneath my shirt and bent down beside the river. "First you have to touch this," I said, holding out the amulet, "and after that, you can teach me how to use your ability."

Tully swam over and touched the amulet with his paw, and the symbol of the otter lit up with a jolt.

"OOOoooo," he said, staring at the green glow, "I like that!"

"Now you should be able to show me how to change the elements."

"Okay!" Tully said, swimming back into the centre of the river and clapping his hands. "All you do is point at a rock and"—he pointed at a large stone sitting on the riverbank—"turn it into water." The rock disappeared with a pop. "And if you want to turn the water into rock, you . . . well . . . point at the water and"—he turned a part of the river into stone and hopped out onto it—"turn it into stone."

"That's it?" I asked. "Aren't there any tricks or tips on how to do it?"

Tully shrugged. "That's how I do it. I just point."

I pointed at a rock on the riverbank but had no idea what to think or do. Not surprisingly, the rock didn't change.

"There has to be more to it than that," I said.

Tully thought for a moment, scrunching up his face and twitching his nose. "This game involves too much thinking," he said. "I'm going to play a different one."

He ducked under the water and disappeared.

We resumed our silent walk through the forest, Tully playing a game that involved spraying water in the air like a fountain and turning it into pebbles, Proctin mumbling on and on about acorns, and Aurora humming quietly beside my ear.

Half a kilometre from Mount Skire, the forest came to an abrupt end, and we ducked behind some low bushes. Ahead was a large clearing. Dead stumps were scattered around the area, with piles of logs placed along the edge. The area had been stripped of its trees. Although it was poorly lit in the shadow of Mount Skire, I could still make out dark figures walking across the clearing.

"Tully, get down," I whispered, hoping he hadn't been seen.

The figures were unmistakable: large, powerful beasts skulking around and snarling.

Wolves.

Hundreds of them.

Getting close to Mount Skire would be harder than I'd expected.

Chapter 56

I PEERED OVER THE BUSH AT THE CLEARING. MANY OF THE WOLVES were stalking back and forth, scanning the woodpiles and surrounding area. The rest were herding a long line of creatures single file up the mountain.

"Humans!" Proctin said. "What are they carrying?"

"Boxes of some sort," I said, straining my eyes, "and they're getting them from inside that building."

I pointed to a large steel structure along the far side of the deforested area. It looked like a windowless barn that had been thrown together in a hurry. The front door was open, and a yellowish light shone from within. One line of humans came out of the building carrying boxes, while another entered empty-handed.

"Where did all the trees go?" Proctin asked, disappointment in his voice.

"They've been cleared for the roadway," I replied, nodding toward a raised path of dirt running parallel to the mountains. Along it sat several horse-drawn wagons and a few cars. None of them were moving, and it appeared construction on the roadway had halted.

"But the acorns," Proctin whined.

"Never mind the acorns," Aurora snapped, appearing suddenly by my shoulder. "Where are the Guardians? They should be—"

CRACK!

A flash of lightning zigzagged through the sky and struck Mount Skire near the top. The accompanying thunder made us jump. Tully scrambled from the water and gripped my right leg, while Proctin held tightly to my left.

"What was that?" I asked, looking up at the sky. There wasn't a single cloud.

"Fulgarem," Aurora replied, "the power of the Sky Guardian of Speed. Fantom must be up there."

Another bolt of lightning illuminated the clearing, and I got a closer look at the boxes the humans were carrying. On the side of each was printed one word: EXPLOSIVE.

"Oh no, Fantom had better stop or else—"

A third bolt of lightning struck, and this time the side of the mountain exploded into a ball of flames that sent large fragments of rock hurtling through the sky. A chunk of the mountain split and fell away, crashing down like an avalanche on the open plain. The humans and wolves went into a frenzy. Boxes of explosives were thrown aside as the line of people fled toward the woods, while the wolves lunged left and right to block them.

The lightning must have awakened a murder of crows, because a stream of black birds rose around the mountain peak like a dark halo. Cries and caws and shrieks filled the air, turning the scene into chaos.

"Aurora, can you fly up there and find out what's happening?"

Aurora disappeared from my shoulder. "I'll have a look," she said.

No sooner had Aurora gone than the earth began to shake. A powerful growl echoed through the trees, and the sound of splintering wood drew nearer. An enormous creature barreled from the forest on the far side of the clearing, knocking whole trunks out of its way.

"Arctos!" Tully cried excitedly, though I can't say I shared his enthusiasm.

The bear stood at the edge of the clearing, his dark-crimson eyes surveying the area. The people that had been fleeing in his direction quickly turned around, while the wolves formed a pack in front of him. There must have been a hundred wolves, but even they didn't seem like much of a threat to the giant bear.

The first of the wolves charged at Arctos and he lifted his front paws high in the air to meet them, bringing them down with a crushing blow. The ground shook with so much force I fell to my knees. When I stood, the wolves that had been in front of Arctos had disappeared.

Was that Arctos's ability? The power to make whole animals disappear?

No sooner had the thought gone through my head than I saw the large chasm that had opened in front of the bear. The wolves that had not fallen in clung to the sides.

So that was it? The ability to break the earth? It seemed like an odd way of protecting Terra.

More wolves poured into the clearing—some from the mountain, some from the trees—and they surrounded Arctos on all sides. Crows joined their efforts, swooping at the bear from above.

"I'd better go help Arctos!" Tully said, letting go of my leg and taking off toward the clearing. I grabbed him by the scruff of the neck before he got very far.

"It's too dangerous," I said, putting him down beside Proctin. "You stay here. I'll go."

"But I'm a Guardian!" he complained.

"I know. That's why I need you to stay here and protect Proctin."

Truthfully, I couldn't imagine a scenario where Tully took anything seriously enough to avoid getting hurt.

Tully nodded. "Okay," he said. "I'll look after the pregnant one." He turned and patted Proctin's tummy.

"For the last time, I'm not pregnant!" Proctin cried, attempting to swat Tully as he scampered around in circles.

Good, I thought, *they're occupied.*

I scanned the clearing once more, plotting my route, when something shot from the woods opposite Arctos that sent the wolves flying in all directions. It was like the world's fastest bowling ball, and when it stopped, there was a deafening snap that left my eardrums vibrating.

"What was that?" I said, placing my hands over my ears to stop the ringing.

"Kanetis," Tully said with a happy chirp, "the power of the Land Guardian of Speed! Felinia is here!"

Sure enough, in the path now cleared of wolves stood the slender frame of a cheetah, looking around with a calm poise as if she'd just strolled in for dinner.

If Felinia had arrived, that meant—

"Vulpeera!" Aurora's voice suddenly shrieked beside me. "She's at the top of the mountain! She's in trouble!"

Chapter 57

"STAY HERE!" I YELLED OVER MY SHOULDER AT PROCTIN AND Tully, as I took off running through the clearing.

I weaved through discarded crates and tree stumps toward Felinia, hoping she'd stay put long enough for me to reach her.

A group of wolves had surrounded her, but she looked surprisingly relaxed, licking her front paw as she eyed them.

"Felinia!" I yelled, and she turned at the sound of my voice.

She looked at me as if I were a ghost running toward her. Had she forgotten who I was?

"Winter?" she said, one moment twenty feet away, the next standing directly in front of me. Her yellow eyes narrowed as she looked me up and down. "I-I thought you were dead."

"Dead? No, not dead," I said. "Very much alive. For now, at least."

I hugged Felinia around her neck, and she lifted a paw to rest on my shoulder.

"But how?" she said. "I don't understand."

"I'll explain later. Right now, we have to help Vulpeera. She's in trouble at the top of the mountain."

"Trouble? Where's Catharia? She carried her up there."

"I don't know, but Aurora was just at the top and said Vulpeera needs us. Can you clear a path to the base of the mountain?"

As I let go of Felinia, I noticed the wolves had surrounded us.

I lifted my hands and summoned the fire before waving them at the wolves, forcing them back.

"Follow me," Felinia said, and with another loud snap she took off toward Mount Skire.

I followed in the path she cleared until the ground began to slope upward at the base of the mountain. Felinia was waiting, looking up the narrow trail that led to the top.

"I won't be any help up there," Felinia said. "I need space to run or my ability is useless. I'll stay down here and hold off the wolves. It will give you time to get to the top and help Vulpeera. Fantom and Catharia are already there."

"Alright," I said.

Felinia smiled. "I'm glad you're okay," she said. "Go help Vulpeera."

She turned and took off, sending another crowd of wolves flying.

I stared at the mountain. The path zigzagged back and forth up the steep slope until it reached the flat peak. A thick cloud of crows circled that peak, so I knew that's where I'd find Vulpeera. I took off running, but stopped when my foot hit something soft and a grunt came from below.

I bent down to find a man lying on his side, half buried beneath the rock.

"Are you okay?" I asked, removing rocks from around his head.

He groaned but didn't answer.

"I'm going to move you off the path, so you don't get trampled." I grasped him beneath the arms and pulled him toward the wall of the mountain.

Once he was propped up, I brushed off his face. He wasn't much older than I was—maybe eighteen at the most, and he looked terrified.

"It's okay, I'm not going to hurt—"

I stopped when I saw a shadow moving slowly over his body. I didn't have to turn around to see what it was; only one thing was that large.

"So," the bear's deep voice rumbled from behind, "it is as I expected. You are helping them destroy our mountain."

Chapter 58

I turned and came face to face with Arctos.

Well, more like face to chest.

"It's not what it looks like," I said. "I was only helping him move aside."

"Helping? These humans are here to destroy Terra!" he roared.

"Arctos, I—"

The bear stood on his hind legs and raised his arms. I knew I'd have no chance in a fight, so I ran up the path as fast as my legs would carry me. The narrow trail zigzagged often and wouldn't be easy for Arctos to follow. With luck, I'd get to the top of the mountain before he caught me, and maybe Vulpeera could reason with him.

As I ran, I came across several wolves on the path, all heading down the trail to the clearing. I heard them before they saw me, their claws making loud scraping noises against the rock. When they were close, I pressed myself against the wall, called my Evanestium, and hid. I waited for them to pass before reappearing, surprised at how easily the abilities came on Terra's mountain.

In the few short breaks I took to catch my breath, I looked down on the fight in the clearing below. Felinia and the wolves were tiny figures in the distance, and the chasm Arctos had left was an ugly scar on the battlefield. The occasional snap echoed up the mountain as Felinia performed her sonic assaults, which sent wolves flying in all directions. I watched in awe as she single-handedly took on an army of wolves. But I couldn't stand around, because I needed to help Vulpeera. I needed to keep running.

I was nearly at the top and growing hopeful that I would make it unscathed when suddenly, the whole mountain seemed to explode around me. I was tossed sideways, barely grabbing the cliff's edge as the stone shook. A wave of heat washed through the air and burning chunks of rock flew into the sky as if they'd come from a volcano. Rocks plummeted like meteors toward the clearing. Several must have hit boxes of explosives, because they blew up on contact, leaving craters in the earth. One giant piece landed on the steel barn, and seconds later it exploded, sending flames in all directions, igniting the surrounding forest.

Tully and Proctin! They were still in the woods!

I tried to scan the trees below, but the explosion had triggered a rockslide, and boulders bounded toward me. I pulled myself onto the ledge and danced around the first few, but the rocks kept coming and soon there was nowhere left to dance. I was going to be crushed or knocked off the mountain.

In a moment of panic, I raised my hands in front of me and pointed at the oncoming boulders. A large one was only a few feet away when a familiar sensation rose in my chest and spread down my arms. It was like my Imperia, except it felt cold rather than hot. The rock exploded into a wave of water that splashed over me, drenching my clothes. I pointed at the next rock and it dissolved into a burst of water, as well. I continued until all the rocks were gone before leaning against the wall, breathing heavily. Wisps of steam rose from my mouth into the cool mountain air. On my chest, the symbol of the otter glowed a bright green.

I guess Tully's explanation wasn't so bad after all, I thought. *Just point at the rocks, and voilà!* Nearly having a heart attack might have helped, as well.

As I stood, panting, I noticed Arctos lumbering along the path below. He was still a long way away, but the rocks didn't appear to have fazed him. They had probably bounced off his shoulders like small pebbles.

There was no time to rest. I had to keep moving. I turned and sprinted up the rest of the mountain, not passing another wolf as I went. As I rounded the last bend to the peak, I realized I had no plan for what I was going to do at the top. I didn't even know what to expect, but I supposed a pack of wolves headed by Lupora and Alectus would be a good guess.

Chapter 59

I DUCKED BENEATH A LEDGE, HOPING I HADN'T BEEN SPOTTED, BE-fore peeking out to survey the wolves.

I was at the top of Mount Skire's lower peak—the flat one—and a large plateau spread out before me, some fifteen metres across. On the far side of the plateau was a slender ridge of rock running up to the second peak, the higher, pointed peak where Aurora had said Terra's pool was located. Along that ridge, a line of men carried boxes of explosives.

As much as I wanted to run and stop them, I couldn't. Not without facing an entire pack of wolves. The pack was looking up at a steep rise of rock on the other side of the plateau, and it only took me a second to find what they were looking at: Vulpeera, huddled on a ledge near the top, her body half wrapped in her tail as she stared down at the wolves.

Where were Catharia and Fantom?

The sky held an ominous cloud of crows. There appeared to be thousands of them, moving like ink in water, a flowing smear of black. Catharia and Fantom moved among them, Catharia in slow circles, her body nearly twenty times the size of the crows, while Fantom whizzed in and out, his feathers sparking like static electricity. The crows near Catharia seemed to be having difficulty flying, as if some unseen wind current were tossing them around, while many that approached Fan-tom dropped from the sky in a ball of sparks. But for all their efforts, Catharia and Fantom had their talons full. Any time they attempted to come closer to Mount Skire, the crows flocked in front of them, driving them back.

There was no time to waste. I was going to have to help Vulpeera myself.

The wolves took turns jumping up at the fox, and it wouldn't be long before one of them nabbed her.

I was readying myself to run out from behind the rock when I heard a familiar voice coming from the far side of the plateau.

"You can't hide up there forever!" it yelled, and I looked around the ledge to see Alectus and Lupora standing side by side behind the pack of wolves.

Alectus held a large double-barreled shotgun aimed at Vulpeera, while Lupora stood beside him looking frail but as nasty as ever.

Before I could move, Alectus pulled the trigger, and the rock where Vulpeera had been sitting exploded into a thousand shards. The shot had narrowly missed her tail as she leapt to a lower ledge, now inches away from the pouncing wolves.

"You're fast," Alectus jeered. "I'll give you that." He flipped open the barrel of his gun and placed shotgun shells in each chamber.

While everyone was looking up at Vulpeera, I moved out from behind the rock, creeping quietly along the back of the plateau. I managed to get behind Alectus and Lupora without being seen.

Alectus finished loading the gun and snapped it shut, then aimed it at Vulpeera. "I've got more shells than you've got places to jump," he called.

I ran at him.

I'm not sure what my plan was—jump on his back and wrestle the gun away from him? Throw him over the edge? Beat him mercilessly for what he'd done to Pteron? It doesn't matter, because none of it happened. I got three steps away from Alectus, and he spun around and smashed the butt of his gun into the side of my head, catching me off guard and sending me toppling sideways.

Sirens blared in my ears while knives stabbed at my brain. Everything went dim and hazy. A moment later Alectus was there, staring down at me with his cat-like eyes.

"You know," he said, "ever since you came to visit me on Pitchi, I've developed this uncanny ability to see behind myself." He let out a low, guttural laugh and walked back to Lupora.

"We were hoping you'd show up," the white wolf said, stepping forward. "News arrived last night of your escape. Tantum, that fool"—she shook her head solemnly—"but no matter, he has been taken care of. I won't make the same mistake he did." She smiled slyly and came closer, lowering her head and pulling her lips back to reveal rows of broken, uneven teeth. I could barely sit up, let alone fight back. The world spun and wobbled around me. "I won't underestimate you."

Lupora looked ready to pounce, but Alectus stepped between us. "Not yet," he said, blocking her path.

The white wolf snarled. "The girl is mine! We agreed on that!"

"Yes, yes," Alectus said, waving his hand nonchalantly. "But I want her to see something first."

Alectus turned and walked to where the ridge extended up toward the second peak. My head was slowly clearing, and I saw Vulpeera over Lupora's shoulder. She was no longer huddled behind her tail, but standing and staring down at me with a bright expression.

Alectus bent and picked up a small wooden box from the edge of the plateau. "When we first arrived here, we had no idea how we were going to destroy an entire mountain," he said, "but then that stupid owl showed us we wouldn't have to." He looked over at me, smiling. "Up there," he said, pointing to the top of the second peak, "is a small pool of water. It doesn't look like much. I'm not even sure what it does. But that damn owl wouldn't let us get within thirty metres of it before it started screeching and squawking. The fool couldn't have made it more obvious." He lifted the top of the wooden box and clicked something inside before pulling out a long metal lever and setting it back on the ground. There was a wire running from the back of the box toward the second peak; it was some sort of detonator. One push on that lever would likely trigger all the explosives they had piled on the second peak, and Terra's pool would be gone.

"Destroying Mount Skire will hurt you as much as it will hurt the Guardians," I croaked.

Alectus shook his head. "This mountain means nothing to *me*."

"It means everything to you. It's the source of Terra's energy and She is the one who brings you life. The Guardians are the protectors of Terra. They are not your enemies; they're your friends."

"Friends?" Alectus growled. "They took my leg and killed your father and you still call them friends? Don't be so naïve, cousin. They are trying to steal your powers—that's why they brought you here."

"Steal my powers?"

"These powers!" Alectus said, raising his hand in front of him and igniting a small flame on his palm.

"Alectus, they're not trying to steal those powers. Those powers come from Terra."

"No!" Lupora snarled, stepping forward. "The powers come from the amulet. The same one you have around your neck."

My hand went instinctively to my chest. "This isn't the source of the power. The power comes from the earth. It comes from Terra."

"Then why do I have these powers after touching the amulet?" Alectus asked. "Why can I create fire and see with my eyes closed? The Guardians are lying to you. The source of the power is the amulet. That's why they're trying to steal it. They took it from your father. And now they're trying to take it from you."

"No one is trying to take it from me but that wolf," I said, pointing at Lupora.

"Lies! I read your journal—I know the truth! The bear and the whale tried to kill you for the amulet. And the wolf pack told us how the turtle willingly handed you over but refused to give up the amulet. He wanted to keep it for himself until Tantum forcibly took it."

"Alectus—"

"You see? You can't even deny it! The amulet belongs to our family, not these Guardians. That's why your father was trying to get it back before they killed him."

"The amulet belongs to Terra!"

"And Terra gave it to you, a human. She knows we are the leaders of this world. Not these *pests*!"

"They're not pests! They're Guardians! A long time ago, the world was almost destroyed. Terra created the Guardians and this amulet to prevent that from ever happening again."

"A long time ago? Maybe back when humans were uncivilized barbarians, but things have changed. We have evolved, and they haven't. We're the only species that's moved forward. That's why Terra made you—a human—their leader and gave you the amulet. That's why the animals are angry and trying to take it from you."

Alectus moved toward the detonator.

"But we won't let that happen, Winter. We'll send a message to these Guardians. These *animals*," he said with a sneer. "We will remind them of their place."

My mind scrambled for a way to stop Alectus. I couldn't move, but maybe there was another way. "These wolves," I said, "are they below us, too? Are they not lowly, primitive animals?"

The pack of wolves turned to Alectus, growling.

"I see what you're trying to do," he said, waving his finger at me. "But the wolves are too smart for that. They're not like the other animals. They understand how the world works. They know power is earned, not given. They've fought for what they have. And once the Guardians are gone, they will be given their rightful share. I'll make sure of it." This seemed to appease the wolves, and Alectus turned back toward the detonator, wrapping his fingers around the lever. "But before anyone can have a share, we have to remove the relics. Before we can move forward, we have to destroy the past."

Chapter 60

Two things happened as Alectus went to push the detonator.

First, Vulpeera leapt from the wall and rushed at him from behind. He must have seen her with his inner eye, because he turned quickly, firing his shotgun at her, but missing as she sank her teeth into his leg.

Second, I managed to crawl toward the detonator while Alectus was occupied and kick it toward the edge of the plateau.

I had meant to kick it off the edge, not considering the possibility that the lever could hit something and detonate, but the wire hooked around a rock and stopped. Before I could finish the job, teeth sank into my shoulder.

Pain shot up my neck. It was piercing but at the same time helped clear the fogginess from my head. I acted quickly, reaching a hand up to my shoulder and grabbing the snout. It was crooked and white and belonged to Lupora, and that thought fueled my anger as the heat rose in my palm and singed her fur.

She let go, but the damage was done—to both of us. Her nose was red and burnt, my shoulder damp with blood.

Lupora pounced at me, but I rolled out of the way and got to my feet. Vulpeera weaved in and out among the other wolves, while Alectus crawled toward the detonator.

I ran at Alectus and jumped on his back, rolling us over so that he was on top when Lupora pounced again. She landed on him, and he cried out in anger, pushing her off while I held onto him from behind.

I forced the heat into my hands and directed it at his shirt, but he laughed.

"You think that's going to hurt me?" he said, elbowing me in the stomach and forcing me to let go.

He stood and looked down at me, holding his hands up beside his head and lighting them. The fire reached into the sky like two blazing torches.

"I've touched the amulet, too, remember?"

A sharp yelp turned our attention to Vulpeera, and I saw the tail of a wolf disappearing over the edge of the cliff. Vulpeera had made short work of the wolves, and there were only two left circling.

Lupora let out a grunt and ran to join the remaining wolves, leaving Alectus and me alone. I moved toward Vulpeera, but Alectus grabbed me from behind, wrapping his arm around my neck and putting me in a chokehold.

"Let them fight among themselves," he whispered in my ear, tightening his grip around my throat and making it difficult to breathe.

Vulpeera and the two grey wolves continued to circle, while Lupora stood motionless a few feet away, watching, waiting, biding her time.

I tried to get away from Alectus—stomping on his good foot and biting at his arm—but he didn't flinch. He was too strong, and his hold on my neck was like a vice.

"Just watch," he whispered, "watch as they do our work for us."

One of the wolves leapt at Vulpeera, and she slid beneath its front paws, snapping at its soft belly.

The second wolf lunged just as the first tried to get away, and the result was a head-on collision between the two beasts. There was a crack of skull-on-skull, and the two wolves fell beside each other, dazed.

Lupora stood a few feet away, watching, a calculated look across her snout.

The two wolves slowly got back to their feet, but their legs wobbled like saplings, and their eyes looked dopey. Vulpeera moved to the edge of the plateau and let out a loud, cackling cry.

This angered the wolves, and they barreled toward her. Vulpeera waited until the last second before jumping out of the way, and the wolves went over the edge with piercing, heart-wrenching cries that faded rapidly down the mountain.

"Too bad," Alectus griped into my ear, "I was hoping all three would go over."

He forced me to keep watching as Vulpeera and Lupora began circling each other. Vulpeera moved gracefully, while Lupora limped along awkwardly.

"It doesn't have to be like this," Vulpeera pleaded.

The white wolf snorted. "I don't see any other way."

For another two turns, they watched each other. Vulpeera's face was blank and resigned, while Lupora's eyes burned like molten metal.

"Was it really so long ago that we ran and played together?" Vulpeera asked.

Lupora's hair bristled. "So long, I have pushed it from my memory."

She lunged at Vulpeera, but the fox skidded neatly out of the way, and they returned to circling.

"And our mothers," Vulpeera said, her voice calm and even, "what would they say if they saw us fighting? They loved us equally. You are my sister, Lupora. I will never think of you as anything else."

"Sisters? You are a fox and I am a wolf."

"As were our mothers, yet they loved each other dearly. They never saw each other as different."

"It doesn't matter how they saw each other. Your mother was a Guardian—the separation existed whether they saw it or not. And when she died and you were named a Guardian—where did that leave me? Did you expect me to waste my life in the shadow of a fox? Did you expect me to pad along behind you?"

"I never asked for that."

"How do you think it felt for me—me, a cripple—to watch my sister be given the power to move like the wind?"

"I was given the power to protect Terra and Her creatures."

Lupora threw back her head and laughed. "Forgive me!" she said. "I suppose I should kneel before you, lick your paws, and thank you for all you have done for me."

"That is not what I meant."

"You see, Vulpeera," Lupora continued, "the boy is right. The difference between you and me is that I have earned my power. You were born with the blood of a Guardian, while I was born lame. Everything I have, I have worked for."

"No one would argue that you have accomplished much. You were always driven, even as a young pup, but your motives, your anger, they are misguided."

Lupora snarled and looked at Alectus. "After today, the playing field will be leveled. No more hand-me-downs. No more nepotism. Power will come only to the deserving. Power will be earned." She turned back toward Vulpeera and lowered her head. "You may have a throne in the Cove, but soon that will no longer matter. You will be left only as you are—a smaller, weaker version of me."

And with that, she leapt at Vulpeera.

Chapter 61

Vulpeera had her head down, clearly upset by everything the wolf was saying, when Lupora leapt. The wolf grabbed hold of her hind leg and crushed it like a twig.

The snap echoed around the plateau.

"Ouch!" Alectus said, delightedly.

Vulpeera wriggled free, but her leg bent at an unnatural angle, and she couldn't put it down. She hobbled away on three legs as Lupora crept toward her.

"Fitting end, isn't it?" Lupora taunted. "Now you know how I've felt my whole life."

Lupora leapt again, but this time Vulpeera was ready. Even on three legs, she was able to slide out of the wolf's reach, grabbing hold of Lupora's ear as she passed. Lupora whipped her head sideways, swinging Vulpeera back and forth.

"This is getting good," Alectus whispered.

Lupora managed to free herself from Vulpeera's jaws, but no sooner had the fox released her ear than she grabbed the wolf's tail. Again, Lupora bucked, but again Vulpeera found a new target, this time latching on to the wolf's ankle.

Lupora was thrown into a frenzy, spinning left and right while Vulpeera glided around her. Broken limb and all, she zipped in and out of Lupora's legs and pounced on her back to tear at her ears before retreating below to nip at her ankles and throat. All the while, Lupora spun around and around, getting closer to the edge of the cliff.

"Goodbye, wolfy," Alectus whispered, as Lupora's hind foot came down to find nothing but air. She yelped and slid—desperately clawing at the rock as she slipped toward the edge.

Vulpeera sprang forward, grabbing Lupora by the fur beneath her throat, digging her front paws into the rock and trying to pull her back. But the wolf was too big, and Vulpeera only had three working paws. At most, she could slow Lupora's slide, but she couldn't pull her back up.

"Alectus, let me go!" I screamed, trying to break free to help.

Vulpeera and Lupora looked at each other, their eyes inches apart. For the first time, I saw fear in the white wolf's expression.

"What are you doing?" Lupora growled.

"Trying to save you," Vulpeera said through clenched teeth, as she held fast to Lupora's fur. "Pull yourself up!"

Lupora scrambled but couldn't get any higher.

"You fool! Let me go! We'll both be pulled over."

"I won't let go!" Vulpeera barked.

The white wolf stopped trying to climb. "You can't save me, Vulpeera! You never could!"

Vulpeera's front paws slid forward as she tried to pull Lupora back, but the white wolf's head was barely visible over the edge—her fall was inevitable.

"Let her go, Vulpeera!" I begged. "Please, let her go."

"Listen to the girl," Lupora said. "I won't have you die trying to save me!"

"I won't let go," Vulpeera repeated.

And she didn't.

With one last harrowing cry, both the fox and the wolf went over the edge.

Alectus released me just as the two fell, and I scrambled to the place where they had disappeared. My throat was choked, both from Alectus's grip and the thought of Vulpeera. I sprawled on my stomach and looked over the edge, searching for any sign of my friend.

"She's gone," Alectus said from behind me.

The cliff was a sheer drop, and the trees at the bottom looked like nothing more than moss. It was a long way down. Nothing could survive that fall. Nothing. Not even Vulpeera.

My eyes began to water.

Vulpeera was gone, dragged to her death trying to save her sister. I would never see—

Something moved on a ledge below.

I wiped my eyes and looked closer, barely able to make out the small shape perched on a crag thirty feet below. The sunshine from the east was bathing the mountain, and though I couldn't see what had moved, I saw its colour.

Red.

Tawny red.

"Hang on," I yelled. "I'm coming, Vulpeera. I'll get you!"

"No, you won't," Alectus said.

I turned to see my cousin with both hands on the lever of the detonator.

He smiled, looking me right in the eyes.

"Goodbye, Guardians," he said, and pushed down the lever.

302

Chapter 62

THE TALLER PEAK OF MOUNT SKIRE ERUPTED INTO A BALL OF fire and rock. I was thrown across the plateau, landing shoulder-first against a boulder, and felt my collarbone snap. Fire and ash spat into the sky as my arm went numb. A loud crash shook the plateau as a massive chunk of burning stone landed in its centre.

The pain was unbearable, but it was nothing compared to the noise that followed.

It started as a hiss, sharp and shrill like a kettle, before growing to a piercing shriek that threatened to cut through my eardrums. I covered my ears, but it did nothing to dampen the sound. It only grew louder.

I lifted my head and looked at the other summit—or what was left of it. The towering peak was gone. In its place was a sawed-off mountain not unlike the one I lay on. From the centre of the broken peak rose a stream of mist, visible only with my mind's eye. It filled the sky above like the fog over Olport.

I knew what it was.

It was Terra's energy.

And the sound.

Was this Her last breath we were hearing? Our Mother, dying? The sound was the worst thing I had endured since meeting the Guardians, like the sound of life ending, of death, of nothing.

The mountain became eerily quiet. The mist vanished, and white ash fell from the sky like snow in storybooks.

From across the plateau I heard choked laughter.

I turned to see Alectus lying against another rock on the far side of the plateau—his shoes missing, a streak of blood running down his temple, one eye swollen shut. He was laughing.

Anger boiled inside me, and a low flame seeped from my flesh, spreading over my skin like a thin layer of clothing. I crawled toward him, pulling myself through the layer of soot that was forming over the rock. I was halfway across the plateau when a voice stopped me.

"What. Have. You. Done."

I turned to see Arctos standing at the edge of the plateau.

I was too angry to be afraid, even as he looked down at me with those cold red eyes and repeated the same four words: "What. Have. You. Done."

The bear walked toward the centre of the plateau, cutting off my path to Alectus. "Terra . . . the pool—" he said.

"It wasn't me," I said. "I never meant for—"

"I knew this would happen," he said, shaking his head. "There was too much of him in you. We all saw it. We should have stopped you when we had the chance."

He approached slowly. I tried to pull myself away, but my arm felt as if it were no longer attached to my body. "Arctos, listen to me. It was Lupora and Alectus—I had nothing to do with this."

"You, the boy . . . what does it matter? He is only here because you were chosen."

"No! You've got everything wrong! I didn't bring him here. I came here to—"

"To find out why he's been gaining the powers," Arctos interjected. "Yes, I know."

He stopped and looked up at the jagged rock that had held Terra's pool. His eyes looked less angry and more defeated. He sat down with a deep sigh. A quiet calm permeated the plateau; even the crows were gone. A minute passed before he spoke.

"It wasn't so long ago that I stood in this very spot," he said. "And there, right where you lie, was your father. I had never seen so much anger. He wanted to destroy Terra for what had happened to your mother. He was determined, possessed, consumed. And perhaps he would have succeeded if I had not been here to stop him."

"You!" Alectus bellowed from across the plateau. "You're the one that killed my uncle?"

Arctos turned and looked at Alectus. "I did what I had to," he grunted.

"Oh, please," Alectus said, pulling himself to standing using the rock for support. "Don't pretend you didn't enjoy it. I'll bet you felt mighty powerful killing a human. Tell me—was he armed? You had your claws and teeth, but did he have a weapon? And when it was over, did you take the amulet from his corpse?"

As Alectus spoke, he moved slowly around the edge of the cliff. At first, I had no idea what he was doing. Taunting Arctos seemed stupid, even by Alectus's standards, but then I saw the muzzle of his shotgun sticking out from the layer of soot five feet from where he stood. I forced

305

myself to my feet. It was agonizing to stand.

Arctos made no move to attack. He barely acknowledged Alectus or me as he spoke. "I took no pleasure in fighting Gregor. He was my student, much as Winter is Vulpeera's. His failures as a Guardian were my failures as a teacher. I only did what was required. I thought I was ending the threat. But how was I to know that history would repeat itself? Or I suppose I should say, fulfill itself."

"It was only a matter of time before the Guardians were ushered out," Alectus said. "Humans are the future—my uncle knew it. The Society will make this world a far better place than a bunch of simple-minded animals ever could. Don't get me wrong; the powers you possess are useful. But even without the amulet, we humans can invent and create things more powerful."

Alectus bent and wrapped his fingers around the gun, lifting it and pointing it at Arctos. The bear seemed neither to notice nor to care.

"Tell me," Arctos said, still staring at the broken mountain, "have you not wondered why you have been gaining the powers? You were not chosen by Terra. You are not a Guardian. Yet you have the ability to hold fire. And I suspect you can see Terra's energy."

Alectus aimed the gun downward. "I know why," he said. "I touched the amulet."

Arctos shook his head. "Many have touched the amulet without gaining the powers. Only the Terra Protectorum can gain all the powers, and you are not the Terra Protectorum." Arctos turned to me. "And you, oh Guardian of Wisdom, have you not figured it out?"

Figured it out? I felt my face flush. Wasn't that the whole reason we had come to Mount Skire? To ask Terra that very same question? Did Arctos really know the answer?

"Cheelion and Vulpeera said Terra was the only one who could answer that question," I said. "They said only She knew the answer."

Arctos let out a whoosh of air between his teeth, shaking his head. "That is true, and it isn't. They knew the answer. We all knew. But they couldn't tell you, because they had sworn an oath to your grandmother to keep it a secret."

"Granny?" I said. "What oath? I don't understand."

Alectus scowled impatiently and raised his gun again. "Spit it out, already! Start making sense!"

Arctos appeared unfazed by the threat. He turned calmly toward Alectus. "You said you touched the amulet. Did it glow green?"

Alectus looked skeptical. "Yes. So?"

Arctos nodded. "You see, the amulet could not tell the difference between the two of you. Terra could not tell the difference. So, when one of you gains a power, so does the other. You are connected."

"What? That doesn't make sense," I said. "Why would the amulet not be able to tell the difference? Surely it doesn't work like that."

"No," Arctos said, shaking his head. "It's not supposed to, but in your circumstance, it does. The two of you are too similar to tell apart. To the amulet, you are one and the same—blood of the same blood, flesh of the same flesh, fire of the same fire. Twins, as you humans call them."

"Twins?" I repeated. "What are you talking about?"

"Brother and sister—born of the same litter," Arctos clarified.

"LIES!" Alectus bellowed.

"Not lies," Arctos said. "I assure you."

"How can that be?"

"Tell me," Arctos said, turning to me, "what did Lillian say about your mother's death?"

"Sh-she said she died during childbirth," I said, numbly repeating the words Granny had spoken to me many times before. "She said it was a complicated pregnancy."

Arctos nodded. "It always is when your kind has more than one."

"I don't believe you!" Alectus shouted, gripping the gun so tightly his knuckles turned white. His face flushed and contorted in a way I'd never seen. It wasn't anger. It was something else.

Arctos ignored him. "When your mother died, your father was driven to madness. Lillian was left to raise you both, but she was getting on in years and worried about your future. It seemed unlikely that one of you would be chosen as the next Guardian after your father killed Orcavion, but she worried all the same. So, she decided to separate you, to keep you apart so that if one was ever made a Guardian, it could be kept hidden from the other. One of you would be spared this life."

"B-but Uncle Farlin—" I stammered.

"Your mother's brother," Arctos said. "He had always wanted a son, and agreed to raise Alectus as his own. And we all swore an oath to keep it secret. You would be raised as cousins and visit each other during the dry months. That way, you could remain close, but your lives would be separate. That was what Lillian wanted."

"Why are you telling me this now?" I asked. "After all these years, why break your oath?"

Arctos shrugged his broad shoulders. "You destroyed Mount Skire. You are the greatest threat that exists to Terra—that which I am sworn to protect. I will have to kill you. I felt you had the right to die knowing the truth."

He raised himself from his haunches and lowered his head.

Chapter 63

My mind was too jumbled to think. Alectus and me—twins? I didn't even move aside as Arctos charged at me; all I could do was stand there and watch him come.

A shot rang like thunder from Alectus's gun, causing the bear to veer sideways as the pellets ripped at his flank, preventing a head-on collision. His shoulder connected with my chest, sending me rolling across the plateau with the air knocked from my lungs.

I came to a stop right at the edge, gasping for breath as I stared down at the clearing below. Fire blazed through the trees, the forest nearly gone.

Another blast sounded, and this time Arctos roared in anger. He collapsed sideways, the flesh from his shoulder and chest exposed where the lead pellets had ripped the fur away.

Alectus reloaded the shotgun as Arctos stood. The bear charged and the gun fired. Arctos fell backward with a howl, landing beside the huge piece of rock that had fallen from the other mountain.

"Guardian of Strength?" Alectus jeered. "You call that power?" He hoisted the gun and advanced toward the fallen bear. "This is power!"

Breath slowly refilled my lungs as I lay on my side. Arctos's massive head rested on the ground, wisps of ash blowing around his nostrils as he breathed. His red eyes looked pained as they stared at me.

Alectus stood beside the bear, glaring. Even lying on his side, Arctos was as tall as my brother. This must have bothered Alectus, because he walked around the massive creature and climbed the boulder. When he reached the top, he stood and aimed the gun downward, pressing the muzzle directly behind Arctos's ear. But the bear made no move to get up. He just continued to stare at me.

"Now, we end this!" Alectus growled, his face contorted into a pained expression like someone about to cry. He was angry. Angrier than I'd ever seen him.

"Stop!" I croaked, and Alectus looked over at me.

"Stop?" he sputtered. "This bear killed your father—*our* father—and you want me to stop? Because of him, you grew up parentless and I grew up on that forsaken island!"

I looked at Arctos. The bear *had* killed my father. Did he deserve to die? Was Alectus right? Because he had wronged us, did we have the right to wrong him?

No, that was Malum.

"Let him go," I said. "Killing Arctos won't bring our father back."

Even Arctos looked surprised by this.

"It may not bring him back, but it will give him retribution!" Alectus shouted.

I shook my head. "Arctos only killed Father because he had to. Father was consumed by Malum. By killing Arctos, we'd only be going down the same path."

Alectus gritted his teeth. "You're a disgrace to our family," he spat, turning back to the bear. My mind whirled. I had to do something. I couldn't lie there and watch this happen. I focused all the energy I had into one thought.

Alectus pushed the gun further against the bear's head, forcing Arctos's nose into the ground. "This is for *my* father. At least one of us is willing to stand up for his memory."

I pointed toward Alectus, my arm turning cold and clammy, and the rock on which he stood dissolved with a splash before he could pull the trigger. He fell to the ground, dropping the gun so that it landed beside him, firing harmlessly into the sky on contact.

Before Alectus was back on his feet, I was on mine.

"Alectus, we don't have to fight," I said, approaching with my good arm raised. "Just listen to me. Arctos killed Father—it's true—but Father wasn't right. He had gone mad with grief."

Alectus grabbed the empty shotgun and thrust his hand into his pocket, looking for another shell. I ran at him before he could find one, and grabbed the gun. We wrestled it back and forth before he threw me aside.

I stood and charged at him again.

This time he swung the shotgun at me, and I ducked beneath it, kicking him in the side of the knee. He fell to the ground in pain and was slow to get up. Flames flickered over his skin as he stood.

"You didn't have to live on that island," he growled, swinging at me.

I ducked again and kicked him in the same spot, causing him to cry out in pain and fall. His head slumped forward, chin resting on his chest. I watched, waiting for him to spring back up.

But he didn't.

Instead his head remained slumped, and I noticed a slight quiver to his body. A quiet, stifled sob rose from his chest, and I realized he was crying.

"Alectus," I whispered, cautiously approaching. I got a foot away and reached out, placing a hand on his upper back. "Let's stop this. I know you're hurt—I was too. But blaming the Guardians for what happened to Father is not the answer."

Alectus stood, and I jumped backward, landing a good six feet away. I raised my hand in defense, but he made no move to fight. Instead he stood with his back to me, looking out over the distant mountains before turning around. His face was flushed, and tears had cut two streaks through the soot on his face.

"You're right," he said, wiping his cheek and smearing the soot. "We shouldn't fight with each other."

He walked toward me and held out the shotgun across his two palms, offering it to me.

"Here," he said, "take it. I'm done fighting you."

I went to take the gun from my brother, and in one quick motion he rammed it forward, crosschecking me in the throat.

Chapter 64

EITHER THE PAIN OR LACK OF OXYGEN MUST HAVE KNOCKED ME out, because I opened my eyes to find Alectus standing over me.

"I never was very good at playing fair," he said, grinning.

I tried to respond, but my throat felt tight, as if my windpipe had been crushed. I tried to tell him to stop, but nothing came out.

Alectus turned to face Arctos. "Now, where were we?" he said, opening the gun to reload. "Oh right, I was in the process of removing another Guardian from the world."

Arctos still hadn't moved. His chest rose and fell, his eyes were open, he was alive, but he hadn't moved. Why not? Had he lost the will to fight? To live?

"It's a humans' world now," Alectus said, putting a shell in each chamber and snapping the gun closed. "It might take some getting used to, but sooner or later everyone will fall in line. 'Wild' will be a word of the past, heard only in storybooks." He pointed the gun and looked down its barrel. "You will all be nothing more than a bunch of domesticated pets."

It seemed like Arctos's eyes were burning holes through my chest. He hadn't stopped staring at me, not once looking at Alectus. It was an unblinking glare that pierced my clothes and skin, and looked straight into my soul.

I turned away. I didn't want to see Alectus's final shot. Or maybe I didn't want to see Arctos's eyes anymore.

Below me the fire raged, like an inferno trying to bring the world to an end. It had spread through the forest like a plague, leaving behind a trail of blackened twigs. Soon it would reach Procynia and the rest of the gaze. Soon the whole forest would be gone, and their newfound home would burn just like their last.

A swell of heat simmered in my chest. I looked at the long scar of earth that had been cleared for the roadway. There were wagons moving along it—racing in the other direction as the men that had managed to escape rushed away.

Why had they come in the first place? What good had there been in building a road to nowhere? The Society wanted to build a path through the mountains, but for what reason? To say that they could? To colonize the other side of the mountain as they had colonized Nacadia? Had they even for a moment thought about the animal homes destroyed in the process? Had they thought of the migratory paths that had been cut off? Or how their garbage poisoned the waters and their factories polluted the air?

The heat in my chest grew, spreading into my arms and legs. I looked down at the amulet, and it was glowing brighter than ever—all the symbols shining in a halo of green.

A shot whistled through the air, and Arctos cried out. I turned to see the right side of his face bleeding, his ear torn and his scalp opened. One eye was now closed, but the other continued to stare at me.

"Why won't you just die?" Alectus growled, raising the gun again.

No, I thought, *NO!*

In that moment, I forgot that Arctos had killed my father. I forgot that he had hunted me when I'd been chosen as the Land Guardian of Wisdom. I forgot all those things and saw him only as he was right there—a creature of Terra I was sworn to protect.

A sensation crept through me like fresh air. The amulet was now a powerful glow that shone across the plateau. Lines of swirling mist flowed toward me, the same lines I had seen with my Aminoculus.

How were they so clear? What was happening?

Alectus's finger tightened on the trigger, and Arctos winced in anticipation. Instinctively, I lifted my hand, and a great splinter of rock

sprang from the ground between the bear and my brother, blocking the bullet as Alectus fired the gun. It ricocheted away, and Alectus spun around to face me, his eyes wide with fear, his face bewildered.

I waved my hand, and the wind howled in response. I pointed at the gun and it was swept from Alectus's hand, lifting into the sky and blowing over the side of the cliff.

My body felt weightless as I stood, my head clearer than a mountain spring. I turned toward the burning forest. "No," I whispered, and my breath left my mouth in great gales that blew over the landscape. The flames in the trees flickered like candles on a windowsill, bending and wavering before extinguishing. Wisps of smoke trickled up toward the sky.

I heard footsteps behind me. My mind's eye clearly saw Alectus approaching. I turned toward him, and he charged at me with a look of rage and fear and pain. I looked back at him with only pity.

A faint shudder moved through me—the same sensation I felt when I used my Evanestium, except this time the world didn't disappear. My body vibrated, but everything remained solid around me.

"Alectus," I whispered, raising my hand to stop my brother, but he passed straight through me as if my body were made of mist and light and nothing more.

I heard him screaming as he went over the edge. I heard him screaming as he fell.

And then, I heard nothing.

Chapter 65

Soft fur beneath me and a rhythmic, rolling motion told me I was being carried. My eyes were closed and my body hurt—my throat, my collarbone, every muscle. I was consumed with pain.

I stirred, and whatever was holding me gripped me closer. "We're nearly down the mountain," a deep yet soothing voice whispered.

I opened my eyes a fragment to see Arctos. His face was torn and bleeding, his one eye swollen closed, and his fur matted. His movement was labored and his breathing fast as he held me to his chest with one arm, working carefully to make his way down the mountain. Behind his broken face, the sky was a pale shade of blue.

"Where are we going?" I asked.

"Away."

I closed my eyes again. "Alectus?"

"Gone."

"Are you going to kill me?"

"No."

I was too drained to think of trying to get away. If Arctos was lying, there was nothing I could do. Did I trust him? No. But did I have another choice? No.

"I'm sorry, Winter," he said, as if sensing my concern. "I misjudged you. My thoughts were clouded by my anger—at your father and at myself. When you were chosen as the Land Guardian of Wisdom, I saw only him. It was like reliving a terrible nightmare. You are like him in many ways, but you are even more like your mother. I see that now."

The wind picked up; warm air mixed with the sound of wings above. I opened my eyes as a white bird landed on a nearby branch.

"Scanda," I mumbled.

The owl said nothing, but something about her presence was calming as she looked down at me.

I closed my eyes.

After a few minutes, I heard voices—whispers not meant for my ears.

"What will happen now?" Arctos said.

"I don't know. The energy has been growing weaker for years, and with Mount Skire gone, it might be the final blow."

"But the girl at the top—you must have seen it."

"Yes."

"She controlled the wind and the rock. She blew out an entire forest fire. Could it have been . . . ?"

"It seems so."

"But it contradicts everything we know. The prophecy states that Unomnis will only be granted to the Terra Protectorum who has given themselves completely to Terra. To do that, they must master all twelve of Terra's abilities. That is what we have always believed."

"Perhaps what we believed was wrong."

There was a long silence.

"Perhaps."

I stirred in Arctos's arms, trying to get comfortable.

"She wakes," Scanda whispered.

"Let us talk of this no more. We must get her home to Lillian so she may begin healing. Once she is well, we can ask her what happened. If it is true, if she can truly access Unomnis, then perhaps we are not doomed. In the end, it may be a human that saves us from the humans."

"Perhaps Terra was not such a fool," Scanda said.

"No, perhaps not. With the pool gone, we may never have another Terra Protectorum. But with the power this girl possesses, perhaps we won't need one."

Chapter 66

WHEN I AWOKE, IT WAS WITH A SOFT MATTRESS AND PILLOW BEneath me. A wet nose pressed against my chin, and I opened my eyes to see two black eyes staring back at me.

"She's awake!" Proctin cried. "She's awake! She's awake! She's—"

"Will you cut that out?" Vulpeera snapped, her ruddy face appearing beside Proctin's. "The last thing she needs is you screaming in her ear the moment she wakes up."

Proctin scowled and scampered off the bed and out the door, still calling out that I was awake. I tried to sit up, but a sharp pain shot through my shoulder.

"Just rest," Vulpeera said, "you're not ready to get up."

"I'm so happy you're alive," I said, wrapping my good arm around her and pulling her tightly to my neck.

Vulpeera gave a gentle laugh. "I'm beginning to wonder if I'm part cat," she said, holding up her back paw to show the white bandage and splint wrapped around it. "Though I think my nine lives are nearly up."

"Yes, we're all indebted to Lillian." I turned to find Pteron splayed across the chair in the corner of my room. Over each of his wings was a large gauze, while another covered his chest.

I heard footsteps on the stairs and Granny entered, followed by Uncle Farlin in his stained overalls.

"So, it's true," Uncle Farlin said, smiling. "Our little princess is awake. You gave us quite a fright."

Granny sat down on the side of my bed, placing her hand on my shoulder.

"How do you feel?" she asked.

"Fine," I said. "Sore, but fine."

"I mended your collarbone, but it will ache for a while. I have become quite a medic these past few days."

Granny swept her hand around the room and we chuckled. It looked like a hospital ward, not a house.

"Thank you, Doctor Granny, you've healed everyone," I said, then a thought occurred to me. "Well, everyone who could be healed."

A solemn silence fell over the room, and my uncle's eyes grew glassy as he turned away.

"Is it true?" I said. "Is Alectus . . . or should I say, *was* Alectus my brother?"

Granny's lips tightened, and from the corners of where her eyes once were, tears began to form. "Yes," she croaked. "Yes, he was."

I shook my head in disbelief. "But why? Why didn't you tell us?"

"You have to understand that I was looking out for your best interests. Both of you. I thought I could spare one of you this life. Keep you hidden from the thing that had already taken so much from our family." Granny's hands shook as she spoke. "I'm sorry, Winter. I don't expect you to understand. I'm not even sure that I do."

"No," I said, taking her hand, "I do understand. At least, I think I do. I just wish things could have turned out differently."

"I'm mostly to blame," Uncle Farlin said, sitting beside Granny so that the bed sagged another foot. "I wanted so badly to have a son. I thought I had it in me to be a good father. But Alectus had so much passion and drive; I should never have kept him on the island. It drove him mad. It made him feel trapped. Once he found the Society, I thought he had turned a corner, but it wasn't enough. I see now that I was blind as a parent. I was blind to his cruelty. Perhaps I was never meant to be a father after all."

"Don't say that!" I said, tears running down my face. "You were a great father. I often wished you were *my* father. Alectus was just—"

"Too much like *his* father," Granny said. "Passionate and driven, but in the end, taken by Malum."

I lay my head back on the pillow, thinking of Alectus. His last look. That look of anger. That resolve to destroy. "Alectus is gone," I said, "and so is Mount Skire."

"Yes," Granny agreed.

"What will happen now? Am I done being the Terra Protectorum? Are the Guardians finished?"

"No," Vulpeera said. "If anything, we are needed more than ever. Terra has taken a heavy blow, but at the same time, there is hope. Lupora is gone, her dark army disbanded across the continent. The other animals will hear of what happened, and faith in the Guardians will be restored. We will come together as a united front. No one has heard from Cheelion, and Cano is still angry, but the rest of us will rally behind you. We will use our powers to stop the wane of Terra's energy." Vulpeera looked at me curiously. "Speaking of powers, how much of what happened on top of Mount Skire do you remember?"

"On top of Mount Skire?" I said, thinking. "I remember my fight with Alectus. And the mountain exploding. And you falling. And Arctos. And then . . ."

"Yes? What next? Do you remember what happened next?"

I rolled on my side and looked out the window. In the garden below,

Tully was running around in circles while Proctin chased him with a stick. Arctos and Felinia sat at the far end of the yard, looking up at the mountains.

"I remember a little," I said.

"Arctos claims that he saw you control the elements. He says you moved the rock and blew out the forest fire. Do you remember that?"

"Sort of," I said. The memories all seemed like a dream now.

"What was it, Winter? What power did you call?" Vulpeera asked, inching closer to me on the bed. Pteron leaned closer from his place on the chair, watching me intently.

"I'm not sure. I remember feeling something. It wasn't like the other powers I've used. It wasn't a single feeling. It was different. It was everywhere. I felt light and complete and . . . one."

Vulpeera and Pteron shared a long look. Did they know something I didn't? Did they understand what had happened?

"Unomnis," Vulpeera whispered.

"Let's not get ahead of ourselves," Pteron said, straightening up in the chair. "We cannot be certain of what it was. Unomnis is only supposed to be granted to the one who has gained all twelve of our Mother's abilities. Only then can they become one with Her."

"But you heard what she said."

"I'm not doubting what she says; I'm just trying to be reasonable."

"There was a lot of energy in the air," I said. "When Mount Skire exploded, I saw huge tides of Her energy around me. Could that have something to do with it?"

Pteron nodded. "Perhaps. Whatever it was, it was a power we have not seen before. But it is there, inside you, lying dormant. You only have to learn to control it. No doubt it is linked to the other abilities, and further mastering them will help. But Mount Skire is gone, and Terra's energy has now weakened further. It will not be easy. You will have to train again. You will have to give yourself to learning. But if it is true, if you can call upon Unomnis, then perhaps there is hope that you can not only slow the decay of our Mother, but heal her completely."

"You think so?"

"I hope so," Pteron said. "But I know this: if ever there was a Guardian who could save us, it is you."

Vulpeera nodded. "I have faith in you."

"As do we all," Granny said.

"So?" Pteron asked. "Will you do it? Will you find this power hidden within you and heal Terra?"

I looked around the room at the hopeful faces. "I-I'll try," I said.

Vulpeera smiled. "That is all anyone can ask of you."

Chapter 67

I<small>T WAS A SLOW CLIMB UP THE MOUNTAIN</small>. I <small>HAD REASSURED</small> Granny that my body no longer hurt, but that wasn't exactly true. It had only been a few weeks since I had come home from Mount Skire.

"These mountains looked a lot smaller from the house," I said, panting, "but I'm glad you asked me to come. I've always wanted to hike up here. I used to watch these mountains from my window at night. It sounds odd, but sometimes I felt like they were trying to tell me something. Like they were calling to me." I laughed at myself. "I sound crazy, don't I?"

Arctos let out a low grunt to let me know he was listening, but continued walking ahead. Sometimes he didn't answer my questions. I had initially thought this was a sign that he was unfriendly, but I'd learned over the past few weeks that it was just his way. He wasn't sweet like Vulpeera or chatty like Proctin, but he had a good heart—of that I was sure.

"When I learned about Mount Skire," I continued, "I thought I had my answer. I thought it was Terra's mountain that called to me. But Mount Skire is gone and the mountains still speak to me. Every night, I hear them."

We rounded the last bend in the path and came to the summit, a rough peak with many jagged rocks. It had taken us hours to climb to the top, but the view was worth it. We were higher than most of the other peaks.

"Wow!" I said, "I can see my house from here." I pointed to a small cluster of dirt roads and houses in the distance. "It's hard to appreciate how big these mountains are until you're standing on one."

"They were built by my ancestors," Arctos said.

"They were?"

The bear nodded. "After the Almost End, the lands to the south became inhospitable, and there was fear that the toxic environment might seep into the fertile lands up here. The Land Guardian of Strength at that time—my ancestor—built these mountains to seal off the threat."

"I had no idea your gift was so powerful."

"It was," Arctos said.

"Was? But not anymore?"

"No. The Weakening has reduced my gift to little more than the ability to move rocks. Terra is fragile."

"Fragile? You mean you weren't trying to make that hole in the ground during the fight in the clearing?"

"No," Arctos said, shaking his head.

The conversation ended, and we sat quietly, watching the view. The sun was low behind us, causing the shadows of the mountains to reach across the landscape. Fields of orange and yellow blanketed the ground between small towns and glades. The gentle rolling of the hills gave the entire scene a sense of motion, as if we were living on the waves of Terra.

"It's beautiful, isn't it?" I said, breaking the silence. "It's worth protecting."

"Yes," Arctos agreed. "But even for one as gifted as you, it won't be easy."

My eyes followed the road leading from Dunvy toward the ocean in the distance. I couldn't see Olport, but the heavy smog showed me its location. I thought of the scum in the water there. Near the base of our mountain

was a charred patch of earth with blackened trees—the remnants of the Red Woods. There were so many reminders of our destruction.

"We're killing Terra, aren't we?"

Arctos didn't answer. He didn't have to. I knew I was right. The humans *were* destroying the earth. The signs were everywhere.

"I can fix this," I said, more to myself than Arctos. "I know I can. I just need to talk to the Society. I'll make them understand what's happening. Once they realize their inventions and pollution are destroying the earth, they'll stop. How could they not? We're one of the smartest species on earth. We wouldn't knowingly destroy ourselves, right?"

I looked up at Arctos. He was staring down at me with an expression I could not read beneath his still-healing face.

"You sound so much like your father," he said. "He, too, had many ideas of how he would save Terra."

"He did?"

Arctos nodded.

"Come with me. I brought you up here to tell you something about your father."

I followed the bear to the far side of the summit. The view was different to the south. There were no rolling hills or sun-touched fields, only endless peaks. A heavy fog lay over the mountains, blocking any view of the Forgotten Lands.

"Before I tell you," Arctos said, "I need you to understand something."

"What?"

"Your father was like a son to me."

"I know," I said. "You told me, up on top of Mount Skire."

"But I need you to appreciate it. I need you to know that what I did, I did out of necessity. I did not wish to fight with your father, but Malum's grip was too strong. There was no saving him. He could not be forgiven and he could not be let go. The anger was too great. The destruction would not have ended."

"If you're looking for forgiveness," I said, "you've already got it. I don't blame you."

"I'm not seeking forgiveness. I need you to understand that the man I fought that day was not your father. He was gone. Just as Lillian says— Gregor Wayfair died the day your mother died. I was fighting Malum."

"I've come to terms with what happened," I said, tears spilling down my face. "I know what my father tried to do."

I looked away from the bear and wiped my cheeks with the back of my hand.

"I'm sorry," he said. "I needed to be sure you understood that before I told you. I needed to be certain you would not go looking for him."

"What?" I said, turning abruptly back to Arctos.

"It will do you no good, Winter. It will only bring you pain. Your father is gone. You must understand that."

"What are you talking about? Why would I go looking for him? He's dead!"

Arctos and I locked eyes.

"He's dead, right? You told me yourself. You said you killed him."

Arctos shook his head. "I never said I killed him."

"Yes, you did! On top of Mount Skire! You told me!"

"No, I told you that I did what needed to be done—I did not say that I killed Gregor."

"What do you mean? I don't understand."

"Everything I said was the truth. I told you that your father and I fought—the truth. I told you that I won—the truth. But when it came time to strike the final blow, I could not do it. So, I made him a deal. He would leave Nacadia and never return. He would be banished to the Forgotten Lands, where he could do no more harm." He pointed his paw to the south. "In the end, I think he was happy to go. His soul was troubled."

I could hardly speak.

"So, my father is still alive?"

"I don't know," Arctos said, "and I do not tell you this so that you will go looking for him. I merely wanted you to know the truth. No more secrets. No more lies." He sat down heavily, his eyes wet. "I do not know what is calling to you, but perhaps it is not the mountains as you have thought." He turned his powerful eyes toward me, holding me with his gaze. "Perhaps it is what is left of the man who was once your father."

Epilogue

HIGH ATOP MOUNT SKIRE, A SNOWY OWL SITS PERCHED ON A rocky crag. The mountain is no longer as it once was. The pool is gone. Her link to Terra's heart is gone.

"What will become of Terra Creatura?" she asks, shaking her head back and forth slowly.

The wind blows and her feathers ripple, but there is no answer.

"Can the girl heal us? Is it as You predicted? Can she stop this decay?" The owl looks around at all the destruction: forests burned, mountains crumbled, caverns opened. There will be no answers. She must simply have faith.

With one last look around, she takes off into the night sky. As she flies over Mount Skire for the last time, she does not see the boy. How could she? He is half buried beneath the rocks at the bottom. His clothes are torn, his body bruised and broken. If he were an ordinary boy, he would be dead.

But this is no ordinary boy, and he has no intention of dying.

He has but one thought. One so strong he can taste it—a sharp, biting flavor that mixes with the iron taste of blood in his mouth.

It is a single word.

Some call it Malum.

But the boy knows it by a different name:

Revenge.

Acknowledgements

To Wiz, the biggest influence on my writing, thank you for your countless readings and re-readings. To David, for the patchwork quilt and your cartography skills. To Sydney and Aidan, for your amazing illustrations. To Jess, for being a wickedly thorough editor. To Jacob, my biggest online supporter and fan. To my amazing beta readers from the Teen Committee—Adelyn, Dannica, Lily, and Kirk, thank you for your invaluable feedback. To Pip, my only sibling to read this book, and to my other two siblings that will not be named as they did not read this book. To Mom, for championing my marketing team and being so supportive. To Dad, for reading the back of all my books. To Auntie Janie for being my biggest fan in the family. To Uncle Steve, for reminding me that eagles can't lift people but perhaps condors can. To Carol, for your research and help with cover ideas. To Mimi, Scott, Marek, Nana, Barb, Jenn, Chip, and Elara for all your suggestions and support. To all my other friends and family who helped with this book—thank you! Most importantly, to my wife, who stayed up many nights listening to me read, and only fell asleep once; to my kids, for being the most lovable distractions I could ask for; and to Michelle, my brilliant editor, cover artist, marketer, publisher, and all-around book make-betterer, thank you a million times.

About Alex Lyttle

    Alex Lyttle is a pediatrician living in Calgary, Alberta with his wife and four children. His first novel, *From Ant to Eagle*, was based on his experiences as a doctor and won several awards. *The Rise of Winter* steps away from the medical world and enters that of fantasy—a world created during bedtime stories for his eldest daughter. When not working or writing, Alex enjoys . . . well . . . it doesn't really matter what he enjoys, because he mainly just chases toddlers around the house.

Alex Lyttle Talks About
The Rise of Winter

WHY ARE YOUR FIRST TWO BOOKS SO DIFFERENT?

My first book, *From Ant to Eagle*, was written using the adage "write what you know." I drew from my experiences as a pediatrician and wrote a book about a boy whose brother was sick. My second book tosses that adage out the window. *The Rise of Winter* is a story from my imagination, not my experiences. I began creating stories as a teenager working as a camp counselor. I liked to tell stories where the campers were the main characters and could put themselves into the story. I would often start with, "Imagine yourself lying on a grassy hill with the warm sun on your face. Your eyes are closed when you hear a scurrying sound not far off. You open your eyes to see a red fox staring back at you. In a troubled voice, the fox tells you that it needs your help." It was from these stories that *The Rise of Winter* began. When I had my own children, the story evolved further until I had enough to begin writing.

THE END OF THIS BOOK SUGGESTS THERE WILL BE A SECOND BOOK. IS THAT TRUE?

Yes—this book is the first of a trilogy. Without ruining the story, I can tell you that the second and third books will answer a lot of the questions that went unanswered in this one. You will learn why Penny is mean to Winter, what happens to Cheelion and Cano, and whether or not Winter's father is alive. You will also learn more about the world in which Winter lives, the Society that runs it, and why Winter and Alectus have cat-like eyes.

HOW MUCH OF THE SECOND BOOK HAVE YOU WRITTEN?

At the time of writing this, I have written approximately one fifth of the second book. When I write, I tend to work on several chapters before setting them aside for a few weeks to reflect on them. This allows me to return with a fresh set of eyes that will find mistakes I missed before. It also gives me time to decide where the story will go, as I do not map out my books before I write. While I know the major plot points and how the story will end, the rest is decided as I write. *The Rise of Winter* took me four years to finish, but I hope to have the second book ready in a year. You can follow my progress on the website: alexlyttle.com.

WERE THERE ANY BOOKS THAT INSPIRED YOU TO WRITE *THE RISE OF WINTER*?

While there isn't one book that inspired this one, there are several that inspired my love of the genre and desire to write a fantasy series. My favourites include Philip Pullman's His Dark Materials series and J.K. Rowling's Harry Potter series. I also love dystopian novels with which *The Rise of Winter* shares elements; one of my all-time favourites is *The Giver* by Lois Lowry.

WHERE DID YOU GET YOUR IDEAS FOR THE GUARDIANS' ABILITIES?

When I was imagining the Guardians' abilities, I tried to think of things that were magical but still rooted in science. For example, humans can't create fire by snapping their fingers, but the principle behind energy transference is true. Likewise, the idea that you could become invisible by moving quickly back and forth like the blade on a fan is theoretically possible (a bit of a stretch, but possible), and Vulpeera's discussion about movement and proprioception is something I learned in medical school. I had a lot of fun trying to think of ways to use science in a magical way, and I think the powers give credit to how truly magical our world is.

WHO ARE YOUR FAVOURITE CHARACTERS IN THE NOVEL?

My favourite characters are Winter, Proctin, and Vulpeera. I like Winter because she faces challenges with a mix of confidence and humility. When I was training to be a doctor, I always admired staff that were knowledgeable but willing to admit when they didn't know an answer. I tried to write Winter with this same characteristic. Proctin was an enjoyable character to write because he shares my sense of humor and love of food. Vulpeera is special to me because she is gentle, sweet, and wise, like my grandmother.

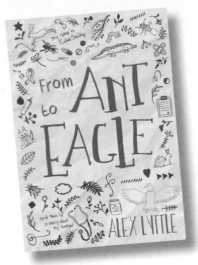

FROM ANT TO EAGLE

Alex Lyttle

Middle Grade - 978-1-77168-111-7

It's the summer before grade six, and Calvin Sinclair is bored to tears. He's recently moved from a big city to a small town, and there's nothing to do. It's hot, he has no friends, and the only kid around is his six-year-old brother, Sammy, who can barely throw a basketball as high as the hoop. Cal occupies his time by getting his brother to do almost anything: from collecting ants to doing Calvin's chores. And Sammy is all too eager—as long as it means getting a "Level" and moving one step closer to his brother's Eagle status.

When Calvin meets Aleta Alvarado, a new girl who shares his love for *Goosebumps* books and adventure, Sammy is pushed aside. Cal feels guilty but not enough to change. At least not until a diagnosis makes things at home start falling apart, and he's left wondering whether Sammy will ever complete his own journey...

From Ant to Eagle.

"Tender, direct, honest." *Kirkus Reviews*

"A moving and ultimately hopeful book." *Booklist*

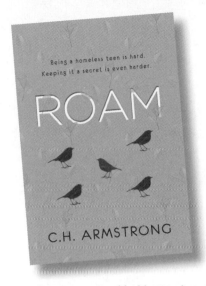

ROAM

C.H. Armstrong

YA - 978-1-77108-151-3

Seventeen-year-old Abby Lunde and her family are living on the streets. They had a normal life back in Omaha but, thanks to her mother's awful mistake, they had to leave behind what little they had for a new start in Rochester. Abby tries to be average—fitting in at school, dreaming of a boyfriend, college and a career in music. But Minnesota winters are unforgiving, and so are many teenagers. Her stepdad promises to put a roof over their heads, but times are tough and Abby is doing everything she can to keep her shameful secret from her new friends. The divide between rich and poor in high school is painfully obvious, and the stress of never knowing where they're sleeping or finding their next meal is taking its toll on the whole family.

As secrets are exposed and the hope for a home fades, Abby knows she must trust those around her to help. But will her new friends let her down like the ones back home, or will they rise to the challenge?

"Treats homelessness with respect and makes it visible." *Kirkus Reviews*

"An inspiring and heart-wrenching message." *Booklist*